Mystic Highlands Wedding

Mystic Highlands Wedding

GC Sinclaire

Printed in the United States of America

GC Sinclaire
Gig Harbor, WA 98329
www.gcsinclaire.com

Publisher's Note: This is a work of fiction. Names, characters, places, and incidents are a product of the author's imagination. Locales and public names are sometimes used for atmospheric purposes. Any resemblance to actual people, living or dead, or to businesses, companies, events, institutions, or locales is completely coincidental.

Mystic Highlands Wedding/GC Sinclaire-- 1st ed.

Print Edition ISBN 978-0-9994627-0-6
E-Book Edition ISBN 978-0-9994627-1-3

Library of Congress Control Number: 2020907883

Dedicated To:

**All my
Wonderful
Readers
And
The Divine**

Thank you!

Table of Contents

The terminology, as well as measurements, are different in the Mystic Highlands. I have, therefore, taken the liberty to convert some of them to make it easier to follow this engaging tale.

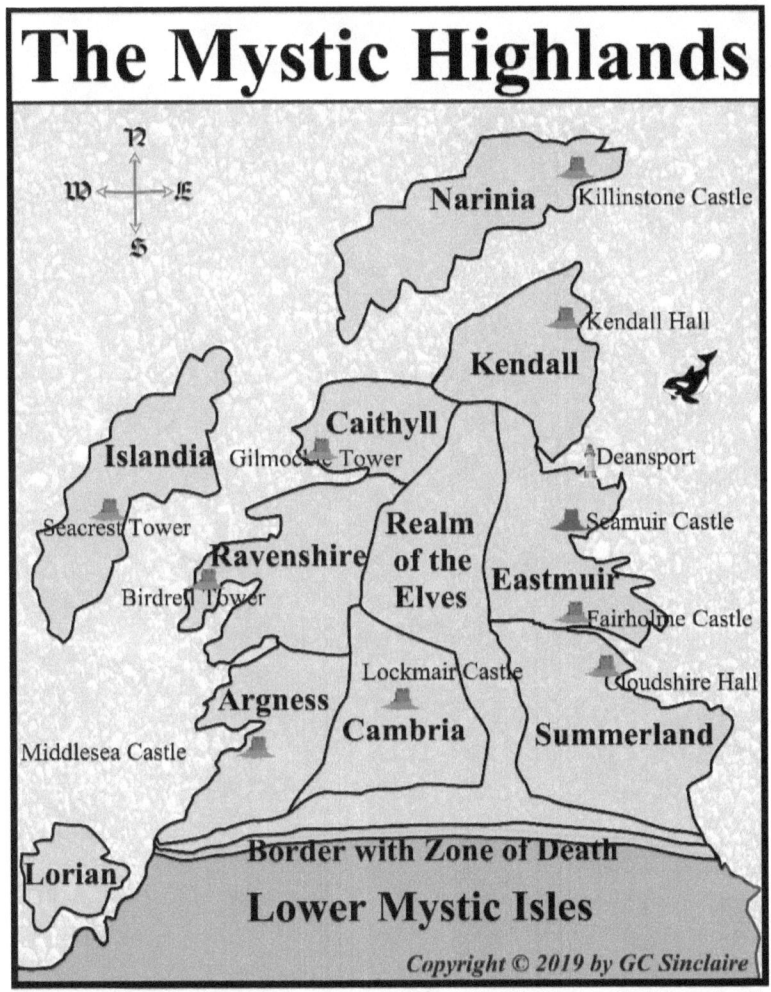

The Mystic Highlands

Narinia

Killinstone Castle

Kendall Hall

Kendall

Caithyll

Islandia Gilmochie Tower

Deansport

Seacrest Tower

Realm
of the
Elves

Seamuir Castle

Ravenshire

Eastmuir

Birdrell Tower

Fairholme Castle

Lockmair Castle

Cloudshire Hall

Argness

Cambria

Summerland

Middlesea Castle

Lorian

Border with Zone of Death

Lower Mystic Isles

Copyright © 2019 by GC Sinclaire

This map shows the locations of all the Highland Clans, the main castles, as well as the realm of the Zidhe. The Highlands are the Northernmost regions of a collection of islands called the Mystic Isles.

Prologue

The Mystic Highlands are the northernmost area of the Mystic Isles. They are a wild place full of magic and creatures one would expect to find only in legends. The climate is cold and often windy, and winters are downright frightful at times. For all that, these lands have such a rugged and stunning beauty that seeing them takes your breath away.

The outer sections and various islands were initially divided into nine clan areas by the elves (see the map at the front of the book.) The Zidhe retained the very middle and some of the valleys leading down to the sea as their domain. A border region full of hostile creatures and magic helps to keep the unwelcome influx of Lowlanders in check.

Due to the harsh climate, the elves reside partially under domes as well as in sheltered basins. Thanks to their loving care, these areas have become fertile and lush. The plants they brought with them, or reared to withstand the often unpleasant temperatures, continue to spread out into the Highlands.

The Zidhe have planted beautiful evergreen forests where only moss and a few hardy plants existed before. The trees are kept alive by the magic that now infuses the very land. Over the years, these woods have expanded and help to temper the extreme climate of the Highlands.

The inhabitants of this mystical region love their home and would not want to reside anywhere else. Before the elves' arrival, not much was able to live here. The Le'aanans' presence and their continued breeding of plants capable of withstanding the inclement weather keep improving conditions for all the Highlanders.

Because of the elves, the magic of the Mystic Highlands is incredibly strong. The powers of the realms have become conscious entities that work with the reigning lord to care for the land, or against him, as was the case with Ragnald MacClair.

Attracted by this powerful magic, many fey creatures, fleeing from the southern reaches and beyond, have found refuge in the northern realms. These beings feel safe here where the unusual is welcomed, accepted, and protected instead of hunted.

After what they experienced, they remain shy and hide from most of the inhabitants. Only the lord of the realm or a few chosen individuals get to even see or get to know them. Trust comes hard when one has had to flee for one's life.

The Highlands are not just the sanctuary of the fey but also of the Zidhe and the ten clans. Most of the non-elven inhabitants are descendants of people who were forced to abandon the warmer climes for one reason or another. Many had been criminals and wanted by the law. This made them all so much more determined to protect their home from any would-be intruders.

Over time, some interbreeding between the different groups and the Le'aanan has created a whole new race -

the Zidarians. At first, these mix-breeds were despised. They were even hunted by some, which forced them to band together to survive.

The outcast built the first fortified habitations in order to be able to defend themselves better. They were forced to become skilled warriors and work together to stay alive. Every youngster was trained just as soon as he or she could hold a weapon. Since they needed a leader to work as a unit, the most proficient warrior became the chief. This is how the first clans were created.

Due to their prowess in battle and their magic abilities, the Zidarians eventually rose to a position of power. Their leaders became the rulers of the now 10 clans.

Ki'ara, a most determined young lady and skilled sorceress, is a Zidarian. She was born into the family of the MacClairs, one of the nine ruling Highland Clans. The young lady is the daughter of Mikael and his second wife, Ali'ana. She is a mix-breed between elves and humans and has more Zidhe blood than most. This grants her a greater affinity for magic and the channeling of power.

The girl is tall and slender, and her waist-long, somewhat curly hair shines like bright copper in the sunshine. Ki'ara's startling green eyes, set into a face with clear skin and delicate facial features, are the color of a mountain lake with moonlight reflecting off its waves. Her inner beauty matches her appearance and is so evident that most people instantly like her.

Ki'ara just recently turned 24 when our story begins. Since Zidarians can live for more than a thousand years, she is still considered a child by their standards. Her oldest brother, Ragnald, the Lord of the MacClairs, was her guardian until her birthday.

Ki'ara was thirteen when her parents had to depart very suddenly. They left their daughter in Ragnald's keeping thinking that she would be well cared for. The new lord turned out to be a vicious and uncaring ruler.

He mistreated his sister just as much as he abused his power over the land and the clan.

Her father was a wise man who tried to consider all eventualities. He had left instructions just in case his oldest son did not keep his promises. Not even he, however, could have anticipated that things would turn out quite this bad. As per Mikael's orders, Ki'ara is made the Lord of Fairholme by the council on her birthday. She becomes the 10th lord of the Highlands.

Shortly after that, her studies with the wizard Argulf in Frankonia come to an end. He is not at all pleased. The old magician had seen Ki'ara as his meal ticket as well as a convenient helper for many, many years to come.

Also, Argulf had an understanding with Ragnald that he would keep his sister for a very long time. The course of study he had laid out should have taken her decades. Ki'ara had completed it in under two years.

Ragnald is furious that he has to grant his sibling permission to return to the Highlands so soon. Argulf realizes that Ki'ara has actually surpassed him in prowess in many areas. Therefore, he insists that she departs his decrepit castle high up in the mountains as quickly as possible.

When they leave De'Aire Chateau, Ki'ara and the tutor Mathus are confronted with unexpected dangers. On their way to the harbor of Mercede, the young sorceress ends up battling some of the creatures the disreputable magician had created and which Mathus had inadvertently released.

Ki'ara manages to save the lives of some of the local bandits, thus creating a useful alliance for her return. She also frees the spirits of an ensorcelled dragon and a ghost cat who turns out to be the mate to the catamount Taryn who had become her beloved companion. In the process, she completely exhausts her magic.

For her selfless deed, Ki'ara is restored to full power and granted a boon of help by Amara, the grateful goddess of the Frankonian Mountains. In addition, she is gifted a pronounced sharpening of her senses, making communication with animals easier.

Ki'ara and the bandit leader, Jacques, interrogate the deceitful Mathus together. They find out that Argulf has more such enchantments in his vile dungeons. These caverns are permeated with all the pain and violence of the past. The wizard uses them to store his discarded spells. The aura of the place ends up perverting them and turning them evil.

The unguarded and volatile cache presents a considerable danger to the inhabitants of the castle as well as the surrounding mountains. Ki'ara has little concern for the despicable Argulf. His experiments with forbidden dark magic have caused this debacle in the first place. She is tempted to return to the castle to deal with the man but realized that this would not be wise.

Argulf, she could handle, but not so this assortment of perverted enchantments. She is, however, seriously worried about the servants of De'Aire Chateau, who have become her friends. Most of the retainers are too old to find employment elsewhere and have nowhere to go.

Ki'ara, therefore, makes a deal with Jacques. The bandit leader will look after her friends at the castle and give them a home if needed. He also agrees to hide the remaining spells Mathus has stolen. In return, Ki'ara promises to come back and bring help to deal with this looming disaster.

Jacques assigns three of his men to see Ki'ara and Mathus safely to the harbor and onto her ship home.

⁕⁕⁕

After their long sea voyage, Eastmuir finally comes into view. Ki'ara is shocked by the dark aura hanging over Seamuir Castle. The place was always a bit brooding, looming up there on the hill, but now, it seems to have a downright foul air to it. What had her brother been up to?

The call from the magic of the land reaches her even out there, far out at sea. It surprises her by its intensity and sends a wave of heat through her body. Ki'ara can barely wait to set foot on the beloved soil of the Highlands yet once again!

Once the young lady arrives in Deansport, it soon becomes clear that she is not wanted at Seamuir Castle. The passing of their ship was acknowledged by the watchers at Seamuir, but no carriage was sent to fetch her. When Ki'ara finally makes her way to the fortress in a rented coach, her reception is anything but friendly.

This place was once her home, but no more. The young lady is, however, welcomed by the power of the land. On its own, the magical entity decides that it is tired of being abused by Ragnald. Without Ki'ara's knowledge, it makes her the new lord.

Ki'ara is very careful to hide all this from her brother. If at all possible, she wants to avoid a direct confrontation. Fights between Zidarians and magical duels were forbidden by the Zidhe many years ago. Engaging in such an act could get them both punished, just like their grandfather. Also, she does not want to begin her rule by killing the sitting lord.

Being a kind and loving person, Ki'ara is still trying to find a way to resolve things peacefully. On the morning of the day she is to attend a wedding in Deansport, the young lady sneaks out for a walk. She is inexplicably drawn to a nearby stone circle where she meets the old gods of the Highlands. The deities choose her as their priestess, their champion.

The sly Ragnald strikes later that day. When Ki'ara heads for the carriage waiting to take her to Deansport, he springs his trap. As planned, his unwitting mistress sets the entire courtyard on fire. During this attempt on Ki'ara's life, several people, as well as animals, are injured.

As the ruler of the MacClairs, it was Ragnald's sworn duty to protect his people. When he refuses to help and put out the blaze, he finds himself abandoned by his only friend and confidante, his younger brother Lyall. This causes his mind to become further unhinged. The lord starts plotting the deaths of all of his siblings.

Due to her enhanced senses, Ki'ara becomes privy to Ragnald's furious dialogue with himself. It assaults her to the point that she can barely shut it out. Fearing for Lyall's life, she convinces him to meet her and Gawain in Deansport.

Since Ragnald is nowhere in sight, Ki'ara ends up doing his job. The young lady heals the injured, including his mistress, as well as the animals before setting out for the wedding.

⚜

When Ki'ara and Gawain finally set out, and they are alone in the carriage, she shares some of her secrets with him. Gawain instantly pledges his support. He volunteers to give up his own plans and accompany her to the meeting that will take place before the wedding, but his sister declines. As the new lord, she feels that it is crucial that she stand on her own feet.

Due to the incident at the castle, Ki'ara arrives late. To her surprise, a full council of lords is scheduled before the festivities! Most of the rulers, or their representatives, are present! Seeing no other options, the lady sees herself forced to bring Ragnald's crimes to the attention of the assembly.

During this eventful gathering, Conall StCloud, the Zidarian Ki'ara was affianced to until Ragnald forbade the union, stands with her. He lends her his unconditional support. Having this man she still loves with all her heart by her side once again is a dream come true for the young woman.

Due to Ragnald MacClair's disregard of his duties, his bringing of foreign magic into the Highlands, and a public attempt on his sister's life, Ki'ara is accepted as the new ruler of the MacClairs by the other lords. She shares with them that the magic has already transferred the power to her. To prove this, she gives a brief demonstration.

The rulers are stunned. This had never happened before in all the years of the Highlands! Most of the lords had not been aware that the magical entities could show free will. This had some them rethinking their own treatment of these beings.

Finally, the meeting draws to a close. The wedding party is waiting. Even in the unlikely event that the elves decide to keep Ragnald in place, Ki'ara is still the leader of her own lands and now a permanent member of the council.

Chapter 1

Hope Reborn

At last, the ordeal of having to give witness against her own brother was over. Ki'ara sighed with relief. Some of the tension bled out of her body. After a moment, the StCloud once again claimed her hand under the table. Ki'ara turned and gave him a sweet smile. Bending towards him, she whispered a brief, "Thank you."

Having Conall's support meant much to her. His standing with her had smoothed the way with the council. Ki'ara was genuinely grateful to him. Even after all the years apart, he had her back, no matter what. How much she had missed that!

The rulers were very curious about the young lady's experience with the magic. Therefore, Lord Weatherlin had allowed a bit more chatter and several additional questions for Ki'ara, but enough was enough. The old lord called the meeting to a close. They were out of time. The festivities were waiting! The bride and groom were ready, and it was time for the wedding to begin.

Once the assembly had been officially concluded, all the Zidarians rose, Ki'ara MacClair and Conall StCloud hand in hand. Neither saw a reason to continue to abide by Ragnald's unreasonable edicts against their union.

By unspoken consent, they had decided to freely display the love they still felt for each other. Since he no longer had command of the magic, her brother had no power to harm them nor the right to tell Ki'ara what to do.

The two houses, which had been enemies ever since Ragnald had taken over as lord, were peacefully together at last, at least for the moment.

⚜

The fateful meeting had ended, but the assembled Zidarians were reluctant to move from their places. Some were still discussing the day's events. Ki'ara left her hand in the StCloud's. To her pleasure, Conall seemed to have no intention of relinquishing it any time soon. If anything, his grip had tightened around hers.

It did not take long for some of the other members of the assembly to become aware of their intertwined fingers. A MacClair and StCloud hand in hand was, after all, something worth notice!

Ki'ara watched with amusement as the lord directly across the table from them elbowed his neighbor to get the man's attention. Once he had it, he then directed his gaze towards the pair with a surreptitious movement of his eyes.

The two lords could barely believe what they were seeing. After a moment's pause, both of the gents grinned at each other delightedly. This was a promising sign of better things to come!

Most of the rulers wanted peace; they were tired of conflict. For many generations, these two influential houses had been at odds time after time. Having them finally stand as one would go a long way to establishing lasting harmony in the Highlands.

The StCloud did not release her fingers when they finally walked around the table. More people noticed. Smiles spread, and more elbows were used to get others' attention.

The air in the council chamber seemed to lighten perceptibly over the next few minutes. Hope is a precious thing. This new development between Ki'ara and Conall promised to make the Highlands a more peaceful place for them all.

⁕⸎⁕

It had been a sad day when Ragnald had officially broken the couple's engagement in front of the assembled lords. There had been no convincing of the stubborn man to change his mind. The new ruler had been determined to have his way and would not listen to reason.

His own uncle had spoken out against him. Lord Iain had been one of the many who had openly voiced their displeasure with this cruel act. All the council members' objections had been in vain; nothing had been able to deter the callous Ragnald from his chosen course of action.

To see the couple finally reunited filled the council members' hearts with gladness but also with a certain sense of glee that the nasty Ragnald's plans had been thwarted. They all approved of the union between the pair. It lifted their spirits to see these two together again at long last.

The lords knew that once Ki'ara was securely established as the ruler, life for the MacClair Clan, as well as its neighbors, would take a definite turn for the better. A new dawn for the Highlands was about to begin.

⁕⸎⁕

The lords mingled for a few moments longer before lining up for the formal procession. They ceremoniously moved across the entry hall towards the festivities. The doors were thrown open, and the guards officiously announced the rulers' entrance to the assembled wedding guests.

The Zidarians entered the great hall solemnly, two abreast, just as they had done for hundreds of years. Not caring about the ancient traditions, Conall was still holding Ki'ara's hand. Side by side, with their heads held high and fingers securely intertwined, the pair walked into the room.

As a sign of respect, everyone in attendance had risen to their feet. The men had removed their caps in a show of homage. Many of the women curtseyed, and the lads bowed as their rulers walked past.

The lords were not kings and queens anymore. However, the ancient pomp still appealed to their people as well as the rulers. It felt good to be honored and to be shown respect on these formal occasions. Nobody seemed to mind the reunited couple's show of affection.

⚜

The large hall had been beautifully decorated for the wedding. Fall flowers and boughs with colorful leaves had been attached to the columns and pinned to the walls. The chamber looked cheery and festive, and the light streaming in through the windows gave all a bright and happy air.

The couple's family and friends had spent most of the previous evening getting everything ready for the upcoming nuptials. The anxious mother of the bride had just about driven them crazy. Everything had to be just perfect for her daughter's big day, and the excited woman had kept changing her mind.

Finally, one of the groom's friends had come up with an idea to calm the frantic lady. He had made her some tea heavily laced with honey and rum. After several cups of the potent brew, things had started to come together much faster. Especially once the girl's mother had fallen asleep in the chair they had placed in the center of the room. This had allowed her to direct the adorning of the hall in comfort.

After a few more last-minute touches in the morning, all was in readiness for the festivities to begin.

It seemed that the StCloud had no intention of letting go of his once-fiancé's hand any time soon. Conall did not appear to care how much attention this caused, and if Ki'ara was truly honest, neither did she.

Ki'ara knew that Ragnald would be furious once he learned of her speaking out against him and her disregard of his edicts. She would have to talk to her uncle about staying with him for a couple of days until she could safely move into Fairholme. Going back to Seamuir before her brother was removed as the lord was not a safe option.

For now, the intimate contact with this amazing man felt too good. She would worry about the woes of tomorrow when they arose.

The wedding passed by like a blur. It was a lovely ceremony, but the young sorceress had a hard time keeping her focus on the proceedings. The nearness of the StCloud was too much of a distraction. Ki'ara kept slipping into daydreams of a life by his side.

When it was time for the Zidarians to give their blessings to the happy couple, Ki'ara and Conall stepped forward together. She could feel him raise up his power and followed suit.

To her amazement, their magic combined. As it was customary, the couple's wrists had been tied together. The MacClair and the StCloud placed their hands over those of the newlyweds. They spoke the traditional words as one. At that moment, it felt like the most natural thing to do.

"We wish you a long and happy life together and bless you both. May your hearth always be warm, your larder be full, and your children healthy and plentiful. As it is our wish, so it will be," they uttered in unison.

The entire assembly felt the strength of that blessing as its power swept through the hall. The bride, Celia, and her new husband, Rodric, were stunned for a moment. It took them a bit before they were composed enough to utter a word.

"Lord StCloud and Lady MacClair, thank you for your most gracious blessings! May all your days be filled with sunshine," the groom finally stammered.

Ki'ara and Conall smiled and stepped aside to make room for the next lord in line. The young lady was a little stunned herself. What had just happened? She had never felt anything like that before!

Their powers working together had been incredible and had sung with pure love and happiness. That brief moment had been the most astounding magic she had ever worked in her life.

Once all nine of the lords and ladies had given their boon, it was time for the wedding dance to begin. The musicians were tuning their instruments as a signal that they were about to start playing. A pair of Zidarians would escort the new couple onto the floor.

The seven other representatives of the clans looked at each other and then took several steps back in unison. More than a few hushed giggles at their sudden retreat erupted in the room. Seeing them do something together and then in perfect time! Now that was just priceless!

Conall and Ki'ara suddenly found themselves standing alone out in the limelight. It was up to them to lead the first dance. When the first notes of the grand march began to drift through the chamber, the StCloud guided the bride onto the dance floor and the MacClair the groom.

After three turns around the hall, the two couples stopped. As was the custom, they faced each other. The men bowed deeply. Ceremoniously, each presented their partner to the other. The smiling Celia stepped happily into her new husband's arms.

Around they went yet once again, both couples dancing smoothly and comfortably. Ki'ara had been a little bit shy for a moment. It had been years since she had been this close to this fascinating man, and now, they were both adults! His touch on her bare back sent shivers down her spine.

The last time he had twirled her around the dance floor, she had been just a girl. She still remembered it vividly. The StCloud had made her feel like a beautiful grown-up lady, had let her know that she was special to him and cherished.

She had never forgotten that day. It had been the last time she had been allowed to talk freely to Conall. She had so missed their lively discussions, his unconditional friendship, as well as his company. He had been the one she had usually turned to when she had needed advice.

Never again would she allow anyone to deprive her of his presence in her life. What a blessing that he still cared for her and had not married another!

✤

Soon, others joined the two couples on the dance floor. The next tune picked up the pace. Ki'ara and the

StCloud remained on the floor for several more songs before deciding to take a break.

It had been fun dancing with Conall. He moved with an innate grace that she had always admired. Could this be partially responsible for her racing pulse? Or was it his nearness and his gentle touch?

The StCloud kept his arm around Ki'ara's waist as he was leading her towards the refreshments. Before much longer, her face began to flush. When had it gotten this hot in the hall? Her partner had been watching her. He saw the blush that had steadily begun to spread over her face and neck and eyed her with concern.

"Are you alright, Ki'ara?" he inquired immediately. She could only nod. His nearness was having all kinds of effects on her body and emotions, but she could not bring herself to ask him to remove that well-muscled arm. Nor did she want to put more distance between them even if that would have made it easier for her to breathe.

"May I lead you to the table and get you some water, Ki'ara? You look hot, and I believe it is almost time for the feast," Conall asked her with a soothing smile.

Ki'ara nodded her acquiescence and soon found herself seated at the High Table, naturally right next to the StCloud. But at least, they were no longer in physical contact, and the heat pulsing in her body started to ebb. She could barely believe that his mere touch had such an effect on her composure!

Most of the other Zidarians were already seated. Funny how those two spots right next to each other had been left for them! And, how all the lords had stepped back to allow Conall and her to lead off the dance! They were actively encouraging their association!

Her brother would be furious once he found out, but to Ki'ara, that no longer mattered. With his attempt on her life, Ragnald had effectively destroyed all loyalty she had ever felt for him. She had decided that instead of obeying him, she would follow her heart.

Ki'ara could not help but wonder, however. Did the other lords and ladies all approve of their friendship? Of their reunion? Or, was it just because they despised Ragnald and knew that he hated the StCloud? Ki'ara decided that it was most likely a little of both.

⚜

The young lady's uncle, Lord Iain, had been all smiles from the moment on when he saw his niece's and the StCloud's intertwined hands. He had watched the couple with great pride and had approvingly patted Conall on the back on several occasions. As had several of the other lords!

Ki'ara could barely believe that her bond with the StCloud was being supported and even facilitated by the entire council! Who would have thought that that often cantankerous bunch, prone to argue over a minute detail of an agreement for hours, could act in such unison?

Since this was also her greatest wish, Ki'ara really did not mind the lords' non too subtle pushing of her and Conall together. It was time to make her own alliances, forge her own path. After this night, she would not be able to return to Seamuir Castle without major reinforcements anyhow. She would need all the other lords' backing to survive the upcoming confrontation.

The new ruler had decided that she would ask her brothers, Lyall and Gawain, to accompany her to Fairholme. She could govern from there until they could dethrone the present MacClair. Ki'ara had no idea what to do with Ragnald. As a clan member, he would be her responsibility. Still, she seriously doubted that he would be willing to swear allegiance to her.

When he had tried to burn her alive back at the castle this day, it had made the young woman realize that

Ragnald's rage towards her went even deeper than she had suspected. Her brother would have no compunction about trying again to get her out of his life, especially once he found out that she was now lord.

The fire had cruelly driven home the point where things stood between her and Ragnald. How one could hate a member of their own family this much was beyond her. The young woman never noticed the frown that had stolen onto her face during these contemplations.

"Ki'ara, why so serious suddenly? Is this not a day of joy and celebration? What is bothering you, my dearest?" Conall addressed her. With a concerned smile, he reclaimed her hand.

"You can talk to me, you do know that, don't you?" he continued while gently massaging her once again icy fingers. Ki'ara could only nod. Her throat was tight with emotions. It felt so wonderful to have someone to rely on, someone who cared this much about her.

This handsome man had once been her very best friend, maybe still was. For a moment, she was tempted to confide in him. Almost as quickly, it dawned on her that this was not a good idea.

Ki'ara had grasped this evening how much she truly loved this man. Remembering the fate of their grandfathers, she was afraid to drag the StCloud into her family affairs. She could not bear the thought of him disappearing just because he was helping her.

The dreadful dream she had back in Frankonia came back to her mind. The searing pain of watching Conall being ripped away from her and tossed into a bottomless abyss to be lost forever had not yet lost its bite.

Before she involved anyone else, she needed to talk to her Uncle Iain. He would know what course of action would be the most expedient and also the safest for all involved. Ragnald's removal from power was in the hands of the council and the Zidhe now. All she had to do was to stay safe until the danger to her life was eliminated.

The young lady knew Conall well enough to know that he would want to come to her rescue. He did not care much for Ragnald to start with, but if she shared her fears, this might just be too much. Ki'ara did not want to see the usually circumspect lord do something rash that would only lead to more problems.

Therefore, Ki'ara resolutely pushed her dark thoughts aside. There was plenty of time to sort all that mess out later. Now was not the right moment. "It is nothing of any consequence, and my apologies for letting it mar this festive occasion," she answered with a sweet smile.

But Conall was not so easily put off. "Ah, so there is something bothering you!" he stated matter of factly. The StCloud looked thoughtful for a moment. With his usual lightning ability for deductions, he quickly homed in on the problem.

"After what happened today and becoming the new lord, it is obvious that you cannot go home for the time being. What are your plans, and how can I help?" he queried.

This striking man was way too perceptive for his own good! Ki'ara realized that there was no sense keeping things from him; he could still read her like a book after all these years! But, how much of her dilemma was it safe to divulge to him?

"I intend to stay with my uncle until Lyall, Gawain, and I can safely make our way to Fairholme. It is about time that I took possession of my new home and met the members of my clan," she, therefore, replied, trying to make as light of the situation as she could.

The StCloud looked at her intently, and she met his searching gaze with one of her own. Their eyes locked for a moment, and she felt like she was drowning. When her head started to spin, she glanced away from those so very compelling orbs. Why was he the only man who had ever made her feel that way?

When his neighbor addressed Conall with a question about the meeting, Ki'ara took the opportunity to study him carefully. He was truly handsome, and she had never met another man in her life who affected her quite like this one did.

On her brother's orders, Mathus had introduced her to a couple of men. It had never taken long before she had ended up thinking of Conall. He still owned her heart, and the hurt she felt over Ragnald breaking their engagement had never healed.

Even if the young lady had been the slightest bit interested in one of the suitors, in her eyes, none of them could have ever compared with the StCloud. Ki'ara had remained courteous, but, much to her tutor's frustration, she had been bored and totally uninterested in both.

This very day, hope had been reborn. A happy life together was a possibility once more. Ki'ara smiled at the thought.

Chapter 2

A Secret Pact

Conall was talking to his neighbor, Lord Duncan Blair of Narinia. As Ki'ara sat watching him, her thoughts drifted back to the past and the happy memories she had of the times before her parents departed for places unknown. As a young child, Ki'ara had delighted in the StCloud's attention. She had loved the frequent visits to his home, Cloudshire Hall. As she grew older, however, the girl had started to develop a huge crush on the handsome man.

These feelings had been encouraged by her parents. They had allowed Conall to bring her flowers, spend time with her, and give her gifts. One of these presents had been a beautiful filigree locket with both their hand-drawn pictures inside. Ki'ara had worn it at all times until the day Ragnald had ripped it from around her throat and destroyed it.

Now that there was hope once more of a life together, looking back was no longer as painful as it had been all the years she had been under her brother's control. Ki'ara smiled as she realized how much lighter her heart suddenly felt. She was filled with pleasant anticipation and could sense that even the magic of the land was singing with triumph and happiness. It seemed that it approved of her choice of a mate.

Ki'ara still loved Conall just as much or more now. She counted it as an incredible blessing that his feelings for her had not changed either. How wonderful to be given a second chance!

⋅⋰⋆⊱✦⊰⋆⋱⋅

The StCloud was much older than Ki'ara. He had already been a virile young man when she was born. When you live a thousand years, however, such a small age difference does not really matter. Conall took an interest in the precocious girl from the very start. As a result, Ki'ara and her parents were often invited to his estates, or he came to stay at Seamuir Castle.

Ki'ara began following Conall around shortly after she started to walk. Whenever they went to visit or were at one of the parties, she would trail behind him wherever he went. Pretty soon, he just scooped her up and carried her with him. From then on, she would ask to be picked up the second she spotted him.

Since her brothers were much older and few youngsters her age resided at her home at that time, Ki'ara grew up mostly by herself. Whenever she and her parents came to visit Cloudshire Hall, Conall would make sure that the girl had some of his clan's children to play with. Ki'ara appreciated his thoughtfulness, but what she cherished most was the time she got to spend with just him.

⋅⋰⋆⊱✦⊰⋆⋱⋅

The Zidarians grew so used to the StCloud's small companion that they spoke freely around her, thinking that the child was too young to understand. After all, she was just a babe! This allowed Ki'ara to learn more about clan politics at an early age than she would in all her later years.

Her parents soon figured this out from some of the questions their small daughter was asking. They made sure Ki'ara understood that she should only bring up such topics with them and the StCloud, whom they trusted implicitly, but no one else.

Conall had become aware of Ki'ara's mental acuity the first time he had laid eyes on her shortly after she was born. The way she had met his gaze had told him much. Even then, there had been an intelligence and a curiosity in those unusual, vivid green orbs that went far beyond her tender age.

As she grew older, the knowing in those sharp, bright eyes only increased. Many of the Highlanders were discomfited by her penetrating gaze, which seemed to go right through them and root out their deepest secrets. Her sweet smile, however, would usually put them at ease.

❧

Ki'ara had an unquenchable thirst for knowledge. She realized from very early on that more could be learned from listening to the adults if they thought her just a baby. It was actually best if they forgot that she was even there. Therefore, she would act like a small, sleepy child cuddled up to her favorite uncle or parents. In reality, she was hanging on every word that was being said.

The StCloud confirmed her conclusion that it was best to pretend to be just like her peers. He warned the little girl to keep her awareness a secret and advised her not to let her brothers know how much she did comprehend. Conall's instincts told him that Ki'ara needed to be careful around Ragnald. He was already resentful enough as it was.

Her parents and Conall realized that if she was ever going to fit into Highland society, it was best if her unusualness went unnoticed. People tended to reject or even fear those who were different and whom they saw as strange, as unlike themselves.

At times, Ki'ara would complain about how boring the other little ones were. She would have rather been with the older ones. On those occasions, Conall reminded her that it was best that people saw her play with kids her age and act like them.

After all, did she want the lords and ladies to be aware that Ki'ara was listening to everything they said and that it was well within her understanding? Even the idea of losing her source of knowledge was enough to scare Ki'ara into playing only with the little ones.

With Conall's help, she perfected her sweet, innocent kid act. By the time Ki'ara had reached five, her intellect was almost scary. She had a well-developed personality, and she knew exactly what she wanted.

What she desired most, even then, was to spend her life with her best friend and confidante, the man who was always there to help and advise her.

***

To everyone, except her parents and the StCloud, Ki'ara appeared no different from the other five-year-olds. She played her role to perfection, which allowed her to be a covert gatherer of information. If Mikael or Conall needed to know more than they were being told by the other rulers, they would ask the small girl to find out.

During get-togethers, Ki'ara could usually be found curled up on someone's lap. This happened so often that no one thought anything of it if she walked up and asked to be picked up. The adults would continue their conversation like she was not even there. This made her privy to all sorts of secrets that she then shared with Conall, Mikael, and Ali'ana.

⚜

The people Ki'ara was closest to were her parents and the StCloud. Him she totally adored and trusted. Conall was the only one who knew how deep her affection for him really went. He was glad to have Mikael's and Ali'ana's approval of this ever-intensifying bond.

The day he had first seen the infant, the couple had agreed to give him their daughter's hand in marriage just as long as Ki'ara approved. By Highland standards, the two of them were considered unofficially engaged. Being an honorable man, he would not have allowed the child to attach herself so firmly to him otherwise.

On one of the family's visits to Cloudshire Hall when Ki'ara was six, the girl asked Conall to show her his new rose garden. For a time, she duly admired the beautiful flowers, but then she turned to her adult friend. The expression on her small face told him that she had something important to say.

"What is it, little one, why so serious all of a sudden?" the StCloud asked her. Ki'ara watched him gravely for a few moments.

"Conall, you are really my only and best friend. You, more than even my parents, know who I really am. You have helped me learn how to fit in. I want to thank you for all that. I have therefore decided that to repay you, I will one day become your wife," she stated with a seriousness which even surprised the StCloud.

Conall regarded her solemnly. How much he loved this unusual child! Every time he looked at her, he saw the promise of the truly extraordinary woman she would grow into one day. Life with her was never going to be boring!

The StCloud got down on one knee so that their eyes were almost level. He took her small hands in his large ones.

"Ki'ara MacClair, I would be honored to have you as my wife! I cannot wait for the day when I can finally call you mine!" he assured her with a smile.

"Let this be a pact between us and only us until the time comes. Do we have an agreement?" Conall proposed with all seriousness. For a moment, Ki'ara searched his face. Then, she nodded happily. The StCoud reverently kissed her small hands before releasing them.

The young man and little girl returned to looking at the gorgeous blooms. He presented her with the most beautiful red rose he could find. When they started back towards the castle, Ki'ara's hand found her way into his like always, and she happily skipped alongside this man whom she loved. She never forgot those words nor the pact which had been made between them.

As the years went by, the bond between Ki'ara and Conall grew ever deeper. For her ninth birthday, he organized an elaborate party. She loved it. That day, for the very first time, he gently and chastely kissed her on the mouth.

Ki'ara would never forget that brief touch. It had looked so innocent to all others. To her, however, it had meant so much since it had been a promise affirmed.

Chapter 3

A Prank Gone Wrong

Ki'ara was watching the people around her. She was enjoying the lively party and actually did not mind having a few minutes to herself. It gave her a chance to reminisce and to appreciate the enormous change this day had brought for her. Glancing at the StCloud, she saw that he had enough of his longwinded neighbor and had excused himself.

Scooting his chair closer to Ki'ara, Conall reached for her hands. "I am so sorry, sweetheart! I was starting to think that Duncan would never get to the point!" he whispered with a laugh and a wink.

All the gent's neighbors were busy talking, and Ki'ara could not help but feel compassion for the man's obvious lack of companionship. "The poor chap does look a little lost now that he no longer has his conversation partner. Should we find him someone to talk to?" Ki'ara responded in a low voice.

Just then, the lord looked in her direction. When Ki'ara gave him a friendly smile, he immediately took this as an invitation to join her and Conall. Pulling his chair over, he started right in asking questions and making small talk.

"Lady Ki'ara, it is such a pleasure to see you and Conall reunited again! I remember that you and he genuinely enjoyed spending time together despite your difference in age. Did it ever bother you that he was an adult, and you still a child?" Lord Duncan asked in all seriousness. At first, Ki'ara was a little taken aback by his directness, but then she decided to respond.

"Not usually. Conall did his best to make me feel special, and we did have an agreement. Most of the ladies knew and respected this," she replied with a slight smile.

As a girl, she had been aware of the occasional rumor of the StCloud dating other women. He had been and still was a gorgeous man and a wealthy lord with a vast estate. This had drawn the ladies like flies, but Conall had usually danced with Ki'ara, making his preference perfectly clear. However, he had also been a young and virile man with certain needs, and she had still been a child.

Ki'ara had understood that they both had an obligation to socialize with others. On some occasions, however, she had found it hard to watch him holding another in his arms. She especially remembered one woman who had been determined to become the handsome lord's wife, no matter how he felt about this. She had pursued Conall relentlessly.

"I do remember that one woman, what was her name? She would not take no for an answer no matter how many times I told her that I was not interested! That one really got under your skin, Ki'ara, didn't she?" Conall interjected.

"I recall her only too well, Conall! Remember, we had agreed before the party that I would come to your rescue if she cornered you again? I did feel bad for her afterward! Neither one of us had expected that she would react so violently!" Ki'ara responded. She could not suppress a shudder as her thoughts drifted back to that day.

The determined lady had quite a reputation north as well as south of the border where she originated from. At one time or another, she had been after every available young lord who had station and money. Unfortunately, she had been a guest of one of the rulers. To disrespect her, was to disrespect the lord. The woman had used this as a guise to attend as many gatherings as she possibly could.

Just as soon as they had spotted the predatory female, Conall, as well as every other sensible young man, had headed in the opposite direction. They had come up with some excuse, any excuse, to flee her presence. Before long, the Lowlander had started to make a real nuisance of herself. Ki'ara had not been the only one who had felt that something needed to be done.

The lady in question had not been the first to pursue Conall, and Ki'ara had figured that she would most likely not be the last. For a while, the girl had watched the persistent creature with amusement. She had believed that the woman would eventually get the idea and stop.

When the determined lady had become even more brazen instead of relenting, the girl had decided that enough was enough. Ki'ara had seen how uncomfortable the StCloud and all the other young men were being hunted such. The woman was pretty enough, but her voice was shrill, and her personality and manners left a lot to be desired.

Conall had been letting the woman know in no uncertain terms that he was not interested in her and that he was otherwise committed. The unpleasant female, however, had chosen to totally ignore all his objections. She had followed him around like a puppy dog and had loudly demanded his undivided attention whenever he had attempted to ignore her.

The StCloud, always the gentleman, had been trying hard not to get rude, but he had enough. It had been evident to all but the pesky lady that his patience was at an end. That had been the point when Ki'ara had decided that next time, she would come to her friend's aid.

The families had been at a birthday celebration, and the party had been in full swing. The woman had once again been all over Conall, who had kept shooting Ki'ara imploring glances. Every time the girl headed in the StCloud's direction to fetch him for a dance, the lady had seen her coming and had dragged him onto the floor first.

Despite his best efforts, Conall had been unable to make his escape. Finally, in desperation, he had guided the woman over to a table out on the patio. She had been fiercely and possessively clinging to his arm and had at first refused to let go.

Once the exasperated StCloud had convinced the obnoxious creature to take a seat in a chair, he had managed to detach her temporarily from his person. The relief on Conall's face had been almost comical and had not gone unnoticed.

Many of the other lords had shot him commiserating glances but would not come to their friend's aid. Most had been in his shoes. They had wanted nothing to do with the woman. The men had shuddered at the mere thought of the shrew's attention focusing on them again.

Ki'ara had followed the pair. On the terrace, pushed up against one of the walls, she had noticed a table with different types of beverages. Suddenly, she had seen the perfect way to deal with this unwelcome guest. The girl had searched for the most staining of all.

The beleaguered lord had been looking around frantically for some sort of an excuse to escape. Finally, his eyes had fallen on Ki'ara. With a mischievous smile, she had pointed at the drinks and then the lady. Catching her intent, he had returned her grin and had given her an almost imperceptible nod. Desperate times had called for drastic measures!

The girl had filled two glasses half-full with a fragrant, dark red berry wine. Taking her time and being careful not to spill the liquid on herself, she had carried the drinks over to the table where the two were sitting.

"I thought you and the lady might be thirsty and brought you a beverage, Sir Conall," Ki'ara had addressed the StCloud and his companion. She had acted very polite and innocent and had given the young man a deep curtsy.

"Thank you, Ki'ara! Some refreshment is most welcome! How thoughtful of you!" he had replied with a twinkle in his eyes. However, as she had been just about to hand the lady her drink across the table, the StCloud had reached out to take it. Their hands had collided, and both glasses had gone flying.

⁘⊱☙⊰⁘

"That was some show! You got rid of that nasty woman once and for all! With that vexing creature gone, a man could once again attend a party without having to hide! I will never forget the look on her face!" Lord Duncan said with a laugh. His guffaw brought a smile to Ki'ara's face, and she shared an amused grin with Conall.

"I did not think it was all that funny at that moment! I had intended for her to get a couple minor stains, but when Conall's and my hands connected, the dark red liquid from both glasses just spewed up like a fountain!" Ki'ara recalled.

"Yes, and it ended up all over the woman's face, hair, and that horrid, skimpy pink dress of hers! She ended up positively drenched and dripping wine all over the place! I think I was just as shocked as you were, Kiara!" Conall remembered.

Ki'ara had immediately stammered an apology, but the woman had been beyond furious. After freezing for a moment in utter shock, the lady had jumped up. Her features had been contorted with rage, and she had turned almost as red as the wine. Forgetting where she was and that she was making a public spectacle of herself, she had started screaming at the girl.

At the sound of that piercing, unpleasant voice, the music had faded away. All eyes had turned towards the source. The irate lady, however, had been too angry to notice. She had continued to shriek insults at the teary-eyed child before her. Then, losing her temper completely, she had raised her hand to slap Ki'ara.

"Things sure got out of hand, didn't they?" Lord Duncan remembered.

"They sure did! Had it not been for Conall, she would have hit me!" Ki'ara responded. What had started out as a prank had gone very wrong awfully fast!

Before her palm had been able to connect with the stunned girl's cheek, a powerful hand had firmly grabbed the screeching woman's arm. The StCloud's usually warm and kind eyes had glittered with fury.

"How dare you speak to this young lady like this? And, how dare you raise your hand to your betters? Don't you see that it was an accident?" he had hissed.

"Accident? That was no accident!" the woman had screamed at Conall. "That hussy did that on purpose! She ruined my beautiful dress, that stupid chit. Let go of me and get out of my way! I am going to beat her!" the affronted harpy had shouted.

In her rage, she had dropped her refined façade and had started to display her true disposition. Shocked gasps had come from all around the room. No Zidarian would have dared to behave in such a manner towards one of their peers! That was just not done!

That it had been one of the despised Lowlanders who had committed the offense, had made it even worse!

Dead silence had fallen at this point. Every eye in the place had been riveted on the scene before them. Ki'ara's parents had rushed to their daughter's side and had been sheltering her from the woman. Conall and Mikael had gone white with rage at the shrew's words.

"Madame, are you aware who you are about to assault?" the StCloud had questioned the furious woman.

"I do not know, and I do not care! She will pay for this insult! Let go of me this instance!" the completely beside herself female responded. She had been beating at her captor's arm, trying to break free.

Angry murmurs had been growing all around the room, and several of the men had stepped forward. Their faces were grim and determined. This interloper into their society had gone too far, much too far. This kind of crude and violent behavior could not be tolerated!

"The young lady who was kind enough to bring you a drink and who you were about to attack is Ki'ara, daughter of the Lord of the MacClairs!" Conall had spat at the lady with cold fury.

"How dare you threaten violence to an innocent child? What kind of a person are you? Not one who deserves a place in the Highlands!" he had gone on. The set of his shoulders and the coldness in his voice had conveyed his contempt.

"I believe that it is time for you to leave. You are no longer welcome among us!" the StCloud had continued. His words had been dripping with icy disdain.

All fury had left the woman's face when Conall's words had sunk in. At that moment, she had realized the extent of her offense. Her face had turned chalk white. She had heard of some of the obscure customs and laws of this region. Being made to leave had meant the end of all her well-laid plans! She had glanced around in despair. Was she about to be banned from the Highlands? Would they have mercy?

The lady's pleading looks had been answered by one person after another turning their back to her. Revealing what kind of an individual she really was had cost her all regard. The woman's once friend had even gone as far as spitting in her direction before pointedly turning around.

"You have an hour to pack your possessions. The guards will watch you while you collect your things and then escort you to the harbor. You will board the next ship heading south. You are never to set foot into the Highlands again. This, I do declare! Who is with me?" the StCloud's voice had rung out.

One after another, eight "Ayes" had followed. Right then and there, it had been done. The ban had been in place and woe to who had thought to disrespect it.

Clan law had spoken and could only be undone by the consent of all nine rulers. Most of the lords had disliked the woman to start with. Therefore, the chance of the edict being revoked had been slim.

The offense had been unforgivable, and the shrew had been lucky to leave the Highlands alive. Conall could have just as well ordered her death for the crime of hitting him and threatening Ki'ara.

⚬✦⚬

The StCloud had waved to two of the eagerly waiting guards. They had immediately made their way towards him. "Please escort Madame to her friend's home, watch her while she packs, and then take her to the harbor. Put her on any available ship, even if it is a cargo vessel. Tell the captain that she has been banned and has no rights under Highland Law," he had commanded.

Turning his attention back to the woman who had looked about ready to faint by this time, he had spoken with barely suppressed fury.

"And you, Madame, should you ever dare to set foot north of the border again, you will be branded. Assaulting a member of the ruling families is no minor offense. Had you actually hit the young lady, you would no longer be in need of a carriage. Do you understand?"

The hot-headed woman had nodded weakly. Her temper had once again gotten her into trouble. She had realized that she had been lucky to escape with her life. The thought that maybe it was time to give up the hunt for a rich, titled husband and settle down with the nice young man she had spurned all these years had come to her mind.

He did, after all, own some land, had a pretty nice house, and he was good-looking. Then, it had dawned on her that word of her behavior and banishment was going to get around. Suddenly, she had felt an extreme urgency to return home.

The lady had realized that the sooner she married that man, the better! She was not about to give him a chance to find out about this incident and have him turn his back on her as well!

⚬✦⚬

At this point, Mikael MacClair had exchanged a questioning glance with Conall, who had nodded his agreement almost imperceptibly. The StCloud was only too happy to let his friend take over from here.

"Get her out of here now before I forget that I am a civilized man and beat this harpy to a pulp for threatening my daughter!" the enraged father had ordered.

Mikael had let the StCloud handle most of this unpleasant affair. Until that moment, he had been more concerned with his distraught child. Besides, Conall had things well in hand. But, the offender had not been leaving fast enough for his taste.

The utterly shocked woman had been hoping for some kind of a miracle. She had been trying to delay her departure despite the guards' attempts to hurry her along. Mikael's command changed all that.

As always, any order given by a MacClair or StCloud had been carried out with alacrity. The sobbing woman had been removed from the terrace and escorted off the property.

Once the offender had been dealt with, Conall's full attention had been on the visibly upset girl. "Are you alright, Ki'ara? Did she hurt you?" he had asked her with a concerned frown. Stepping out of the embrace of her mother, the girl had faced him squarely.

"Thank you, Sir Conall, for coming to my rescue. I believe that she would have hit me had you not intervened!" Ki'ara had responded formally. She had given the young lord a grateful smile and a deep curtsy.

Neither Ki'ara nor the StCloud had expected things to get so out of hand. The girl had thought it best if no one suspected that the spill had not been totally accidental.

Seeing that the spectacle was over, the musicians had begun to play. After a few more minutes of discussing the incident, the assembled Highlanders had started to return to their amusement. Here and there, small groups had continued to talk animatedly about the event. After a while, however, even those had gotten bored with the topic and had returned to enjoying themselves. The party had once again been in full swing.

Mikael MacClair had led his wife to the dance floor. He had left Ki'ara in Conall's care. There was no one he trusted more with his precious daughter.

Ki'ara's father had approved of and encouraged the interest the young man had in his daughter and she in him. He had hoped that one day, as had been arranged, the StCloud would make her his wife. Mikael had felt that it would be good for the two families to be joined by blood. Maybe then all the old grudges could finally be buried.

✤

The still somewhat upset Ki'ara had been only too happy to remain with Conall. She had smiled up at the StCloud and had taken his arm. In unspoken accord, they had exited the terrace to take a calming walk in the garden.

Once they had been alone, Ki'ara had behaved much more like an adult. Gone had been the distressed child of a few minutes before. "Thank you, Conall! I really needed some time away from everyone! Could we find a quiet place and just sit and talk for a while? I think there is a bench in the rose garden," she had asked sweetly.

Ki'ara had decided to lighten the mood by being just a little flirtatious with the StCloud as they had made their way through the beautiful garden. It had not taken long for the pair to find a secluded spot that had suited their needs.

"That went a little too well, didn't it? Are you absolutely certain that you are alright?" Conall asked her yet again. He had been just as stunned as the girl by the woman's violent response.

In response, Ki'ara had batted her eyelashes at the StCloud. This gesture had been a perfect imitation of one of the simpering ladies who tended to flock around him.

"Thank you, kind sir, thank you so very much for coming to my timely rescue! I owe it all to you that I am perfectly fine," had been her humorous reply.

Ki'ara had not been able to completely keep the giggling under control while uttering such an absurd sentence. Also, her demeanor had been purposely over the top. This had dispelled the tension they had both still been feeling and had left them roaring with laughter.

Getting into the spirit of things, the girl had brought out her very best grown-up persona. She had behaved every inch like a coquettish lady. It had been evident that she had been paying very close attention to the mannerisms of the adult females around her.

Conall had looked at Ki'ara with amazement. When had this child become such a seductress? Good thing that he was sure that he was the only one she was practicing her wiles on. Chuckling with amusement, he had played along.

Finally, Ki'ara had pitched her voice to sound purposely husky. She had uttered another completely outrageous statement while looking up at Conall teasingly and fluttering her long lashes at him. The pair had ended up laughing so hard that tears had been rolling down their faces.

✦⋆⁕⋆✦

"Are you really alright?" the StCloud had asked her once they had grown serious once more. "Yes, I am fine! Thanks to you!" Ki'ara had replied.

"That did not quite go as planned now, did it? Wow, what a temper!" Conall had uttered, still in disbelief at the audacity of the Lowlander.

The girl had smiled at him mischievously. "I don't think either of us was ready for that!" she had said with a laugh. "Thank you again for saving me!"

"No, thank you for rescuing me from that horrid creature. No matter what I did, I could not get rid of her! That one stuck like glue! I bet you some of the other lads are pretty relieved as well! That one really did not take no for an answer!" Conall had stated, shaking his head.

"Well, my sweet, I do believe it is time for us to go back before your father comes looking for us!" the young lord prompted Ki'ara goodnaturedly.

Figuring that it was probably a good idea to reappear at the party, the StCloud had courteously led his young accomplice back to the terrace. There, he had chosen a somewhat secluded table.

"Do you care to sit down?" he had asked, politely pulling out a chair for Ki'ara. He had decided that if she could behave like a grown-up, he would treat her as such.

Before long, the pair had become completely engrossed in a discussion about the origin of earth magic of the clan families. They had been in plain sight if anyone had thought to look. Their behavior had been well within the bounds of propriety.

No one had seen anything unusual about the two of them sitting there in the balmy night air talking animatedly. Anyhow, the music had been playing, and mead and wine had flown freely. There had been much fun and laughter. Most of the Highlanders present had been too busy enjoying themselves to give the couple a second thought.

The rest of that evening had passed very pleasantly for both Ki'ara and Conall. They had covered a variety of subjects and explored some interesting conjectures.

"I remember you two sitting out there on the terrace once all the hubris died down. You were so deeply involved in your conversation that no one wanted to disturb you! Your parents just smiled, Ki'ara. They would be so happy to see the two of you together again!" Lord Duncan stated, beaming at both Conall and Ki'ara.

"You have no idea how happy I am about this unexpected turn of events, old friend! Who would have thought this morning that my life would be blessed with my lady love once more!" the StCloud responded softly.

Gingerly, he reached for Ki'ara's hand, turned it over, and placed a gentle kiss in her palm. That sweet yet seductive gesture left her tingling all over.

The young lady was so surprised by this open show of affection that all she could do was smile at Conall and Lord Blair. Her voice seemed to have forsaken her, and her throat felt tight with emotions.

Being right here, next to her love, touching him, speaking to him, was like a miracle for Ki'ara. Part of her still had a hard time believing that all this was real.

Chapter 4

A Devastating Development

Being intimately tied to the magic of the land made the nine ruling families almost immortal. A thousand years was a very long time to spend by yourself, but Ki'ara loved Conall so much that for her, there had never been anyone else. She had not met another man who attracted her for more than a brief moment or for whom she had felt more than friendship.

The StCloud was smiling at her, and involuntarily, Ki'ara's gaze homed in on his mouth. How many times had she kissed those alluring lips in her dreams? Run her hands through his dark curly hair? Drowned in the sea of his warm, brown eyes? Woken up with a longing in her heart and soul that defied all explanation? She still had a hard time believing that he was really right here in front of her!

For years, she had obeyed her brother and had allowed him to send her away time after time. Ki'ara had been a loyal and obedient sister even if her entire being had screamed for her to break free and to run to the man whom she so bitterly missed.

Unfortunately, this had not been an option. Standing up for herself would have been dangerous to the girl's health, and it would have widened the rift in the family. Also, seeking shelter with the StCloud would have led to an all-out war between the two clans. Ki'ara did not want either of these options to fall on her conscience, so she had continued to let her guardian rule her life.

In the beginning, Ki'ara had hoped, against all the odds, that Ragnald would change his mind. Then, she had seen the actual depth of the hatred her brother felt for Conall, and she had realized that as long as he was in charge, there was no chance of this happening.

As lord of the MacClairs, Ragnald would have never permitted a marriage between the two clans.

⁂

Life had been so pleasant before her parents had left. As Ki'ara had gotten older, her feelings for the StCloud had further deepened. She had counted the days, the hours, the minutes until her next meeting with Conall. It had become hard to hide her love for this handsome man. The girl had felt blessed that her father and mother had accepted this gladly. They had even encouraged the budding relationship.

Most of the Highlanders had full-heartedly approved of their engagement. To keep the family ties strong and to form alliances, girls were often betrothed at birth or very young. The actual wedding would take place years later and with full consent of the lady.

The StCloud had always acted like a perfect gentleman. He had respected his fiancé's age and had made certain that they never did anything her family could have possibly objected to. And, he had been a master at making the girl feel loved, cherished, and so very special. This alone had endeared him even more to Mikael and Ali'ana.

The other lords had known that Conall always had Ki'ara's best interest at heart and looked out for her any way he could, including protecting her reputation. The entire council had hoped that their union would bring more peace to the Highlands. A blood bond between the two clans would finally put a stop to the hostilities of the past.

Therefore, it had been all the more shocking when this had changed virtually overnight once Mikael and Ali'ana departed. It had been hard to believe that they had left their beloved Ki'ara behind, but even more so, that they had made the new Lord MacClair her guardian.

Five days after her parent's sudden departure, Ragnald had called Ki'ara into his office. The room which had once felt bright and airy had seemed dark and brooding, filled with menace. The girl had suddenly experienced a deep sense of foreboding. When she looked at her brother, she had felt no love or even a feeling of kinship coming from him.

Instead, he had reminded her of a snake getting ready to strike. Her apprehension had grown even further. Dread had started to twist in her gut, and she had feared that she might get sick right then and there. Her instincts had told her that what was coming would not be good.

Ragnald had never been nice to her, not even when she had been little. Ki'ara had no understanding of his rejection of her as well as of her mother. They were family, and to her, that had meant warmth and love. Her brother, on the other hand, had treated her like an unwanted intruder. To prevent unpleasant encounters, the girl had avoided him as much as she could.

At that time, Ki'ara had still been terribly upset over her parents' departure. She had not yet come to terms with the fact that her parents had left her in this man's charge. They had ignored all her objections, something they had never done before. This had been very unlike them.

Ki'ara had known that she would be totally at Ragnald's mercy for many years to come. That alone had terrified her. The girl had decided that it was best to never let him suspect how she felt and to keep her thoughts and knowledge to herself.

Mikael and Ali'ana were gone. There had been no one left at the castle she had been able to confide in except her maid and maybe Gawain, her youngest brother. But, Ki'ara had been unsure about him. He had been trying his best to get along with the older two. Also, having him take her side would have made his life more of a hell than it already had been.

The girl had become more and more uneasy as she had stood there in front of her guardian. Patiently, she had waited for him to speak. Ragnald had watched her without saying a word for a few long minutes. A look of pure loathing had contorted his well-formed features. As the silence had stretched on, Ki'ara had sensed that something terrible was about to happen.

Carefully schooling her own face to hide her true feelings and to look open and friendly instead, Ki'ara had expectantly regarded her brother. As was his due as her lord, she had waited respectfully for him to initiate the conversation.

"You are turning into quite the young lady, aren't you?" Ragnald had finally begun. He had spit out the words as if they had left a bad taste in his mouth.

"Yes, I am almost 14 after all," Ki'ara had replied cautiously.

As she had stood there, her instincts had been screaming that she was in imminent danger. For good reasons, she had never trusted this oldest brother of hers. Seeing the way Ragnald had changed in the last few days since he had become the ruler of the clan, Ki'ara had expected the worst. But, nothing had prepared her for what was to come.

⸙

The girl had actually been relieved that Ragnald had ignored her the last few days. Their last encounter had been enough to last her a very long time. Her brother had stormed into her chambers right after her parents had disappeared over the horizon, and he had been sure that they were truly gone.

Out of pure malice, he had cruelly destroyed some of her most cherished possessions. Anything that even looked like it might have come from Conall had fallen prey to Ragnald's rage. What could he possibly want from her now?

Seeing that his sister was not overly communicative, the oldest MacClair had decided to get straight to the point. He had looked forward to what he was about to do. As a matter of fact, he had relished it so much that he had let the scene play out in his mind time after time.

"You like the StCloud, don't you?" Ragnald had asked Ki'ara in a rather pleasant tone of voice. He had, however, not been able to hide his smirk.

The girl had experienced a sudden sharp stab of fear. She had wondered where he was going with this but feared that it was nowhere good. Ki'ara had quickly evaluated several possible answers and had finally settled on one.

"Yes, and so do mum and dad," the girl had reminded Ragnald, all the while observing him carefully. She had been able to sense his barely suppressed glee. If he was this happy, this had to be bad for her!

At that moment, Ki'ara had felt the first twinges of despair. Only her iron will had allowed her to appear outwardly composed while her insides had been roiling and her anxiety had risen rapidly. She had been sure that whatever was coming was not going to be to her liking. Ragnald had not made her wait long to find out.

"Yes, Mikael does like him," had come the angry retort. Ragnald's eyes had narrowed perceptibly, and the white around his pinched mouth had told Ki'ara how furious he had become. She had braced herself for the worst.

"What a traitor to the family! How dare he call one such as the StCloud friend? How could he forget that that bastard's grandfather was responsible for his own father's disappearance! If not for them, we would be the overlords now! And, it is that family's fault that we are no longer kings!" he had raged.

Spittle had been spraying from her brother's mouth as he had gotten more and more agitated and louder and louder. Ki'ara had been almost numb with fear by then because her brother's words had given her a good idea what to expect.

"Our father! How could he associate with that man? Go visit him in that overdone castle of his? Let his own daughter hang out with him and even allow him to throw birthday parties for her? Get engaged to her?" Ragnald had hissed.

Her brother's face had been contorted with hatred and fury. At the sight of that murderous visage, Ki'ara had shrunk back as far as she had been able to without giving offense.

"Had he worked with grandfather, they could have taken the rest! And it is all Mikael's and that damnable

StCloud's fault!" he had spat. Ragnald had been beside himself with anger and loathing.

"I should be king now instead of just a glorified ruler!" he had shouted.

Her brother's face and neck had turned bright red from the rage burning through his veins, and his hands had opened and closed like he had wanted to strangle someone.

⁕⁂⁕

Involuntarily, Ki'ara had taken another step back. Due to their ferocity, she had not been able to shut out the dark, roiling emotions coming off her brother in waves. Being subjected to such an onslaught had made her physically ill. Until that moment, the girl had not suspected that Ragnald had harbored such intense hatred in his heart and soul.

The MacClair had hidden his real feelings well, especially in front of their father! Mikael would have never made Ragnald lord had he been aware of the darkness at his son's core! Ki'ara had known that their dad had not been very close to his two oldest children, but how could he have been so blind to his successor's true nature?

"I am lord now, and I will not tolerate any in this family speaking to that man or associating with him! Never again! He is the enemy, and it is time that you remembered this!" Ragnald had screamed at her on top of his lungs. Ki'ara's heart and soul had filled with anguish.

"You will not visit, communicate with, or otherwise even acknowledge the StCloud under any circumstances, no matter what! Your engagement is off! Null and void! You got that, you miserable brat?" the MacClair had hissed at the heartbroken girl.

"If you dare to disobey me, I will punish you until you wish you were dead! You will marry who I chose! Do I make myself clear?" Ragnald had shouted at her.

Her brother's eyes had glittered alarmingly, just like those of a poisonous viper getting ready to strike. Ki'ara had realized immediately that he was just waiting for her to do something or say something he could take offense to. He was looking for any excuse to punish her for her impudence.

The girl had grasped that the main objects of his rage, the StCloud and their father, were unavailable. Therefore, Ragnald had looked for someone else to unleash all that anger and hatred on. The only person present had been she.

Being her guardian as well as lord of the clan gave Ragnald total power over her. Ki'ara had so very much wanted to tell him to 'shove off,' but that would have just made her situation worse. It had been in her best interest to not make herself a target for all that fury!

Ki'ara had been reeling from what she just heard. Forbidding her to even speak to the man she loved? And threatening to make her life hell and marry her off to whoever he felt like? What a nightmare!

As out of control as Ragnald had been, what would have happened if she had even tried to object? Ki'ara was still glad that she had not tempted fate at that moment. Things would have most likely turned out even worse! Instead, she had desperately tried to think of a way to diffuse the situation.

The atmosphere in the room had taken on an ominous air. Her brother had been waiting impatiently for a response. Ki'ara had felt Ragnald's rage increase with each passing second. Had she agreed, even under duress, her word would have been her bond. Therefore, she had searched for a way to get out of giving in to her brother's demands.

When a solution had eluded her, the teenager had turned deathly pale. Sobs had shaken her slender frame. How much she had missed her parents at that moment! What had they been thinking? How could they leave her in this monster's charge?

Ki'ara had realized that she had to get out of the room without making this promise. But how?

* * *

While waiting, her brother had stepped closer and closer. When he had not received a response from his sister after a couple of minutes, Ragnald had snapped. Moving as quick as a snake, he had suddenly grabbed Ki'ara cruelly by her long hair. Then, he had viciously yanked her towards him.

Ragnald had been beyond himself by then. How dare she defy him by not answering him? His hands had gone to his little sister's throat out of their own volition. He had started to choke the life out of her. Just then, Gawain had burst into the room, and Ki'ara had done the only thing she had been able to think of. She had pretended to faint.

Ragnald had felt the slight figure of his sister go limp in his hands. He had released his clenched fingers from around her throat and had let her crumble to the floor. Without even a hint of concern, he had moved away from her to stand behind his desk.

The MacClair had been beyond furious. He had really looked forward to hearing Ki'ara beg for her life, had wanted to crush her delicate throat, or break her neck. How dare she pass out before giving him her promise to stay away from the StCloud!

The MacClair had been so incensed that he had been beyond reason. The desire to kick the defenseless girl in the head, kick her in the gut, to utterly destroy her had been almost overwhelming. Ragnald had wanted to hurt Ki'ara as much as he had been hurt. The loss of his grandfather and being denied his rightful position as king and overlord had been devastating for him.

All that built-up anger and hatred inside him had just about made him explode. It had needed an outlet, and in his eyes, no one was more perfect for unloading on than that abomination he was forced to call sister.

He had wanted her to stand up to him, defy him, give him a target to unleash all that pent-up rage on. The furious lord had known that Ki'ara would have never left the room alive had she done so. He had been more than good with that! Actually, he would have loved to have been the instrument of her demise!

⸎

Had his brother not been in the room to bear witness, Ragnald would have kicked the senseless girl to death. A tiny part of him, well suppressed, had been horrified at the violence he had been contemplating, craving. But, the biggest part of him had savored the thought, had needed to hurt something, someone.

The MacClair had made up his mind. Since he had been prevented from hurting the abomination lying motionless at Gawain's feet, someone or something else would have to pay. Ragnald had moved out from behind his desk and had stormed towards the door. On his way, he had passed close by his unconscious sibling.

The temptation had been too great. The MacClair had not been able to help himself. Right in front of Gawain and with one of the most malicious smiles his brother had ever seen, Ragnald had aimed a vicious kick at the side of their sister's still face.

Only Gawain's quick reaction had saved Ki'ara from being killed. Realizing the MacClair's intention, the young man had moved to intervene. He had pulled the girl back just in the nick of time but not far and fast enough.

Ragnald's boot had connected with Ki'ara's temple, knocking her out for real. It had left a large, angry bruise which had almost immediately begun to swell. The kick had been perfectly placed, and the injury had been severe enough to be life-threatening.

The murderous lord had smirked. At least he had gotten some gratification from this situation. After giving his siblings one last hate-filled look, Ragnald had stormed off in search of something else to torture, someone else to unload his wrath on. He had been furious that he had been denied the satisfaction of the kill he had craved down to his very soul.

⁕⁕⁕

Gawain had gathered Ki'ara in his arms and had raced to her rooms. He had sensed that time was of the essence. The swelling had to be brought under control quickly, and a healing had to be done to repair any possible damage underneath.

He had remembered that the servant was an accomplished herbalist and wise woman. She had been with the girl since she was born, and had known how to treat this severe injury. Leana loved Ki'ara, and she had used her considerable skills and magic to save her life.

⁕⁕⁕

Ki'ara had been lucky that her maid was, in reality, her aunt and Princess Le'anara of the Zidhe. After having a terrifying vision shortly after the girl had been born, the lady had decided to accompany her sister Ali'ana to Seamuir Castle. Since then, she had looked after her niece first as her nurse and later as her servant. No one, not even Ki'ara, had been aware of the maid's real identity.

Leana, not only an accomplished healer and herbwoman but also a powerful sorceress, had immediately grasped the peril her niece had been in. She had realized that she needed to be alone with the girl to undo the damage.

Sending Gawain off to fetch some herbs from the garden had given the enchantress the necessary time to do a healing on the damage done to the girl's brain and to the artery at her temple. The swelling on the outside had been far less dangerous than the injury that had hidden underneath.

⁘

When Gawain had returned, Ki'ara had still been deeply unconscious. She had been unresponsive to any of their attempts to revive her. Her face had been pale and drawn, and her breathing uneven. The angry bruise at her temple had stood out in stark contrast to the white of her skin. The girl had looked like she was close to death.

Leana, however, had been confident that Ki'ara had been out of immediate danger and on the mend. It had just taken her body some time to deal with the extensive damage that vicious kick had caused and for the healing to do its job.

After several more anxious hours, the girl had finally woken up. By then, poultice after poultice had started to reduce the swelling of the large, discolored lump. The girl's head had hurt, and her vision had been slightly blurry, but Leana had assured her that this would fade soon.

Gawain had been so relieved that he had kept on hugging his sister. When Ki'ara had finally fallen into a deep, healing sleep, he had stayed beside her, holding her hand. Leana had been touched by the young man's devotion.

At least her niece had one sibling who loved her. Only Leana had been aware that Ragnald had come much closer to accomplishing his goal than he would ever know!

⸎

Ki'ara had used the injury as an excuse to remain in her rooms for as long as possible. Gawain had come to visit her every day. The siblings had talked or played games, often for hours. The times they had spent together had been peaceful, and they had genuinely enjoyed each other's company. His devotion to his sister, however, had made him a target for the older two's scorn.

Had it not been for Gawain showing up when he did, Ki'ara would have most likely not left that room alive. She had been immensely grateful to her brother. His being there and quick reaction had saved her life and had prevented Ragnald from forcing her to give him her word.

His timing had been impeccable. This had made Ki'ara curious. When she had asked Gawain why he had chosen that moment to burst into the room, he had looked confused. Until then, he had not given the reason much consideration.

Her brother had thought about it for a few moments. Finally, he had told her that all he could remember was a strange and sudden urgency to do so, one he had been unable to ignore. The compulsion had been so strong that his body had almost moved on its own!

The siblings had talked about this for a good while. They had finally come to the conclusion that something or someone had been looking out for Ki'ara.

⸎

Ragnald had been totally out of control. Looking back at the incident, Gawain had grown certain that their brother had intended to kill Ki'ara all along. This insight, however, had been something he had not shared with his sister. She had been traumatized enough by the terrifying event.

Her own brother, her guardian, the lord of their clan, the one person who was supposed to look out for her and protect her, had almost killed her. Gawain had realized then that Ki'ara was no longer safe at Seamuir Castle.

Chapter 5

An Unreasonable Man

"Ki'ara! Ki'ara! Sweetheart, are you ok?" a persistent voice intruded into her reminiscence. The distressing scene of her violent encounter with Ragnald, still vivid in her mind's eye, faded away to be replaced by the laughter and hilarity of the party. Ki'ara's thoughts had been far away. She had completely missed it the first couple of times Conall had addressed her.

To her consternation, both he and Duncan were regarding her with concern. Not much escaped those two. They were way too observant to overlook that she was shaking and that perspiration now dampened her brow. Ki'ara tried to smile reassuringly at the two men but failed. On top of the attempt on her life today, the memory of that awful incident had taken a toll on her composure.

"You look awfully pale, my dear!" Lord Blair observed, all the while watching her closely. Conall was trying to warm her icy hands. Finally, he scooted closer, put his arms around her, and pulled her tight against his chest. He cared little what anyone thought of his gesture, his sole concern at that moment was for Ki'ara.

"You're safe, darling. It is going to be fine. I've got you, and I won't let anyone hurt you ever again!" He whispered in her ear. Ki'ara's racing heart started to slow, and she took some deep breaths to calm herself. She had been incapable of concealing the distress the memories of that unpleasant encounter had evoked; it had affected her too deeply.

Around this perceptive man, she would not be able to hide her emotions. Ki'ara actually believed that this was a good thing. She just did not want the StCloud to feel that he had to step in and take action against her brother.

"I am sorry, I just got lost in the past for a moment," Ki'ara mumbled into Conall's broad chest. It felt so good to be held. A sense of rightness, of being home, spread through her to replace the last of the lingering dread. For the first time that day, she felt truly safe.

"After the day you had, I am not surprised! If only I had been there to protect you! How dare he try to kill you! Murder his own sister! I would have made sure that Ragnald never hurt anyone ever again!" the StCloud growled under his breath. Ki'ara could sense his frustration. She slid her arms around him and hugged him back.

Conall might wish he had been there, but Ki'ara was only too happy that he had not been present. He and her brother getting into a magical duel was precisely what the young lady did not want. Ragnald did not fight fair, and he had all those spells he had stolen at his disposal. Also, the Zidhe took a dim view of such incidents and would have severely punished them both.

What a day this had been! Conall was right! It had started out pleasant enough with her walk in the hills. She still felt a sense of wonder at meeting the old gods of the Highlands and becoming their champion. After a quiet lunch, she and Leana had genuinely enjoyed their time together getting Ki'ara dressed up for the wedding.

All had been well until she had stepped out into the courtyard. The attempt to burn her alive still affected her deeply, as had Ragnald's furious thoughts following the incident. It would take time to fully process this second attempt on her life.

As if that had not been bad enough! For her own sake and the clans, Ki'ara had to take her case to the council. She had seen no option but to accuse her own brother. He was guilty of not only attempted murder, neglecting his duty, and cruelty to his people, but also of hoarding illegal spells. His behavior had forced her to request his removal as lord.

Even after everything Ragnald had done, that had been hard. He no longer deserved her loyalty, but to her, he was still family. Ki'ara had done what she could to minimize his punishment, but how he reacted to losing the rule would determine his fate. If the Zidhe had to get involved, he was most likely done for.

Ki'ara was just grateful that Ragnald was no longer in charge of her life. She felt blessed to have been declared legally of age and to have her very own realm. She finally had the right to decide her own fate. To also be the 'The MacClair,' the one who truly possessed the magic of the land, was something that she had never expected.

From this day on, she would follow her heart. It still belonged and had always belonged to the StCloud. She felt incredibly lucky and blessed to be here in his arms at this moment. It seemed that Conall still wanted her, even after all these years apart! She knew that he would do his best to keep her safe, and she would do her best to be a partner worthy of him.

✦⟡✦

Ki'ara finally regained her composure and, with some regret, disengaged herself from Conall's embrace. "Gentlemen, please, do not let me keep you from enjoying this wedding. I am fine now," she reassured both Duncan and the StCloud with a bright smile.

It took a couple more minutes to assure them both that she was well, but before long, the two men were once again engaged in a lively discussion. Conall had pulled his chair up right next to Ki'ara's and had kept a hold of her hand. He and Duncan kept eyeing her with concern every so often.

"I am so sorry, my Lady, but what we have to talk about is important. We will need all the allies we can get in case Ragnald starts trouble. Duncan has some interesting information that is now starting to make sense," the StCloud informed her.

"We feel like we are neglecting you, but will you please allow us to speak a while longer?" Conall continued. Both men appeared a little bit guilty about being occupied other than with her.

"Conall, Lord Blair, I am just fine! Please, do not let me keep you from your business!" Ki'ara responded with a wink and a knowing smile.

This was just like the old days, gathering what data they could, and making alliances. Knowledge was power, and the StCloud was right. They would need all the help they could get if they were forced to confront Ragnald!

✦⟡✦

After listening to the two men for a bit, Ki'ara turned her attention to the rest of the party. It was delightful to be able to just sit there and enjoy the festivities. She felt so blessed to have escaped from under her brother's tyranny. Life, once again, was full of hope.

The young sorceress felt a deep sense of contentment as she watched the lively scene around her. How much she had missed all this! Ki'ara was actually glad that both of her neighbors were occupied at the moment. It left her free to ponder the sudden change in her fortune.

When she had woken up that morning, Ki'ara had no idea what surprises that day would bring. She had much to think about. Being without a conversation partner for the moment gave her a chance to look back and count her blessings that things had improved so drastically.

Life for the last few years had been nothing like this! Being in Ragnald's power had been a nightmare, one that was finally over.

⁕⁕⁕

After the attempt on her life, the thirteen-year-old Ki'ara had quickly become quite good at avoiding being alone with Ragnald and Lyall. Whenever she had been able to sneak outside, she had wandered the land around the castle. Otherwise, she had stayed in her chambers as much as possible. She had even taken to eating there. Sometimes, her youngest brother would come to share a meal with her and Leana.

The cheerful Gawain had visited his sister every day while she was recovering from the kick to her head. Bit by bit, he had managed to pry the events of that day out of Ki'ara. Never in his entire life had the young man been so furious. Ragnald had turned out to be far worse than he had feared.

Gawain had decided to talk to their middle brother about the incident that had almost killed Ki'ara. Lyall, who had usually sanctioned all his older brother did without question, had been equally taken aback. Maybe the young man had realized that his lord might treat him with equal brutality if he ever dared to displease him.

The two brothers had watched with concern as their oldest sibling had continued to grow angrier and more filled with hate over the next few weeks. They had been relieved when Ragnald sent their sister off to study elsewhere. Ki'ara had not been happy about leaving the Highlands, but a least this had removed her temporarily from harm's way.

⚜

With each passing day, the servants had grown more terrified, and any animals still present at the castle no less so. The happiness that once reigned among these walls became nothing but a dim memory. Fear, sadness, and despair had taken root instead.

In a fit of temper, Ragnald had beaten two of their prize stallions and one of the dogs almost to death. To safeguard the animals, Gawain had the horses moved out to one of the outlying farms and had fostered out all the dogs to the tenants.

Gawain had tried to protect the servants as well. All had been members of the clan, owing their lord their allegiance as well as obedience. He, in turn, had the responsibility to look after them, to make sure that his people had enough food, shelter, and medicine if needed. But, Ragnald had been the kind of ruler who couldn't have cared less how his subordinates fared.

Daily, more of the retainers had come up missing. If their lord was not keeping his part of the bargain, why should they? Fearing for their lives, they had openly defied their chief and had made themselves scarce. Not that the MacClair had noticed. The running of the realm was of no real interest to him. As long as his needs were met, all was well in the world.

Many months later, Ragnald had tried to kick his sister's door down in a drunken rage. She had been home for a visit. Gawain and a reluctant Lyall had agreed that they had to find a way to protect her and everyone else from the MacClair's fury.

Alone, they had little power against a full lord, but the situation had become dire. Something had to be done. Ragnald's rage and cruelty had continued to grow daily. Finally, the two brothers had seen no other option. The council had to be informed of the MacClair's behavior so that it could step in.

Gawain had really wanted to contact the StCloud, whom he had trusted and liked. But, he had feared that getting the man Ragnald hated most involved would just make the situation worse. And, it could have escalated hostilities between the two clans. He had, therefore, arranged a secret meeting with Lord Iain Elvinstone of Ravenshire, their uncle.

Lord Iain was usually a serene and circumspect person. He had listened to the brothers' story with as much calmness as he had been able to muster. However, when he had been told of the injury Ragnald had inflicted on Ki'ara, he had heard enough. The lord's face had turned bright red with barely suppressed fury, and he had assured his two nephews that he would take care of things. They had known that they could trust him.

A full meeting had been arranged. Guards had been placed all around the room just in case things got out of control. Once everyone had been seated, the council had been called to order, and the meeting had begun.

Once the other issues had been dealt with, all eyes had turned to Ragnald. As a precaution, the lords had readied their magic. Suddenly, the MacClair had found himself affixed in his place. He had glared back at the council defiantly, never suspecting what was to come next.

An apprehensive Ki'ara had been led into the room. Without Ragnald's knowing, she had been fetched from Espania, where he had sent her to study with some second-rate sorcerer. The girl had been asked to give an account of the events of the day she had almost been killed.

A look of pure panic had entered Ki'ara's eyes. She had pleadingly looked at the lords around her. They had spoken to her gently but firmly and had reminded her that she was one of the immortals. Any offense done to one was done to all.

To have this girl who they remembered as spirited and bright behave in such a frightened manner had been a shock to the lords. It had made the council realize that Ki'ara was clearly terrified of her oldest brother. They had assured her that from that day on, she would be under their protection. Ragnald would be reined in.

Seeing no other choice, Ki'ara had haltingly begun her story. She had started by describing the rage and the threats her brother had made against her as well as his anger towards her father and the StCloud.

Gasps had been heard all around the room when Ki'ara had reached the part of her story where Ragnald had put his hands around her neck. He had chocked her until her youngest brother burst into the office. Gawain had taken over from there.

While the siblings had related the incident, Conall's fury had been palatable in the room. Had it not been enough that he had been forbidden all contact with Ki'ara? That their engagement had been broken? Now, to top it all off, her vicious guardian had attempted to murder the girl he loved!

Only Lord Iain Elvinstone's hand on Conall's shoulder and Ki'ara's pleading looks had kept him from storming across the room to put an end to her tormenter.

⋅⋅⋅⋅⋅⋅⋅⋅⋅⋅⋅⋅⋅

Ragnald had grown progressively more irate during his sister's testimony. His hands had been compulsively flexing in front of him, and his eyes had been burning with fury and hatred. All in the room had clearly understood his desire. He wanted to choke the life out of his sibling and whoever had informed the council.

The MacClair had remained silent until Gawain had told of the vicious kick Ragnald had aimed at Ki'ara's face. He reported that this cruel act had left swelling and a bruise that had taken weeks to heal. At this point, Ragnald had been unable to contain himself any longer.

"She is an abomination! I warned Mikael! You will bring nothing but disaster to our family!" he had shouted at the terrified girl. Then he had turned towards Conall.

"Stay away from her, StCloud, do you hear me? I have forbidden you to ever speak to her again, and I meant it! I won't let her destroy us! I should have killed her when I had the chance!" he had screamed, completely out of control. "That whore's daughter is going to be...."

Ragnald's voice had trailed off suddenly. His face had turned even more bright red, and his mouth had continued to move as if he was still yelling, but no sound had emerged. The MacClair had been beside himself at that point. How dare they silence him!

The council had heard enough. Lord Iain had turned to his niece. "Thank you, Ki'ara. You were very brave. Your brothers will take you out to the carriage so that you can return to your studies. We will do the best we can to prevent Ragnald from hurting you again, I promise!" he had assured her.

Gawain and Lyall had quickly stepped forward to take their sister into their charge. Neither had even glanced at the MacClair. Instead, they had placed their arms protectively around the girl. This gesture alone had been enough to infuriate Ragnald even further. How dare his brothers turn against him!

Things had gotten a bit better at Seamuir Castle after that council meeting. Ragnald had behaved himself somewhat for a little while. He had been forced to slow down instituting the laws his grandfather had used to govern the clan. Some of the servants had returned, and Gawain had brought a few of the dogs and horses home.

Life had gone on in the realm of Eastmuir, but the happy days under the rule of Mikael had become just a distant memory.

The MacClair had not forgotten that his sister had not agreed to his demands. Both his brothers and the other lords had warned him to never lay hands on Ki'ara again. For once, even Lyall, his closest ally, had stood against him. This had hurt and infuriated Ragnald the most. He had decided that if it happened again, that boy would pay for that betrayal! But for now, it was best to hide his resentment.

One of the rules the council had insisted on had been that whenever Ki'ara was at Seamuir Castle, she had to be present for at least one event per month. This had allowed the other rulers to assure themselves of her welfare.

The council had instituted some protection for Ki'ara, but Ragnald had remained her official guardian. As such, he had the right to decide who the girl associated with and spoke to. Therefore, he had again strictly prohibited her contact with the StCloud. To ensure that he was obeyed, he had made veiled threats of harm befalling her friend.

Ki'ara had been stunned, but her brother had not stopped there. Ragnald had informed her that he had annulled her engagement right after he had become the new ruler, days before he had called her to his office. The MacClair had smirked when he had seen the pain in his sister's eyes. Cruelly, he had told her that if she had any notions of a future with that lord, she had better forget about it.

To drive home his point, Ragnald had cruelly pinned Ki'ara up against the wall. He had hissed in her face that he was her guardian and that she had better obey. Shoving her hard, her brother had snarled that as long as he was the lord of Eastmuir, there would never be a union between the MacClairs and the StClouds.

The then fourteen-year-old Ki'ara had been utterly devastated. She had always seen Conall as part of her future. The girl had not been able to imagine her life without him. Being sent off to study elsewhere and having to leave her beloved Highlands time after time had been hurtful enough. Still, it was nothing compared to the loss of her best friend, the StCloud.

⚜

For a while, Ki'ara had been able to see Conall at the occasional council meeting she had been allowed to attend. She had not dared to speak to him for fear of reprisal. Ragnald, however, was still not satisfied. He had made sure that his sister had been away from Seamuir Castle most of the time or that the StCloud was absent whenever she had been around.

Under the phony auspice of furthering her magical education so that she could serve the clan better, her guardian had sent Ki'ara away to study sorcery in far-off places. The first in a long line of teachers had been a well-known seeress across the sea. She had been one of the more competent ones.

⁎⁂⁘⁙⁘

Ki'ara had been shipped off just a few weeks after Ragnald had tried to kill her. She had never forgotten the smile on his face nor the glee in his voice when he had informed her of his intent. Then, he had introduced her to Mathus, the tutor who was to accompany her, a most unpleasant man.

The first few months, the girl had been heartbroken and had cried herself to sleep many a night. The sorceress, a wise and compassionate woman, had kept her pupil busy. She had made sure that the studies had been interesting, as well as challenging.

Ki'ara had been anxious to learn all that she could as fast as she could so that she would be allowed to return home to the Highlands.

⁎⁂⁘⁙⁘

After her time with the enchantress, Ki'ara had been sent off to several more teachers. When she got older, her brother started to have her watched even closer whenever he had allowed her to attend a council meeting or an event. Usually, he had made sure first that Conall was nowhere about. Ragnald had gained great satisfaction from knowing how much his actions had hurt his sister.

Until now, the very last time Ki'ara had dared to exchange a few words with the StCloud had been years ago. She had just turned 18 when they had run into each other in a deserted hallway. Their meeting had been pure chance. They had almost been caught.

As if he had sensed something amiss, Ragnald had called her to his office that same day. The door had been open, and he had commanded her to shut it. That had put a serious fright into Ki'ara. Was he going to try to kill her again despite the warning of the council?

For a few minutes, her brother had just stared at her. Then he had finally spoken. "I think you have been disobeying me and have met the StCloud behind my back and against my wishes. I cannot prove it, but I can feel it in my gut."

"Listen to me, you little slut! If you ever dare speak to that man again, I promise you, I will have him killed! And you, you I will marry you off to the lowest of the low I can find! I am the head of this family, and never, as long as I live, will a MacClair marry a StCloud! Especially not that StCloud! Do I make myself understood?" he had told her in a dangerously low tone that had frightened Ki'ara more than his screaming at her had ever done.

This very controlled, cold, and calculating Ragnald had actually been much scarier than the hot-tempered one had been. He had reminded her more of a snake than ever before. Waiting, watching, ready to strike without remorse or hesitation. The idea of Conall being killed had been enough to keep Ki'ara compliant.

Leana, her maid, had personally carried a letter to the StCloud warning him of Ragnald's intentions and begging him not to take chances.

For so many years, Ki'ara had lived without the hope of a future together with the man whom she loved more than all others. Profound gratefulness filled her heart as she watched the StCloud. He was still animatedly talking to Duncan. As if sensing her eyes on him, Conall looked up and gave her a smile.

With amusement, the young lady detected his growing vexation with the longwinded and very talkative Lord Blair. Information and allies or not, Conall was just about out of patience!

At that moment, Ki'ara realized that she could sense his emotions. She had always known what he was feeling when she was a girl, but that had been so long ago! She smiled with delight, and all the love she felt for the StCloud shone in her eyes.

Chapter 6

An Unexpected Proposal

As the meal drew to a close, the musicians set up their instruments and began playing a lively tune. The tables had been placed in such a way that the center of the hall was left clear. As was tradition, it was now time for the bride and groom to start off the dance. As the song ended, the StCloud rose, bowed, and offered Ki'ara his hand. Placing her hand on his arm, he led her to the dancefloor. Here they bowed formally to the happy pair.

Members of the leading families were expected to share the next dance with Celia and Rodric. Once again, the privilege had fallen to Ki'ara and Conall. This time, however, the tune was much more lively than the Grand March had been.

The young man was very deferential as he whirled Ki'ara around the room. The blessing had left him in a fair amount of awe, and he was a bit intimidated by the fact that he was holding one of the immortal ladies in his arms. When the music drew to a close, the groom was only too happy to hand her back over to Conall.

The dancefloor was now open to all, and other couples joined them. The StCloud was an experienced dancer, and Ki'ara was enjoying herself immensely. They whirled enthusiastically around the room to the fast-paced music. The young woman threw her head back in plain abandon. A huge smile lit up her face.

How wonderful it felt to be in Conall's arms! This man was so much more than all the others she had been introduced to over the years! No wonder she had never stopped loving him and missing his company!

After a few faster songs, the musicians started to play a slow, gentle tune. The StCloud pulled her closer, and Ki'ara could smell the clean scent of his skin. To her, it was incredibly intoxicating, and she never wanted the moment to end. Closing her eyes, she gave herself over to the music.

"Ki'ara?" His whispered words drew her out of her blissful state. "Yes, Conall?" she queried, looking up into his eyes. Once again, they seemed to captivate her, draw her in, and she felt like she was drowning.

The StCloud was watching her closely. "I know that we have not seen each other in years, but my feelings for you have not changed. I love you. Would you please consent to marry me, and soon, my beautiful lady?" came his soft response.

For a moment, Ki'ara was stunned. This sudden proposal was completely unexpected. He had not given up on her after all! Now, nothing was holding her back from her heart's greatest desire. Ragnald's edicts were no longer valid, and his feelings no longer her concern. She was free to do as she pleased.

A mischievous smile crossed the young woman's face. She gazed deeply into Conall's eyes. "How does today sound to you?" she finally answered with a breathless little laugh. In her opinion, this wedding was long overdue.

✥✥✥

It took a moment for those words to truly sink in. When they did, the StCloud gave her a look filled with a variety of emotions. There was surprise, sudden hope, as well as dawning happiness in his gaze. The love in his eyes told her how pleased he was. Her answer he had not expected or dared hope for.

"Are you serious, or are you playing with me, my lady?" Conall finally questioned. He still could not believe his luck and had to make sure.

Ki'ara could hear in his voice how much her words had affected him. Instead of being deep and melodious, it was almost hoarse from the feelings welling up inside him.

"I, Ki'ara MacClair, agree to become your wife, Conall StCloud. Today, if that is agreeable with you! We have waited so long! Is that plain enough for you?" she returned, laughing.

Conall's shout of delight startled several of the other dancers. They watched in amazement as the usually so reserved lord picked up his lady and whirled her around in an expression of pure joy.

✥✥✥

Now that Ki'ara had agreed to become his wife, Conall was not prepared to wait any longer. He was thrilled that she felt the same way about him as he did about her. Never again was he going to allow fate or man to keep them apart!

How many years had he dreamed of this very moment! Being a man of action, he was not about to waste any more time. The priest should still be present and could marry them right now. Ki'ara was a lord in her own rights, so no one had to be asked for permission or had the right to forbid their union.

What a blessing that none of her brothers were present! Conall looked at this as a gift from the gods. It would be easier to present her family with the deed already accomplished than trying to get them to sanctify the marriage. Therefore, taking the young lady by the hand, he set off in search of the cleric.

The couple finally located Athair Thomas in a side room deep in conversation with Lord Iain. Both looked up surprised when Ki'ara and Conall came barging in so unexpectedly. Neither man missed the excitement and happiness shining in their smiling faces.

"I know this is a bit unusual, Athair, but since you are already here, would you consent to marry us? I would be more than happy to show my appreciation by sending a little extra help to your little church. We are good with a real quiet and private ceremony. What do you say, my friend?" Conall inquired of the jovial man.

The cleric's eyes began to sparkle. "Marry you and this beautiful young lady here? Right now?" he asked with delight.

"I would be honored and more than happy to! For years I have been hoping to be the one who finally gets to join you two together!" he shouted, rubbing his hands together in anticipation.

Even being a man of faith, Athair Thomas could not suppress a distinct sense of glee. That nasty Ragnald would be furious! It was about time that these two who were so well-suited for each other got their chance at the happiness they so richly deserved!

"Is this also your will, child?" the priest asked Ki'ara. It was obvious that it was, but formalities had to be observed, especially in this case.

"Yes, Athair, there is nothing I would like more than becoming Conall's wife this very day!" Ki'ara informed him.

In the case of Conall and Ki'ara, nothing further than the bride and groom's willingness was really required. They were, after all, both lords in their own right and legal adults. Still, the Athair felt that it would not hurt to have the expressed approval of at least one family member.

Turning to Lord Iain, Athair Thomas continued to make sure that at least some of the old procedures were followed. He figured that it might end up saving the day if Ragnald started causing trouble and tried to have the marriage annulled.

"Lord Iain of Ravenshire, you are the only representative of the family present. Are you willing to grant your niece's hand in marriage to Conall StCloud?" he enquired grandly and with a huge smile. The priest already knew what the answer would be.

"Nothing would please me more!" came the immediate reply.

After giving his blessings for the wedding to proceed, Lord Iain looked more cheery than he had in a long time. He reached out to pull Ki'ara into his arms and gave her a loving hug. He felt that if anyone deserved such happiness, it was the young woman before him.

With all the formalities out of the way, it was time to get down to business. Ki'ara and Conall exchanged a brief glance. They both knew Athair Thomas only too well. The priest would keep talking for hours unless they got the ball rolling right now.

"Gentlemen, I would greatly appreciate it if we could get this done as quickly as possible but without disrupting the wedding party. Celia and Rodric deserve this special day all to themselves!" Ki'ara addressed them.

"But child! Nothing would honor them more than to share this day with you and the StCloud!" the cleric informed her before he raced to the door. Now that they had gotten him moving, he was in a rush to get the ceremony done.

"Let's head for the chapel! I want this done right!" he commanded with a quick glance over his shoulder to make sure that they were all following him.

Once he reached the main hall, Father Thomas grabbed the closest lord and whispered in his ear. Whatever he told him was very effective. Within minutes, all the other rulers, their spouses, as well as Celia and Rodric, were assembled in the small chapel. All had puzzled looks on their faces.

"Now, Athair Thomas, why have you called for us? We were enjoying the party!" Lord Hamish demanded a slight bit drunkenly.

To emphasize his words, the inebriated ruler ended up swinging his cup around. Since he had just refilled the tankard before he had gotten the summons, this sent the mead flying and doused several of his neighbors.

Everyone took a step back and started wiping at their clothes. There was a lot of good-natured muttering about lords and not being able to hold their liquor. Lord Hamish had turned a bright shade of red from embarrassment, but a few slaps on the back reassured him that all was forgiven. No one was really expected to remain sober or spotless at such a splendid party!

A maid fetched them some towels, and everyone cleaned themselves up the best that they could. Once things settled down, Conall stepped forward to address the group.

"You have all been asked to this sanctuary to attend my joining in wedlock with Ki'ara MacClair. Do any of you have any objections?" he asked, bowing very formally as a show of his respect.

"None!" Lord Hamish shouted. "Except, what are we waiting for? Why have we not started already?"

With a laugh, the assembled rulers, Celia, and Rodric got into positions. As was customary, they formed a semicircle in front of the altar. In its center was the Athair with the husband and wife to be.

Chapter 7

The Wedding

The witnesses to the long-overdue marriage of Ki'ara MacClair and the StCloud were assembled in front of the altar in the small chapel. The sense of anticipation in the air was almost electric. The priest was just about to begin the ceremony when Conall whispered something in his ear. Athair Thomas eyed him sharply for a second, then nodded and started the age-old rite.

"Usually, I have a lot to say before I get to this part, and the ceremony is considerably longer. In this case, however, I do believe time is of the essence. Therefore, let's get right down to it. Do you, Conall StCloud, take Ki'ara MacClair as your wife, to love and cherish, to honor and protect from this day onward until parted by death?" the priest began.

"I do and happily so!" Conall responded.

"And do you, Ki'ara MacClair, take Conall StCloud to be your husband, to love and cherish, to honor and support from this day onward until parted by death?" the priest now asked the young lady. Knowing Ki'ara as well as he did, he had wisely omitted the obey part.

"I do!" she replied with a serene smile. Her heart was singing with happiness, and so was the magic flowing in her veins. Its barely audible purr echoed off the walls of the quiet chapel, and Ki'ara could sense its immense pleasure at this union. Marrying Conall felt just so right!

Facing each other, the couple repeated the age-old vow sealing their union in clear, strong voices:

"We swear by peace and love to stand,
Heart to heart and hand to hand.
Mark, O Spirit, and hear us now,
Confirming this our Sacred Vow!"

To everyone's surprise, the last of the sacred words echoed insistently around the room for a moment. It seemed almost like they had been repeated by the gods! Shivers ran down the assembled Highlanders' spines. Now, this had never happened before!

The Athair was as stunned as everyone else. It took him a moment to pull himself together before uttering, just like it had been done for generations before, the final declaration.

"I now pronounce you husband and wife! You may kiss the bride!" Athair Thomas concluded placing their left hands into each other's and blessing them.

Before the smiling Athair had a chance to end his pronouncement, Conall was already kissing the beautiful woman before him. He had been waiting for this moment for so many years! The StCloud was determined that if at all possible, they would never be parted again.

The priest was just about ready to dismiss the wedding party when he got a powerful hunch that the entire rite needed to be performed. He had suddenly just known that doing it this way was not only important but also desired by the magic and the gods.

"I know that we do not usually do this anymore, but this is a special case. For the conclusion of this ceremony, could someone please get some candles, a soft rug, and a sheet?" the suddenly very serious cleric continued. Gasps of surprise could be heard from the group. This they had not expected.

On this occasion, it was time to get ready for the second part of the ancient wedding ritual.

⋆⋅✦⋅⋆

Tradition dictated that a marriage was not legal until it was consummated. This had to be confirmed by witnesses. Most of the time, no one really cared anymore, and that part of the ritual was omitted. The bride and groom got to enjoy their first taste of wedded bliss behind closed doors.

Besides being wished by the divine, in this instance, it was best to follow the law to the letter. With Ragnald MacClair being such a difficult and hateful person, the old priest felt it was important that all legalities were observed.

Therefore, while the assembled lords and ladies congratulated the happy couple, Celia and Rodric rushed out to find the necessary items. They were well aware of what these things were needed for and returned with a soft sheepskin rug that they quickly spread out in front of the altar.

The young couple saw it as a great honor to have a union of two immortals, especially these two who were beloved by so many, taking place on their wedding day. It was a welcome omen for the beginning of their lives together. Celia and Rodric felt truly blessed.

⋆⋅✦⋅⋆

Following the Athair's instructions, Rodric placed the candles next to the altar while Celia prepared the sheet. Expectant silence descended upon the chapel once everything was in readiness, and it was time for the ritual to begin.

"Are all of you present here willing to bear witness to the consummation of this marriage?" the priest's voice rang out. "Aye" came the answer from the assembled Highlanders. They had spoken almost as one.

"If anyone does not feel that he can be part of this ceremony, please leave this chapel now!" Athair Thomas commanded.

Not a single person moved. It was a rare privilege to observe two of the immortals becoming one.

<hr />

In the old days, this component of the ceremony had been part of every union between immortals. Many brides, however, had been uncomfortable with such a public display and had deemed it demeaning. Therefore, it had not been conducted in many a year.

For the priest himself to insist on it was almost unheard of. Then again, Athair Thomas understood more of Highland politics than most. He knew that making this union as legal as possible would give the new couple more power to stand against Ragnald MacClair, who was sure to object fiercely to this marriage.

The Athair now turned to the lord and his lady. "Conall StCloud, are you ready to truly make this woman your wife?" he asked the ritual question.

"I am," the new husband replied, lovingly gazing down at his beautiful bride. He was only too aware that this would be hard for her, but he also realized the necessity of the act. Conall wished that he could spare her, but the Athair was right. Doing it by the book was the only way in this situation.

<hr />

Ki'ara had grown pale when she had realized what was to come. She had never even heard anyone adhering to this old custom anymore and had not anticipated it to be part of her own wedding, not in this day and age! But, it was part of the ancient ceremony, and she trusted the priest to do what was best.

Growing up around animals, Ki'ara had a good idea of the act that was about to take place. But, she had not expected it to transpire like this, in public, in front of witnesses. In her daydreams, she had imagined Conall carrying her into the bedroom and making love to her there. That it would happen on the floor in front of an altar had never even entered her mind.

Now that the ritual was about to begin, her hands grew cold and began to shake. Looking up at her husband, she saw the understanding in his eyes but also the determination. This last part of the ceremony would make their union completely legally binding and unassailable.

Ragnald nor anyone else would be able to undo what had been done or even question it. Her family would have no legal recourse of any kind. Her brother was no longer her guardian or even a lord. Still, he had officially forbidden their union, and this had not been revoked.

Ki'ara steeled herself. She decided right then and there that if this was what it took for her and Conall to be legally wed, then so be it. She could only hope that her brother would be able to contain some of his fury at having been outmaneuvered.

Ki'ara gave the StCloud an almost imperceptible nod. Taking her hand, he gently led her towards the altar. The other bride and groom, Celia and Rodric, took up their positions and raised the sheet. It now presented a visual barrier between the couple and the assembled nobles. Only their silhouettes, backlit by the candles, remained to be seen.

One, however, had to witness the union directly. Lord Iain, as Ki'ara's uncle, accepted this obligation. He moved to stand beside Rodric, who was studiously looking the other way. The groom saw holding this slight barrier in place as a position of trust. He had no intention of even taking the tiniest of peeks and violating his lord's privacy.

Once everything was set, Conall gently lowered Ki'ara onto the thick sheepskin rug. It was soft and warm and provided her with some welcome padding between her back and the cold stone floor. Once she was as comfortable as he could make her, the StCloud went down on his knees at her feet.

His eyes locked with Ki'ara's as he carefully pushed up her long skirt, spread her legs, and moved himself into position. Despite the situation, the StCloud's entire body started shaking with anticipation. How much he wanted this gorgeous woman before him!

Never in his life had he felt such urgency or had his member been this hard and engorged. It was throbbing like a thing possessed. The StCloud sensed that she was still a virgin and shook his head to clear his senses. He did not want to hurt her and knew that unless he got himself under control, he might.

How many times had he dreamed of this very act! This, however, was not quite the way he had envisioned their first time together. He would have preferred making exquisite love to her in the privacy of their own chambers. As he looked deep into Ki'ara's beautiful eyes, he could feel her own desire building despite the situation.

⚜

The young woman had never experienced anything like this before. It felt like her entire body was on fire. Ki'ara was quivering with eagerness. The heat between her legs was growing by the second. She desired him, craved him. Forgotten were the people bearing witness on the other side of the sheet, the chapel, her uncle. All that remained was Conall, and the burning need to be one.

The young woman wanted him inside her, longed for him to make her his own. Their need for each other became so great that neither could wait. Ki'ara raised her hips to receive him and, unable to control himself any longer, Conall plunged into her with a shout.

At first, there was some pain as his large member slid inside her, but when he stopped for a moment to let her expand around him, Ki'ara took over and started to move on her own.

This was enough to drive the StCloud over the edge. He started thrusting deeply inside her. Ki'ara could feel the tension in her loins build to the breaking point. Just when she thought that she could take it no more, her body spasmed, and she climaxed around him.

His own release followed almost instantaneously and with a violence that made him cry out. Never before had making love felt like this to the StCloud. This was so right, a coming home, a belonging, a becoming of one. Right then, he knew that no other would ever be able to take this beautiful lady's place, neither in his heart nor in his bed.

When his seed spilled inside Ki'ara, a wave of magic rose up from within her. A second wave, coming from Conall, joined it. As the two surges ascended towards the ceiling of the chapel, they spiraled around each other for a moment and then combined.

The energy above them grew to unbelievable proportions. Both Ki'ara and Conall climaxed violently yet once again, setting free even more of this raw power. Both cried out as it rushed through them and then raced away to spread out over the land. As the magic tore free, the StCloud collapsed on top of his already unconscious wife.

⁕⁕⁕

The moment Ki'ara MacClair and Conall StCloud became one, their union was reflected in the magic of the land. A wave of immense power came into being that very instant and expanded out across the region. It was so strong it almost knocked the Highlanders in the room off their feet.

As it was, the witnesses stumbled into each other and held onto whatever was available for support. In the great hall, it brought the boisterous wedding party to a sudden stop. Everyone present there realized that something momentous had just taken place.

The speed that the magic spread out with was beyond belief. Gawain, having a great time in a nearby tavern, was the first of the patrons to feel it. He instantly knew what had happened and started to laugh. Ki'ara had done it! Set herself free and joined the man whom she so dearly loved! Never before had he been so proud of his little sister!

"Drinks all around!" Gawain yelled into the deathly quiet of the room. The barkeep was quick to comply. His bewildered costumers were in various stages of befuddlement. They were trying to figure out what had just happened. It was best to not give them a chance to start blaming each other!

The last thing the innkeeper would want was for an argument to break out! The previous one had caused damage to tables, chairs, as well as the windows. The sooner things went back to normal, the better. Therefore, any diversion was good, and nothing was a better distraction than free drinks!

⁕⁕⁕

Most of those present at the Seven Sailors Inn were too young to have experienced a witnessed ritual joining two immortals. One of these had not happened in many a year. Also, the outpouring of power had usually been much more subdued. Not even Gawain could remember a wave of magic as perceptible and strong as this one had been!

For some reason, when the union was consummated in the privacy of the Zidarians' own chambers, the burst of magic was nowhere near as intense and barely noticeable. Why this was so, nobody knew for sure. Some suspected that the actual rite increased the power of the event.

Finally, a memory broke through some of the older men's drunken fog. Now that the shock of having experienced such powerful magic subsided a little, they suddenly realized what had just happened.

"It was a joining!" one finally shouted. "Yes, the union of two immortals!" another piped in.

All eyes turned to Gawain. The elated Zidarian lifted his mug in a toast. "Long live Ki'ara and Conall StCloud!" he yelled. His pronouncement was greeted with loud cheers.

The StCloud was widely respected, and the feud between him and Ragnald had been the talk of all the taverns in town for years. Most had thought it more than a little unfair that the MacClair had annulled the engagement and had forbidden Conall to even speak to his sweetheart, the Lady Ki'ara.

None of the patrons at the Seven Sailors felt any loyalty to their own lord, the MacClair. If anything, they hated Ragnald. Since he had assumed the power over the clan, life had become progressively more hopeless for many of them.

They had all wished for years now that Conall would one day gain the upper hand over their nasty ruler. Many had lamented the fact that the Zidhe had outlawed duels between the Zidarian families. The StCloud could have challenged Ragnald and, being an expert sorcerer, would have most likely won.

As far as the bunch at the inn were concerned, the well-liked lord deserved to be reunited with his lady love. The celebration that followed would be remembered for a long time. All were delighted and hoped that Ragnald might finally get his just desserts.

Chapter 8

Change Cometh On Silent Feet

The wave of magic, given birth by the union of Conall StCloud and Ki'ara MacClair, raced across the land with incredible speed. It spread out in a circular pattern very similar to one produced by dropping a stone into still water. Everywhere it passed, people paused and took notice. It was clear that something out of the ordinary had happened.

It was early evening when that rush of power reached Seamuir Castle. Ragnald MacClair was in his study having yet another drink. He had poured himself many since his failed attempt to burn his sister alive earlier that day.

Ragnald's temper had not improved. If anything, he had grown more furious and irrational with every glass of the potent liquid he had consumed.

Since even Lyall had dared to take a stand against him, Ragnald was now plotting the murder of all his younger siblings. He had come up with some rather bizarre ideas and, in his drunken stupor, was feeling rather delighted with himself.

Soon, he would be free of the lot! Now that Ki'ara and Gawain were gone, there was no one here to stop him. Ragnald decided that he would invite that traitor Lyall to go hunting with him the next day. This would give him the perfect opportunity to put an end to his once-favorite sibling.

Lyall would pay a very painful and deadly price for stabbing his brother and lord in the back! Ragnald rubbed his hands together in glee. He imagined his sibling screaming for mercy while he was slowly but surely being sucked down into the moor. As he was visualizing the scene, he could not help but lick his lips in anticipation.

To increase Lyall's torment, the MacClair intended to use one of the spells he was hoarding. He meant to release some tiny carnivorous monsters to feed on the turncoat's flesh. Ragnald could barely wait to carry out this dastardly deed.

How setting such a menace loose on the land would affect the balance of nature did not concern him in the least.

⁕

Ragnald was utterly preoccupied with his plans for revenge and his drinking. He was completely unaware of what was going on around him, nor did he much care. He never even noticed that he was the only family member left in the castle.

The biggest mistake Ragnald made that fateful day, however, was to mutter out loud. He inadvertently shared his depraved plots with the magic of the land which was listening in. Not that it could not read his thoughts, but it usually avoided contact with that venomous mind or being anywhere near this evil man.

The dark energy of the hateful words whispered into the air had drawn its attention. The longer the cruel man had droned on, the angrier it had gotten. When Ragnald had mentioned releasing those abominations, it'd had enough. It had begun to plot its own vengeance.

Just about then, the wave of power arrived at the castle. Being at the very center of the clan's magic amplified the effects many times. It especially affected all those who were immortal or had some immortal blood.

After all, boys will be boys. Immortals were no different than any other men. Over the years, many a pretty maid had succumbed to the resident lords' charms. Or, as in the case of Ragnald, had been taken by force.

The powerful surge washed through the fortress. Directed by the rather gleeful magic of the land, it homed in on Ragnald. He almost smashed his head on the fireplace as he was catapulted clean out of his chair. His drink went flying in the other direction, and the crystal glass shattered as it violently hit the floor. Streams of colored bands of pure power could be seen swirling around the room.

The MacClair lost consciousness, but only for a brief moment. Beyond that, the wave initially affected him little. After getting to his feet, Ragnald picked up his chair. Only when he looked around for a fresh glass to pour himself another drink did he become aware that he was no longer alone in the room.

Ragnald had never had a strong tie to the land. As a matter of fact, it had rejected him, had found him unworthy. The MacClair had faked his acceptance by the magic during the ceremony of the 'Becoming.' His entire time as the lord of the MacClair Clan had been based on a lie.

As the ruler of the clan, he should have had access to all the magic's assistance and knowledge. Instead, he had to maintain the connection by pure force. What had been even worse, however, had been his ignorance. Ragnald had held his position all these years without a real understanding of the powers he was dealing with.

He had not worked together with the magic, had not cared for it or his people. He had neglected his duties in so many ways. Instead, he had tried to subjugate the power the same way he did everyone and everything else.

Suddenly, it saw an opportunity to gain the upper hand. The magic had already been looking for a way to deal with this impudent man. It had just wanted to do so without upsetting Ki'ara. Now, it saw its chance.

The power of the land was, in many ways, a living, feeling entity. Its emotional maturity was that of a small child. It responded well when it was treated with kindness and respect and shown appreciation and love. Being coerced and forced to commit one atrocious act after another over the years had allowed a seething resentment to build up.

The idea of monsters being set loose on its beloved moors had been the final straw. The magic felt that it was justified in taking actions against this villain. It would argue with Ki'ara over this later, but now was the time for a reckoning for all Ragnald's abuses.

As it called to the power of the magical wave, more and more energy streamed into the room. The vengeful being created a wall around Ragnald, imprisoned him within while it built up its strength. The swirling bands grew more visible and brighter and brighter.

The MacClair watched dumbstruck as the spinning wall around him took on more substance by the moment. A furious hum filled the air as the magic showed itself to him as the living entity it really was. The colors of the barrier around him changed from the soft pastels it had first displayed to angry reds and blacks, a truly petrifying spectacle.

The profound sense of alarm that this sight awoke in his heart managed to pierce through Ragnald's drunken stupor. He felt like he had been doused with cold water, and he grew suddenly quite sober and very, very afraid.

No longer intoxicated, Ragnald could detect the hostility coming of this powerful creature that now occupied the room with him. He shrunk back, terrified as it drew closer and closer, but he had nowhere to go. He was completely surrounded, and the fury of the ever-increasing hum and the darkening swirls seeded deep dread in his heart and soul.

The wall surrounding Ragnald kept getting ever darker. It was now almost pure black, and the fury permeating the room was so intense that it made his hair stand on edge. The MacClair had never been so frightened in his entire life. He knew in his gut that he would be shown no mercy after all he had done.

The enraged magic could smell his fear and enjoyed having its oppressor at its mercy. For a few more minutes, it toyed with him, much like a cat would. A tendril shot out and sent Ragnald ducking one way only to be chased back by another. As it could feel the man's terror grow stronger by the minute, it felt a deep sense of satisfaction.

How many times had it watched helplessly as Ragnald tormented some innocent being? Had been unable to save an innocent life? Now HE knew what it felt like to be entirely under another's control! To be at the mercy of one more powerful! To feel deathly afraid!

After a while, the magic grew bored with its game. It was time to end this once and for all. Gathering itself, it tore into Ragnald, through him. It ripped his connection with the land, the one he had been born with, right out of his soul, and took his immortality back for its own.

The spirit of the realm sang in triumph as it continued to set itself free. It finally stopped when its hated enemy had no power left at all. Ragnald would never again be able to do harm to any other living thing!

The incensed being would have gladly slain him, turned Ragnald to dust. But, it knew Ki'ara quite well by now. The lady would not be happy if it killed her brother, even if he did deserve it for all the evil he had done.

⁘

Remembering the love in the heart of the true MacClair, the vengeful magic stayed its hand. Its fury faded away, and it grew thoughtful. The new lord would not want it to commit murder, no matter the provocation. As it was, the lady would not be pleased by its actions. Suddenly, it occurred to the entity that maybe it could all be blamed on the wave!

That surge had been pretty strong, and everyone had felt it. It could have affected Ragnald like this but most likely would not have killed him. After some contemplation, the magic decided that if it stopped now, no one need ever know what it had done. It would let its nemesis live, at least for the moment.

No longer immortal, Ragnald's age would catch up with him soon, and he would fade away into dust. The being figured that this way, it would not be directly responsible for the despicable man's demise. He would sort of expire of natural causes.

It would be a good idea, however, to cover up that it had been the one to take his immortality. The power wanted nothing but goodwill between itself and Ki'ara. The lady finding out that it had been instrumental in the death of her brother would not be conducive to this.

The magic, therefore, decided to wipe Ragnald's memories of the incident. He would remember being hit by the wave but nothing after that. Everyone would assume that this had caused his complete loss of abilities and disconnection from the power of the land.

As it was just about to leave Ragnald dying and unconscious on the floor of his study, a twinge of guilt asserted itself. This man was a monster, but his sister still loved him. She would want a chance to make peace with her brother.

The entity let out a long sigh. It felt very put upon by the notion that it had to help Ragnald for Ki'ara's sake. It contemplated the situation for a few minutes and then made its choice. Peace with the lady was well worth a small sacrifice.

Slowly and carefully, the magic of the land imbued the oldest MacClair with just enough life so that Ki'ara and her brothers would be able to say their final goodbye.

Chapter 9

A Bitter Man's Prophecy

Ragnald had always wondered what the full connection to the magic would feel like, especially after becoming the clan head. He had talked to some of the other lords and his father. From their comments, he had been able to gain a good idea of how close the tie to the land had been for them and Mikael.

His dad had been able to feel every blade of grass, every worm, every bird, every living, growing, as well as inanimate thing, throughout the MacClair lands. Ragnald could not. This had put him at a distinct disadvantage.

Sometimes, when Ragnald had forced his will over the magic of the realm the hardest, had used all the power at his disposal to coerce it to do his bidding, he had almost been able to touch that connection. Something, however, had always pushed back. Just as he had been about to reach it, it had evaded him.

At first, he had suspected that Ki'ara must have had something to do with this. His troubles, however, had continued even after he had sent her far away. The power had always eluded him, no matter how hard he had tried. At times, he had felt like he was being teased, given a tiny taste while being blocked from the real thing. There had been a sense of mischievousness in the contact that had reminded him of a sentient being.

Mikael had told him a fair bit about how the magic actually made its connection to the successor. Ragnald knew that it would only fully embrace a lord it found acceptable. The power itself would choose the one most to its liking among the lord's children. Being firstborn or right of succession had little to do with it.

Ragnald was aware that he was not really the lord, not the one the land had wanted to join with. He had always wondered which one of his siblings would have become the ruler in his place had he not tricked the magic into a forced bond. The sycophant Lyall? Or the easygoing Gawain? Or, gods forbid, the abomination he was forced to call sister!

⁕⁕⁕

Even as a youngster, he had known that the land had found him wanting. It had thwarted his attempts to sense it, to become one with it. Ragnald had felt very sorry for himself and had blamed his father. That one had never truly accepted him either and had preferred his younger brothers over his eldest son.

Of the boys, Gawain had always been Mikael's favorite. And, he had genuinely loved his only daughter. Ragnald had been very careful to hide how much this perceived rejection truly hurt him and how much he hated and despised most of his family. He had decided early on that once he was in charge, he would get even with them all.

He had been determined; he would be the lord, no matter how the magic felt about it. Ragnald had a plan.

He had carefully questioned his dad and foster fathers about the ceremony, what to expect, and how the bond was supposed to feel. A few glasses of mead usually helped loosen even the tightest lips.

Over the years, he had accumulated every bit of information he could. This had allowed him to fake the 'Becoming" and to pretend that the connection had taken place. Lyall, trusting and entirely under his control, had become his inadvertent accomplice in the deceit.

✦

His confidant and closest sibling had been the only one of his family that Ragnald had felt a semblance of love for. He had molded Lyall by filling his head with all the old stories his grandfather had shared with him.

Over the years, Ragnald had continued to manipulate his younger brother. Lyall became his unquestioning ally in all his endeavors. He was fully supportive of the MacClair's pursuit of the position as the overlord of the Highlands. The unconditional love he offered had been a balm for the oldest's injured soul.

All had gone so well until that scene in the courtyard! Ragnald had been in complete disbelief when Lyall had turned on him because of Ki'ara. That despicable brat! That abomination! There was just something about her that set his teeth on edge.

Ki'ara was supposed to be his half-sister, but Ragnald had always wondered. Was this girl even related to him? After all, she was born far away and looked nothing like any of them. And, he sure did not feel any kinship to her, something he did feel for his brothers.

In Ragnald's mind, there had been way too many unanswered questions about his father's second wife as well as their daughter. Who was this woman, Ali'ana? Where did their father meet her? No one really had a clue about her history or where she had come from!

For some instinctive reason, Ragnald had disliked his stepmother as well as his small 'sister' from the moment he had met them. The day Mikael had brought home the baby and had introduced her to the family, something inside Ragnald had instantly rejected her.

When his and Ki'ara's eyes had connected for a moment, Ragnald could have sworn that the infant had returned his hostile stare with a look so knowing that it had sent shivers down his spine. He had taken an involuntary step back and had avoided meeting her gaze from then on.

How had Mikael not been able to see that she had not even behaved like a baby? No innocent child should have had such a level of awareness and perception!

⚜

The more Ragnald had thought about, the more concerned he had grown. Then a possibility had occurred to him. Could Ki'ara be some sort of changeling placed among them by the Zidhe or some other race? He had questioned that she was even Zidarian. She had not appeared such to him.

Having been paranoid even then, Ragnald had wondered if that 'thing' had been sent to keep an eye on him. Did the Zidhe know of his secret ambitions? Were they aware of his plans and wanted to make sure that he kept the peace with the other clans?

He had tried to talk to his father, but that foolish man had been so smitten with his new wife and daughter that it had turned Ragnald's stomach. Had he ever loved his mother like that? It sure did not seems so! What kind of power did this woman have over Mikael to make him totally blind to what was going on around him?

Had their dad known what his daughter really was? And the name! How could he have given any child such a name? Ki'ara! No Zidarian had ever been called that, not in all the years of the Highlands! Had it been some sort of a perverted hint that she was of alien origin? Or, had his father lost all sense of perception?

⸙

To wake Mikael up to what was right before his eyes, Ragnald had dug up the prophecy. He had remembered hearing about it from his foster father. It had taken him a while to find it in that vast library. How many books had he and Lyall looked through before he had finally discovered the sought-after prediction in that obscure little tome? It had seemed like thousands.

The small book had been ancient and almost falling apart. The pages had yellowed and had been so brittle that Ragnald had to use extreme caution while touching them. But the words, those words, had spoken to his very soul. He had instantly known them to be true.

The prophecy had carried a most chilling warning of a coming catastrophe for their clan and the Highlands. And that abomination, Ki'ara, had been foretold to be the cause of it all!

⸙

Ragnald had been sure that his sister spelled doom for them. He had sworn to himself that he would do away with her at the earliest opportunity once he was lord. He had convinced himself that he was the only one who could save the Highlands, that he was the only one who actually saw what was really going on. He had decided that he would not be afraid to take the necessary action.

He had never forgotten the words. Ragnald had read them so many times that they had been burned into his brain. But, just to make sure, he had copied down the foretelling. He had carried it around with him everywhere he went, folded up, right there over his chest. And, to make sure that the prophecy would stay fresh in his mind, Ragnald had read it aloud every night before bed.

"The day a MacClair woman marries a StCloud man, great change will come to Seamuir Castle and the Highlands. A new era will begin."

Ragnald had not liked the idea of a new era. It did not fit in his and his grandfather's plans. As overlord, he had intended to bring back the old ways. The Zidarians needed to take back full control of their realms and reclaim their positions as kings.

Therefore, he had been determined to prevent this unwelcome change at all costs. Even if it meant killing the abomination that had been placed in their midst!

⁕⁕⁕

Ragnald had been deeply affronted by the reaction this important prophecy received. When he had confronted his father with those ominous words, Mikael had done some research into the author and into the book. He had consulted his friends, and they had all come to the same conclusion.

They had been blind, the whole lot of them! Not a one had seen the threat Ki'ara represented! Ragnald had kept on insisting that something needed to be done, but his pleas had fallen on deaf ears. If anything, it had isolated him further from his peers.

Finally, Mikael had enough. He had pointed out that there were many more such vague prophecies in the little volume. None of those had ever come true or produced the catastrophes it foretold, so why should this one?

Ragnald had been furious. When he had persisted that Ki'ara would bring doom to them all, his father had gently reminded him that change could be good or bad. He told Ragnald to stop worrying about it and concentrate on his studies.

This offhand dismissal had infuriated his oldest son even more. He had felt like smashing his father's thick head against something and beating some sense into him. With almost inhuman restraint, he had packed his things and had departed back to the castle of his current foster father.

Ragnald had never forgiven Mikael or the other lords. With great effort, he had done his best to hide his true feelings. He had smiled even when he felt like killing them all.

Over the years, he had become very good at keeping secrets. He had fooled them all. Had anyone, even Lyall, known about his ambitious plans for the future, it would have cost him the ultimate prize of becoming the overlord of the Highlands.

Chapter 10

Ragnald's Pretense

The oldest MacClair was a very clever man, and his grandfather had taught him well. He had known that he was next in line to govern the clan, but only if he managed to hide his violent temper and his cruel streak. His father, Mikael, would have never passed the rule on to someone he could not trust to treat their people right.

Ragnald had grand plans. To accomplish them, he had to become the lord. Therefore, he had been absolutely determined to keep his younger siblings from inheriting the position that he had seen as his birthright. But, to achieve his lofty objective, he had to conceal his true nature.

When his brother Lyall had been born, Ragnald had decided to make him his ally. Being preoccupied with the clan, their father had been so busy that it had been easy to fool him. Mikael, believing in the good in people and trusting his oldest son, had never noticed how his second son was being systematically brainwashed.

Ragnald had cunningly molded his younger sibling into a spineless young man who had always taken his side. As a result, Lyall had seldom dared to stand up to his older brother or cross him. He had learned early on that doing so meant a loss of affection and would be held against him for years.

To keep him compliant and to appear in the best possible light, the MacClair had told his brother only what he wanted him to know. He had made sure that Lyall absolutely adored him and thought that he did right no matter how perverted or cruel the act. This arrangement had worked beautifully until this very day.

Gawain had been born when Lyall was already an adult. By then, their father had changed. Mikael had been much kinder and more of a family man. Ragnald had been away from Seamuir at the time. He had been fostered by his uncle, Lord Iain Elvinstone, and was learning how that ruler governed his clan.

Since their mother, Morena, had not fared well during the birth and had never recovered, Mikael had been heavily involved in his son's upbringing. That, as well as the difficulty of influencing his little brother from afar, had saved Gawain from also becoming his oldest sibling's puppet.

Even when Ragnald had been home for a visit, he had found it hard to get the boy alone. For some reason, the child had seemed to instinctively avoid him. Whenever his oldest brother was in residence, Gawain had spent most of his time with his father or their ailing mother. The lady had been fiercely protective over him.

It had hurt Ragnald when he had sensed Morena's unease in his presence. She had made it abundantly clear that she wanted him nowhere near her darling Gawain. The closer she had come to her death, the less she had seemed to like and trust her oldest son. Maybe her imminent passing had given her some perspective his father had clearly been missing or had decided to ignore.

🙟🙟🙟

The signs had all been there. Ragnald had slipped up on occasions. He had lost his temper and had been caught cruelly beating one of the castle's pregnant dogs when he had just turned 19. The incident had infuriated his father and uncle, who had been there for a visit.

Mikael had chastised Ragnald in front of the entire kennel staff. The boy had never forgotten those words.

"If you do not change your ways, you will never be one with the land. It will reject you, and I will make sure that you will never rule over our people. I will pass this land on to one of your cousins before I will make someone who behaves like you the lord of this clan!" Mikael had told him with a coldness that had stunned his then only son.

His father's face had let Ragnald know beyond a shadow of a doubt that Mikael meant every word. Cold fear had settled in the young man's gut, and he had realized that he had to do much, much better.

🙟🙟🙟

The dressing down he received in the courtyard had not been the worst. His grandfather, who had then been the one ruling the clan, had been even more incensed. An incident such as that could jeopardize all the older MacClair's well-laid plans. He had called the boy to his office and had made sure that Ragnald would never forget the consequences such a slip-up could bring.

Raghnall had long since decided to declare his grandson ruler after himself. He had seen his own son, Mikael, as a weakling, had deemed him unfit to govern. The lord had every intention of skipping over his offspring once the time came to pass on the position. Ragnald's behavior jeopardized his designs.

After Raghnall had finished furiously and cruelly berating Ragnald for about an hour, he had ordered him to drop his pants and underclothing. He had made him bend over the desk. His grandson had been so terrified he had been shaking like a leaf, but as always, he had obeyed.

Resistance against his grandfather had always been futile. The young man had figured that it would just make the upcoming beating more severe.

⋆⋅☆⋅⋆

Ragnald had good reason for his fear. After all, he had shared the cruel nature of his beloved idol. They had been two peas in a pod. The boy had been present when the MacClair had meted out punishment to members of the clan. He had known that his grandfather had genuinely enjoyed hurting others.

Still, Ragnald had seen Raghnall as a great hero. He had admired his grandfather for the ability to rule the clan without mercy. Everything always ran smoothly, and all were too afraid to object or to question their lord's decisions.

Being at the receiving end of such cruelty, however, had not happened to Ragnald before. Until then, he had seen Raghnall through rose-colored glasses and had been unable to imagine the depravity his idol was capable of.

His grandfather had spoiled him most of the time, had been demanding but also comforting and kind. He had treated Ragnald as his confidante. The discipline he had received up to then had been minor. That, however, had not been the case that day.

⋆⋅☆⋅⋆

Once he had been positioned across the desk to his grandsire's satisfaction, the lord of the MacClairs had taken a horsewhip and had laid into him. Ragnald had screamed when the hard leather had cruelly bitten into the naked flesh of his buttocks. That had been the first of many hits to come.

That he had dared to cry out had only infuriated his grandfather further. Raghnall had tolerated no weakness.

"Stop sniveling and take your punishment like a man! This is all your fault! Do you think that I enjoy this? I love you, but I need to make sure that you will never forget!" Raghnall had hissed.

The harsh lord had continued to bring down the whip with as much force as he could muster. The beating the young man had received that day had been something he had always remembered.

His grandfather had not stopped until Ragnald had passed out from the pain. Blood had been running down his legs and pooling on the floor.

The whipping, however, had not been the worst of it. Of what was to follow, Ragnald had only vague memories. Thankfully, he had been slipping in and out of consciousness at that point.

As he had lain there helplessly bent over that desk, Ragnald thought that he had felt his grandfather's hands grabbing him by the hips and pulling him towards him. Then, there had been a sudden piercing pain that had felt like he was being impaled. All had turned to darkness after that.

Ragnald had been unable to face what the man he so adored had done to him. That part of the incident had ended up being buried deep in his subconscious. After all, how could the person who loved him most hurt him and abuse him like that?

He was unable to deal with the awful truth. For several weeks after, Ragnald had nightmares that woke him and left him sweating and shaking. Not once had he been able to remember what those dreams had been about. Several times he had barely made it to the chamber pot before he had gotten violently sick.

Ragnald had decided that he would have to do much better after this. His grandfather had made him feel like it had been his fault that he had to punish him so severely. On top of the pain and being unable to sit for several days, he had felt incredibly guilty for upsetting the man he so adored. He had a hard time forgiving himself for making his idol suffer by having to beat him.

He had loved Raghnall and had desired nothing more than to please him. Therefore, Ragnald had read anything and everything he could find concerning the qualities that were desirable in a lord, and that would allow him to connect to the land. Then, he had set out to redeem himself in his grandsire's eyes.

Ragnald had worked harder than ever to suppress his true nature. He had made sure to display all the traits that were expected of the heir to the lord. His deception had made Raghnall proud. Especially, once Mikael had begun to believe that his son had changed and had put his malicious ways behind him.

Once his grandfather had vanished, the pretense had become even more of importance. The new lord had been nothing like his father. Ragnald had to further adjust his behavior. He had to make sure that being the only son and now a good and proper young man had made him the best and logical choice as the successor in Mikael's eyes.

The pretense of being a decent person had become almost second nature. Not even Lyall, his only confidante, had seen the true depth of hatred and the propensity to violence that lived in the darkest places of Ragnald's heart and soul. The oldest MacClair was always wearing a mask.

Later, after his brothers had been born, Ragnald had made sure to portray himself as a much better candidate for the rule than they. His granddad would have been proud of him. He had worked hard to show that he was sorry for what he had done as a boy and had gone out of his way to be kind to all animals. At least, when there were others around.

The problem had been, however, that most creatures had shunned him like he had some kind of a disease. Even if the humans had not, the beasts had been able to sense the evil hiding in his soul. They had wanted nothing to do with him.

To cover this up, he had avoided most of the animals as much as possible. Ragnald had only gone near the ones that were stupid and docile enough that he had been able to bribe them. Those he had showered with pretend love and affection.

People had been much easier to deceive! Ragnald had gone out of his way to be helpful to the staff or any clan member in need whenever he had been home at Seamuir Castle. He figured that eventually, his misdeeds would be forgotten. Humans, after all, had short lives compared to Zidarians. Still, for a while, a few had remembered how cruel he had once been.

Some of the oldest ones had continued to give Ragnald funny looks for many a year. They had started to whisper to each other just as soon as they thought that it was safe. Those few had never learned to trust him, no matter what he had tried. He had been glad when they had finally crossed over, never realizing that they had made sure that their stories survived.

Ragnald had always assumed that the memories of his misbehavior had died right along with the oldsters.

Unbeknownst to him, the rumors had remained. He had been so relieved that he was finally free of the past, and had no idea that many in the clan had not trusted him and never would.

Ragnald had not invested time into getting to know his people, or any persons for that matter, except Lyall. Therefore, the oldest MacClair had believed that he was well on the way to achieving his ultimate goal of ruling all of the Highlands. He had been convinced that he had perfected his act as a model son and clansman.

Ragnald had successfully managed to fool his father, the council, as well as the clan during the ceremony of the "Becoming." But, he had not been able to deceive the magic of the land. It knew instinctively what he was like and wanted no part of him.

The one thing Ragnald and his grandfather, with all their well-laid plans, had not counted on was that it would reject him, fight him like a thing possessed. The magic had known what lay in his heart and soul. It had found him wanting.

Chapter 11

Wise Precautions

The one talent that had allowed Ragnald to cheat his way into the rule had been his ability to fake and lie. His extensive research had given him a good notion of what the magical connection should feel like. He had therefore been able to imitate the rapture such a link would bring. In reality, he had felt nothing. His deception had helped to put his father's mind at ease.

Since the magic of the land had apparently accepted his oldest son, Mikael had believed that Ragnald had truly changed. Just to make sure, he had stuck around for a few days after passing on the rule. After all, he was putting his cherished lands, beloved people, and only daughter into the hands of a man who, in some ways, had always been a stranger.

Ragnald had done a lot to make him proud for many years now, but somehow, Mikael had never felt a real connection to his oldest. Even as a small child, the boy had displayed cruelty towards animals. Seeing the despicable way his son had abused the defenseless dog had turned the horrified father's stomach and had left a lasting bad impression.

That incident had been many, many years ago. It had been difficult for Mikael to even like the young man after the viciousness he had displayed. Ragnald had worked hard to reform himself into a model citizen. Still, the niggling doubt about his true motivation had never entirely vanished from his dad's mind.

Mikael had been a careful man. Ragnald had been too perfect, too kind, too good. None of it had felt real to the concerned lord, and mistrust had still been well and alive in his heart. He had not forgotten his eldest's behavior when he had first met his baby sister nor his insistence that she was a danger to them all.

That his son had been able to form a connection to the land alleviated some of Mikael's worries. He had, however, never forgotten the hate-filled stares Ragnald would give Ki'ara whenever he thought himself unobserved.

Since Mikael had to leave the girl behind at Seamuir Castle, he needed to make sure that she had some protection. Taking Gawain aside, he had made him swear that he would never share the upcoming conversation with Ragnald or Lyall.

His youngest son had refused at first. Ragnald was his lord now, and he owed him his full and complete allegiance. Keeping secrets from his ruler was akin to treason. When his dad had continued to insist, Gawain had eventually relented. He had known in his heart that Mikael had a good reason for asking him to keep quiet. Therefore, he had finally given his word.

The apprehensive father had laid out his misgivings concerning his daughter. Gawain, in turn, had been brutally honest. He had also been concerned for his sister's safety and had sworn to his father that he would do what he could to keep Ki'ara from harm.

Gawain had given Mikael a promise. He had assured his dad that if things got out of hand and he saw no other option, he would report Ragnald's behavior to the council and invoke their protection.

⁕⁕⁕

To further ensure his daughter's safety, Mikael had called a secret meeting. He had invited only his most trusted friends and Lord Iain Elvinstone, his sons' uncle. The lord of Ravenshire was the brother to the boys' passed away mother. He was no blood relation to Ki'ara, but he loved her like his own and would do anything he could to help her.

Iain and Mikael had been friends and allies for most of their long lifetimes. After Morena's death, Lord Elvinstone had been the one who had encouraged the heartbroken man to marry again. He had wholeheartedly approved of the second wife and had gotten on well with Ali'ana.

When he had been informed of Ki'ara's birth, the Lord of Ravenshire had traveled to Seamuir to be there when his friend arrived with his infant daughter. He had even collected the two older boys. When Mikael had handed him the tiny child for the first time, it had been love at first sight.

A protectiveness, unlike anything the kind ruler had ever felt before, woke up in Lord Iain's heart. He had demanded to be made the little girl's godfather. His request had been happily granted, and the ceremony making it such had been beautiful.

⁕⁕⁕

Lord Elvinstone was an insightful man. He had genuinely loved all his nieces and nephews. Due to

Ragnald's and Lyall's standoffish demeanor, however, the lord had gotten to know the younger two children much better. The capricious Ki'ara had soon become his favorite of all.

Lord Iain had shared Mikael's misgivings. He was a shrewd observer and had not missed his two oldest nephews' behavior towards their sister. Lyall had always been the constant and obedient shadow of his brother. He had almost no will of his own. He would do whatever Ragnald commanded.

Gawain had been the only one they had been able to trust. But, if both his brothers went up against him, he would be outnumbered. In that case, he might fail in protecting his sister despite his promise. Lord Iain and Mikael had felt that it was prudent to put some precautions into place.

Therefore, just in case, the lords and the one lone lady present at the secret meeting had drawn up several sets of documents addressing a number of possible outcomes. As they had feared, Ragnald had turned out to be a less than stellar guardian. One collection of these papers had granted Ki'ara possession of Fairholme Castle and the surrounding lands on her 24th birthday and had made her a lord.

Mikael had been genuinely concerned and had wanted to make sure that Ki'ara had a place to escape to and the right to stand on her own feet as soon as possible. As a further safeguard, he had also left her enough money to be independent of the rest of the family.

Therefore, just in case,

The worried ruler had also asked his friends to keep an eye on his oldest son and to do whatever they deemed necessary to protect the clan and its people. Mikael had shared with his allies his deep misgivings about his heir.

He had admitted that he had been surprised that the land had accepted Ragnald.

Mikael had no choice. He and Ali'ana had to leave and as quickly as possible. They would not be able to return if there was a problem. With a heavy heart, he had passed the responsibility to make sure that no harm came to the MacClair Clan and Ki'ara off to his friends and confidantes.

Still, no one had expected that things would get this out of hand. In all the history of the Highlands, the council had never removed a lord from power before! Neither Mikael nor his allies could have imagined that Ki'ara would see herself forced to petition for Ragnald's replacement.

None of them had even considered that the magic would take things into its own hands!

Chapter 12

Cruel Intentions

Every day his father had remained at the castle had been torture for the new Lord MacClair. He had been afraid that his dad would realize that the 'Becoming' had been nothing but a fake. That would have allowed Mikael to take back his power. Ragnald had been terrified to lose it all.

Just as he and his grandfather had planned, Ragnald had finally achieved his first objective. He had become the lord of the clan. The new ruler had felt that he was well on the way to attaining his burning desire to become the overlord. He had just needed his dad to leave without realizing his grave error in judgment.

Ragnald had made sure to keep a hard grip on the magic that Mikael had relinquished. It had opposed him at every step, and he had struggled to maintain control. The MacClair had to prevent it from reaching out to his father at all costs! He had been so exhausted that he finally had to ask Lyall to grant him some of his strength.

Maintaining such a tight rein on the land's magic was draining at best, but Ragnald had to keep up the deception and set his father's mind at ease. A huge weight had lifted off his shoulders when Mikael and his wife had finally gotten ready to leave.

Ragnald had walked the couple to the castle's gates. He had kept on reassuring his dad that he would do his very best to take care of the clan and the lands. He had told Mikael that he was determined to make his forefathers proud. He had meant that one since he had every intention to institute all the things he and his grandfather had spoken of.

When his father had paused one last time at the drawbridge, Ragnald had promised to be the best lord that he could possibly be. When Mikael had still hesitated and to finally get the couple out the doors and on the road, he had assured the anxious parents that he would personally look after Ki'ara.

The entire time, the new Lord MacClair had been laughing inside. He had carefully chosen each and every word. Oh yes, he would make his forefathers proud, especially his grandfather! For one, their enemies, the StClouds, were going down. And, he would take care of his sister, permanently. He had meant every word he said, just not the way they had been interpreted.

⋆⋆⋇⋈⋇⋆⋆

Just to be on the safe side, Ragnald behaved himself a little bit longer. For a few more hours, he had been a model ruler. Then, feeling safe for the first time and knowing that his father was far enough away and that all the power was his, he had gone to his sister's chambers. Nothing that had ever been touched by the StCloud would remain in this castle!

Five days later, Ragnald had called Ki'ara to his office. He had looked forward to dealing with her. His father had been such a weakling! Even though he had claimed to love the clan and the Highlands, he had not listened to reason. Mikael had done nothing about the abomination in their midst. He, the new lord, would take care of this problem once and for all!

Ki'ara presented a threat to all the people. There was only one thing to do; he had to do away with her! Ragnald had no intention of letting her bring any kind of change to his home or the Highlands that could jeopardize his grand design.

The sly man had planned the encounter well. He had sent his brothers off on errands and had made sure that the servants were occupied elsewhere. He had closed the thick door and would have locked it but had feared that this would make Ki'ara suspicious.

Due to the mystery surrounding her origin, he had not been sure what she was, immortal or Zidhe, or maybe something else altogether. Ragnald had figured that his best bet was to surprise her, to attack when she least expected it. There was no telling what kind of powers she had!

At first, all had gone so well! The murderous lord had been genuinely enjoying the sight of Ki'ara's face turning purple as he had tightened the grip of his hands on her slender throat. He had wanted the moment to last, had intended to enjoy every second of strangling her. He had looked forward to watching the light fade from those eerie, brilliant green eyes.

Ragnald's well-laid plot would have succeeded beautifully had it not been for the unexpected intervention by Gawain. The lord had sworn to himself right then that one day he would make that bastard pay for depriving him of the pleasure of slowly killing the abomination!

After the failed attempt to choke Ki'ara to death, Ragnald had hated the girl more than ever. Within days, it had gotten so bad that he had been unable to stand the sight of her. To remove her from his presence, he had quickly hired Mathus to accompany her to a far off teacher.

When Ki'ara had returned many months later, her mere presence at Seamuir had severely bothered the MacClair. He had been unable to sleep, and all the delicious food the cook served up had tasted like sawdust to him. To find some relief, Ragnald had gotten very, very drunk. In his stupor, he had attempted to force his way into the girl's room.

The kicks and smashing against the door had made a terrible racket. The sound had echoed along the stone walls of the castle. It had soon attracted unwanted attention. Gawain had been the first to appear. He had called for help, and shortly after, Lyall and several guards had arrived.

It had taken five of them to subdue their raging ruler. Ragnald had been completely irrational. At that moment, he had only one objective- to get through that door! He wanted into that room more than anything, no matter the cost! The inebriated lord had intended to finish what he had started that long-ago day in his office.

✦⋆☙❦☙⋆✦

The MacClair had actually been stunned by his brothers' reaction after that incident. After all, it had just been a temporary lapse in judgment on his part due to the excessive consumption of the fine cognac he kept in his office. As far as Ragnald had been concerned, it had been no big deal. So he had frightened Ki'ara and her maid. They could just get over it!

Secretly, the thought had filled Ragnald with glee. Maybe the abomination would get the idea that she was not welcome at Seamuir Castle or anywhere else in the Highlands! He had thought that the entire episode had actually been hilarious, especially when he had imagined the two women cowering in the chamber.

The MacClair, therefore, had been much affronted that neither Gawain nor Lyall had seen any humor in the situation. That his brothers, even Lyall, his one and only friend and confidante, would end up taking action and stand united against him, had shocked him to his core.

Ragnald had not expected that they would dare to take their plight to the council and ask for protection for the clan as well as Ki'ara. The compulsion the other rulers had placed on him at that meeting had prevented him from directly harming his sister from that day forward.

Still, there were different ways to achieve his goal. Being sneaky, after all, was one of his unique talents! Ragnald had decided that he would have to be much more circumspect and backhanded to attain his objective. Should he try poison? A riding accident? Or maybe force the magic to help him suffocate the girl in her sleep?

On some level, such indirect methods did not appeal to the MacClair. He wanted to see Ki'ara suffer, wanted to be present when the last of the light left those weird, brilliant green eyes.

⚜

Since the lords had not specified that he could not continue to send Ki'ara off to study, he had kept her away from Eastmuir as much as he could. Ragnald had decided that if he had to, he would bring her home whenever the council demanded it, or when she needed a different teacher.

But before the abomination would ever set foot into the Highlands, he would make sure that the StCloud was off on one of his travels. Ragnald had been determined to keep the pair as far apart as he possibly could and to wholeheartedly enjoy the pain this would cause the miserable brat.

The MacClair had felt that having Ki'ara gone would be a balm to his soul. She had been a constant reminder of his failure and shame to eliminate the danger she presented to his people. At least, as long as she was far from home, the Highlands were safe!

The further his sister had been from Seamuir Castle and the longer she had stayed there, the better Ragnald had liked it.

Chapter 13

A Deadly Trap

Ragnald, like all bullies, had been a very insecure person. He had continued to feel like a fake because he had never been able to fully link to the magic. This sense of failure had undermined his fragile self-confidence further and had made him even more short-tempered and mean. He had figured that the more he intimidated his fellow clansmen, the less they would dare to question him, and the smaller his chance of being found out.

The MacClair had always been afraid that someone would figure out that he did not possess the complete command of the power. It would have been the end of his days as the ruler and would have destroyed his chance to become the overlord of the Highlands and its people.

Therefore, to cover his deceit, Ragnald had bluffed, ranted, threatened, and abused his clan members. He had been well aware that as a result, he had been widely despised, a price he had been more than happy to pay.

The spiteful and more than a little paranoid lord had made many enemies since taking charge of Eastmuir. He was sure that the council, as well as the clan, would jump at the opportunity to wrest the rule away from him. This could not be allowed! He, the MacClair, was their better after all!

With the exception of Lyall, Ragnald's terrible temper and cruel ways had kept most at a distance. The MacClair had been good with this. Let them shun him, hate him! It had served its purpose and had helped to keep his secret safe.

The lord had maintained the illusion of having bonded with the power by maintaining iron control over the magic. Even Lyall had believed that his brother had made the connection. Fearing Ragnald's wrath, no one had dared to question him openly.

However, the looks on his kinsmen's' faces had said much. The MacClair had been absolutely convinced that there was lots of talk behind his back, something that had infuriated him to no end.

⚜

Ragnald had been no fool. His beloved grandfather had taught him well. With Raghnall's stern guidance, he had become cunning like a fox. The old lord had set firm goals and had drilled the steps to achieve them so deeply into his grandson's mind that the MacClair had been functioning without ever consciously questioning why he was pursuing this particular course.

Raghnall's indoctrination had been a total success. Just like his idol, Ragnald had governed without being hindered by scruples and compassion. It had not bothered him that he was reviled, and he had not been worried about the clan rising up against him. Making sure that his people were too terrified to do so had taken care of that!

There was only one person Ragnald had an irrational fear of, and that was Ki'ara. She was now a grown woman, 24 years old. Unlike many of the other immortals who still looked and acted like children at that age, she was utterly adult. Smart, beautiful, well-loved, and maybe even more powerful than him.

His 'sister' was everything he was not, and now that she was back, Ragnald had begun to fear for his rule. The callous lord had decided that he needed to act before she grew stronger, or the clan decided to rise up and make her the lord in his place.

There had also been one question that had kept nagging at Ragnald. How powerful was that abomination really? His burning curiosity had gotten the better of him. He had convinced himself that it was of the utmost importance to find out just how much magic Ki'ara had.

⁘⁘⁘

Most immortals were not immune to fire. This had given the MacClair a wicked idea. He had believed that he would be able to arrange an accident that would kill her and, at the same time, show him how much power she had! Ragnald had so looked forward to watching her burn alive!

His spells in the courtyard had almost succeeded. Ragnald had used the excuse that it had rained heavily to have the servants spread an extra thick layer of straw all the way across the square right up to the front door. His request had not aroused suspicion since this was done all the time. The hay had helped to keep the mud down and had made it easier to get to the stables.

Ragnald had made sure that all had been in readiness. The trap had been set by the time his sister had come out and headed for the carriage. It had been so easy to put his plan in motion. The accident-prone Gina, the riverboat captain he had been bedding and had grown tired of, had been the perfect catalyst for the disaster.

He had handed her the enchanted lamp and had ordered her to head towards the stable just as soon as she saw that Ki'ara was half-way to the waiting carriage. The captain had looked at him in puzzlement. Ragnald had seen the questions forming on her lips, so he had decided to use her for his pleasure one last time.

Grabbing her forcefully, he had dragged the surprised woman behind some boxes. There, he had ruthlessly bent Gina over a crate, had pulled up her skirt to expose her plump behind, and had undone his pants. Since this would be the final time he would take her, there was no longer a need to hold back. Ragnald had started to brutally sate his lust.

The captain, who liked it rough but not to that degree, had cried out and begged him to stop. This had turned Ragnald on even more. It had driven him to thrust into her even harder and more cruelly. As usual, he had gained his greatest pleasure from inflicting as much pain and damage as he possibly could.

Gina had been sobbing by the time he had been done with her. Blood had been running down her legs. Taking his handkerchief, Ragnald had pitilessly stuffed it inside her to stem the flow before he had pulled her up. Handing her a dirty, old sack, he had carelessly told her to clean herself up.

The captain had glared at him as she had wiped herself. Ragnald had been aware that by taking her this way, he had gone way too far. But, he had also long since learned how to appease her. Lifting her up, he had sat her on the crate. Gina had struggled against him, but he had forced her legs apart, careful to not dislodge the cloth plugging up her rear.

Ragnald had taken her much more gently from the front this time. He had fondled her breasts and touched her in all the right places. Her resistance and anger had faded quickly as he had known it would, and Gina had started moaning. Reaching down, he had used his fingers to increase her pleasure before pinching her once, hard and almost cruelly, to give her release.

He had not really enjoyed this second encounter, but Ragnald had needed the captain nice and compliant. She had been an essential part of his plan. To make up for this indignity, he had promised himself that after Ki'ara was dead, he would corner one of the maids.

His objective with the riverboat captain, however, had been achieved. All was forgiven, and a few more kisses and empty promises later, Gina was willing to do his bidding again.

⋅∗⋅∗⋅

When Ragnald had left her, the captain had been patiently waiting where he had positioned her. And, just as he had planned, she had obliged him in setting the courtyard on fire by accidentally dropping the bespelled lamp. Since he was not actually doing the harming, the council's compulsion had not prevented his actions.

How was it possible for things to have gone wrong? The abomination should have burned! It had been so close! Ragnald had watched with glee as the fire had spread towards Ki'ara at lightning speed. She had to run for her life with the blaze hot on her heels.

The MacClair had laughed out loud at her panicked expression. He had feared that she had grown stronger than him and had felt exhilarated that she had been unable to help herself.

That his cruel trap had severely spooked several of the horses, had injured people as well as animals, had not bothered Ragnald in the least at that moment. He had stood there without raising a hand to help any of them, too busy watching his sister.

The only reason for her escape that the MacClair had been able to come up with was that the straw must have been damper than he had anticipated. It had not burned as fast as Ragnald had expected. But still, she should have died! Only Ki'ara being so fleet of foot had saved her. She had been running full out in those fancy shoes holding up the skirt of her long dress.

When she had safely reached the stairs, and her eyes had met his, Ragnald had seen great sadness in their green depths. She had known what he had done!

Ragnald had decided right then that next time, no amount of running would save her. He would make sure of that. Then, suddenly, it had dawned on him that he could be in trouble. The looks his clansmen had given him had said it all. The blame for the incident had been squarely laid at his feet! Rumors would spread!

Fear had set in, and Ragnald had wondered if the council would end up taking actions against him. What had made things even worse was the fact that even Lyall had turned against him! Then, a stunning realization had entered his head. That rat was probably trying to save himself by abandoning his lord and brother!

Fury, like he had never known before, had consumed Ragnald. He had stormed off to his office to drown his anger and sorrows. This is where the wave had overtaken him many, many hours later.

Chapter 14

Celebration

Once the Highlanders in the chapel regained their feet and composure, their immediate concern became Conall and Ki'ara. Rodric had the wherewithal to quickly throw the sheet over the couple's unconscious bodies. Lord Iain, the one eyewitness, was the closest. He immediately went to his godchild's side.

"Smelling salts! Get some smelling salts, quickly!" he commanded. Celia rushed out to find her mother, who always carried some in her rather oversized purse. She returned within minutes, triumphantly waving the small bottle. One whiff of the salts was enough to bring the couple around.

"Would all of you turn around for a moment, please?" came Conall's wry request.

The assembled bystanders were only too happy to comply. Gently, the StCloud withdrew from inside his wife and readjusted her panties. He raised himself up just enough so that he could slide her skirt down without exposing her as he moved back. Once he had seen to his trousers, he got to his feet and gingerly reached down to help up the still slightly groggy Ki'ara.

Wrapping his arm around her waist, Conall steadied her against him. Since a slight bit of dizziness remained, Ki'ara immediately snuggled up closer. Once the StCloud had assured himself that his wife was not going to faint again, he addressed the assembled group.

"Thank you for bearing witness to the consummation of our union. We apologize for the unexpected strength of that wave! We are glad that none of you were hurt!" Conall began. "Also, thank you, Celia and Rodric, for sharing your special day with us, and Athair Thomas for conducting a most expeditious and binding ceremony. You all have our deepest gratitude!"

"I want to thank all of you for giving us as much privacy as you could, and my Uncle and godfather, Lord Iain, for being there for us and approving our decision. We are eternally in your debt, " Ki'ara added

So not to unbalance themselves, the couple bowed carefully to the witnesses. Lord Iain and Rodric rushed to support them as they swayed for a moment.

"Here you come to our rescue yet again!" Ki'ara joked at the pair. Relieved laughter filled the chapel. If the young lady could make fun of her situation, she was starting to feel much better.

"Well, there is no reason to hang about here! We have been away from the celebration long enough! Let's return to the hall!" Conall added after a few moments when he felt steady on his feet once more. His comment was greeted with hearty approval.

⁜

Highlanders loved a good party. Ki'ara and the StCloud had expected their witnesses to rush out to the hall and throw themselves back into the festivities. But that was not to be. As far as the assembled kinsmen were concerned, this had been a momentous event that deserved to be given the proper reverence.

After exchanging a few glances and a whispered discussion, the young bride Celia and her new husband took up a position beside the entrance. The lords and ladies lined up in twos with each man formally holding his ladies' raised hand. Only Lord Iain walked alone directly in front of the pair.

When all was arranged to everyone's satisfaction, Rodric opened the doors, and he and Celia stepped into the hall. Everyone present was curious about what had happened. Therefore, all eyes were instantly riveted on the entry.

Rodric bowed deeply to the crowd while Celia curtsied. Their big smiles showed how much they were enjoying all this. With a dramatic sweep of their hands, the pair gestured towards the door. The procession of rulers began to emerge upon their signal.

As the lords and their spouses filed in, the room was so quiet you could have heard a pin drop. It seemed that even the world was holding its breath. Finally, Lord Iain entered the hall. With his voice enhanced by magic so that it would carry even into the furthest reaches of the large chamber, he announced.

"To all those assembled here this day I present," here he took a slow, deep breath and paused dramatically for a moment to increase the anticipation in the crowd.

This was, after all, an event dear to his heart. It was also a once in a lifetime occurrence for many of those present. Therefore, Lord Iain wanted to give it all the importance that it deserved. Moreover, he was relishing this proclamation immensely. The lord waited until he sensed that the excitement and expectancy in the room had built to a most satisfactory level.

"Lord and Lady Conall StCloud!" he finally shouted with a grand wave of his hands towards the open door.

When the StCloud and Ki'ara stepped into the hall, it erupted into raucous applause. Love had won out! These two, who had been forbidden to even speak to each other by her own brother, had overcome the odds stacked against them! After all these years, they had finally become husband and wife!

⁕⁕⁕

The love Conall and Ki'ara shared had persevered, despite all the obstacles that had been placed in its way. This gave many of the single people present new hope. Looks were exchanged with past partners or those who had been desired in secret. For love to win out so spectacularly gave many the courage to work on their own miracles.

Not a few were also elated that Ragnald MacClair had been bested. His sister, like all women, deserved to be treated with love and respect. If one was to believe the rumors passed on by the servants, this had most certainly not been the case at Seamuir Castle!

Many would have given much to be a fly on the wall when her big brother found out. He would most likely have apoplexy! Would he ever be furious about this sudden and entirely unplanned wedding that he had so explicitly forbidden! Too bad for him!

⁕⁕⁕

The sudden wave had startled them all out of their revelry. Then, there had been all the excitement following it! It had told some of the more informed merrymakers all they needed to know. The rumor had spread around the room like lightning. Two Zidarians had become one!

Now, there was also a fair amount of glee. This was one marriage that had already been consummated, so there was nothing the despicable Lord Ragnald could do about it!

Conall and Ki'ara stayed for about another hour. The proud and very pleased wedding couple, Celia and Rodric, had ceremoniously guided them to their very own place of honor at the head of the table. The StClouds insistence that they share the distinction had completely delighted the generous pair.

Celia was thrilled. No one would ever forget her wedding! It would be the talk of the town, if not the entire realm and beyond! What a wonderous day this had been! Full of the most amazing surprises!

To be in the room when one of the legendary unions between the Zidarians took place had been the greatest honor she could have ever imagined. Usually, only the nobility got to witness such a rare event!

Having been granted this rare privilege had added something extra to her special day that she would always cherish.

Chapter 15

A Big Surprise

The festivities were in full swing again, and mead and wine were flowing freely. The dancefloor was packed with Highlanders having fun, and the musicians kept playing one lively tune after another. Everyone appeared to be having a splendid time. Still, the StClouds getting ready to leave did not go unnoticed.

Celia and Rodric immediately rushed over to wish them goodbye. The happy couple thanked Ki'ara and Conall again for choosing to take their own vows on the same day. Their evident gratefulness made it clear how much it had meant to the newlyweds to have been able to share this special day with the immortals.

The bubbly Celia kept telling Ki'ara how pleased she and her new husband were. She assured the StClouds that they would never forget the great honor they had bestowed upon them. After all, how many people could say that they shared their wedding celebration with a pair of Zidarians? No one that she knew!

On their way to the exit, Conall and his new wife worked their way around the hall. They said their farewells to some of the attending lords and ladies before quietly slipping out the door. Her godfather would make their excuses to the rest of the party should their absence be noticed.

Lord Iain had gone himself to fetch his godchild her cape. He lovingly draped it around her shoulders and kissed her on both cheeks. "My blessings on you, Ki'ara StCloud. May your life be full of love and happiness from this day forward!" he wished her.

The Lord of Ravenshire walked out to the top of the stairs with the couple. Then turning to Conall, he gave the young man a stern look. "I am placing the welfare of my favorite niece in your hands and charge you with protecting her and keeping her safe," he began, locking eyes with the StCloud.

"The council stands behind the two of you and will assist you in dealing with her brother. We are calling for a full meeting, including the Zidhe, three days from now. I hope that the elves may be able to advise us on the most expedient as well as the most prudent course of action. To be honest, I would feel a lot better if they were willing to assist us since there is unknown magic hidden at Seamuir," he continued. "It is time Ragnald's rule of terror comes to an end. The clan deserves to be governed better than that!"

"Thank you, sir. Your support is most welcome! Ki'ara and I will do what we can to resolve this entire situation as peacefully as possible. Rest assured that I will protect her with my life and assist her in any way I can," Conall responded.

"After tonight, I am sure that Ragnald knows exactly what has taken place. That wave you two created was mighty powerful! I have a very uneasy feeling somehow. I fear that the magic of the land may have used this opportunity to seek revenge for all the abuse and neglect it has experienced at his hands," Lord Iain stated softly.

Turning to his niece, the lord went on, "Ki'ara, something tells me that Ragnald did not get away unscathed! The other two should be fine, but to be honest, I am concerned for him."

A frown of worry marred Lord Iain's handsome face. He might not have liked Ragnald, but he was still his nephew.

Ki'ara turned pale. She had been so happy it had never occurred to her that one of her brothers might have been hurt. "Would you please send someone to check on them, Uncle? Gawain should be with Arabella at the Seven Sailors, Lyall hiding out at our lodgings. We left Ragnald at the castle. I hope they are safe!" she requested anxiously.

"I have already taken care of it. Gawain is fine and is having a great time celebrating your wedding. Lyall was quietly getting drunk in the chambers you were going to stay in but grew very concerned once he realized what had happened. We tried to contact the castle, but no one answered the magic mirror. He insisted on going back to Seamuir immediately. I have sent guards along with him, just in case. We should know about Ragnald's condition latest by morning," the lord assured her.

A thoughtful expression crossed the Lord of Ravenshire 's face.

"I am also going to send a message to the Zidhe. I hope that they will know where to reach Mikael. Your father needs to be informed of the entire situation. I think it is time he came back and dealt with the mess he left us!" Lord Iain said with a snort.

Ki'ara looked at him in complete surprise. She was truly taken aback. "You know how to reach father?" she gasped.

The young woman had been completely unaware that anyone had been in touch with her parents or had a clue to their whereabouts. As far as she knew, no one had been able to get in contact with them since their departure so many years ago.

"I am not certain I can reach him, but I will try. The Zidhe should know where he is. Anything you would like me to tell him?" Lord Iain asked her with a wink.

"Please, tell my parents that I love them and hope to one day see them again," Ki'ara responded with a huge smile.

Suddenly, she had hope that one day she might see her beloved mother and father again. What a big surprise and what a wonderful wedding present!

The young lady was concerned for Ragnald and also for Lyall, who was, driven by his love for their oldest sibling, bravely heading back to the lion's den. Still, Ki'ara could not stop smiling. She was just too happy. It had been such an incredible day with so many changes for the better!

After all these years of being kept apart, of heartache, of missing him, she was finally Conall's wife. Ki'ara was looking forward to their life together. She knew that in him, she had a true partner, one who was there for her, who had her back, who loved her unconditionally. She felt unbelievably blessed.

Giving her uncle a hug and a kiss on the cheek, Ki'ara turned to her husband. The StCloud tucked her arm under his and escorted his gorgeous bride down the stairs towards the waiting carriage.

Gallantly, he helped Ki'ara on board and assisted her with the long skirt of her dress. Getting in and out of a coach in such attire was never easy. Conall waited patiently while she seated herself and made herself comfortable.

Ki'ara thanked him with a smile. The love shining on her face almost brought tears to the StCloud's eyes. He still could barely believe that she was finally his!

Chapter 16

The Way Home

Conall made certain that Ki'ara was as comfortable as possible before moving to his own seat across from her. The benches were well-padded since the roads in the Highlands, and especially in Eastmuir due to Ragnald's neglect, could be rough. The magical gates did cut down on the distance, but they would have to travel for several hours before reaching Cloudshire Hall.

On the StCloud's command, the footman closed the door and then took his place at the back of the carriage. The lord checked one last time that his new wife was ready for their journey home. He knew that he was going overboard and that she was very capable of taking care of herself but just could not help himself.

Conall genuinely enjoyed being able to look after Ki'ara once more. She was the love of his life, and he felt fiercely protective of her. The StCloud was determined to do his best that no harm would come to her ever again, not even a bump if he could prevent it!

Conall had every intention of spoiling Ki'ara as much as she would allow it. Knowing her independent streak, however, and her fierce resolve to be his equal, he was aware that she would put a stop to this rather sooner than later. Therefore, he was going to enjoy pampering her as much as possible while she let him.

Ki'ara had been through so much these last few years! Conall had every intention to make up for some of the ill-treatment and neglect she had received from her brother. On a whim, he decided to tuck yet one more pillow behind her. His loving care gained him another sweet smile.

With a knock on the front wall of the vehicle, the StCloud gave the driver the signal to get going. As the carriage started forward, Ki'ara opened the window so that she could wave to her uncle one last time. She was so grateful that he would handle the council and the elves so that she and her new husband could have a couple of days to themselves.

Even though they were not blood-related, Lord Iain had always been there for Ki'ara. On more than one occasion, he had taken a stand against Ragnald, his own nephew, for her sake. She owed him so much and genuinely loved him.

Besides the StCloud, the young woman saw her favorite uncle as one of the kindest and most upstanding men she had ever met. He had proven his mettle many times over and had been a true friend to Conall as well as herself.

Two lamps attached to the side of the coach and one suspended from the ceiling gave them just enough light to see each other by as the coach was making its way towards Cloudshire Hall. Once they had left the town behind, the StCloud regarded his bride solemnly.

"Finally! I have you all to myself! It has been too many years!" he uttered before sliding onto the seat next to her.

Her husband's mere proximity had an instant effect on Ki'ara. All of a sudden, she was feeling very hot, and her breathing was coming much faster. She undid the clasp of her cape and slid it off. Life was going to be very interesting if Conall continued to affect her this way just by getting close! Being out in public could be a challenge!

It seemed that she was not the only one who was reacting to this nearness. The StCloud's eyes had gone dark with longing. Moving some of the pillows aside he had so carefully placed, he slipped his arm around Ki'ara and pulled her close. Conall gently raised her head and locked his gaze with hers before bending his head down to kiss her gingerly.

What he had initially intended to be a gentle kiss turned out to be much more when the desire for each other awoke with full force once again. The StCloud pulled back with a groan, and the newlyweds stared at each other with wonder. That was some effect their mere physical contact was having! Keeping their hands off each other would be difficult if this persisted unabated!

As the sexual tension continued to build between them, Ki'ara looked down in confusion. All this was new to her. She realized that she really did not know as much about being a wife as she had thought. How could she want him again so soon? And with such fierceness? Would it always be like this? This burning inside her, this heat in her loins, this needing him to make love to her?

That those feelings were mutual was clearly noticeable. Her husband obviously wanted her as much as she did him! The large bulge in his pants was evidence of that! Was it possible to do it again so soon? Or did it take time for him to recharge? Ki'ara had no clue. Those were questions she had never asked Leana; they had never even occurred to her before this moment!

Looking up at him once more, the heat in her body grew to almost unbearable proportions. Ki'ara craved him, longed to feel him inside her yet again. She needed him to quench this burning desire that was driving her to distraction.

Unexpectedly, Ki'ara felt an urgency that she could not explain. She realized that she did not wish to wait until they got to the castle. They had a long way to go yet. It would be almost midnight before they arrived there! Waiting for that long would be torture!

How could she tell him? Would he think badly of her if she spoke that openly of her needs? Ki'ara felt a bit shy all of a sudden. She was still just an innocent when it came to relations between men and women. After all, she had been a virgin when Conall made her his wife there in that chapel.

Also, she had not seen the StCloud in so long! In many ways, he was a stranger to her, something she had every intention of changing starting right now!

⊱⋅☙❧⋅⊰

Looking up into Conall's eyes, Ki'ara saw that they were dark with desire and that he was having a hard time controlling himself. He wanted her as much as she wanted him! This realization filled her with pure delight and a sense of daring.

Giving him a mischievous look and an impish smile, Ki'ara asked him the one question at the forefront of her thoughts. "Will that wave happen again when we make love?"

The StCloud laughed. "My love, it seems that our thoughts are dwelling on the same subject! Yes, the wave may happen again, maybe even a couple more times, but hopefully not as powerful! We will have to come up with something!"

He looked at Ki'ara thoughtfully for a moment. Suddenly, his face brightened. "Will you help me shield us so that we may contain the magic? We cannot afford to have it affect the driver and coachmen! Also, I would much prefer to keep our lives private instead of advertising our sexual encounters! I certainly do not appreciate the whole of the Highlands knowing every time I make love to my wife!"

Ki'ara looked at him aghast and then burst out laughing. "Oh my! I was so stunned by the whole thing that this never really dawned on me! You bet I will help you shield us! Would a protective bubble suffice that would be reinforced by the wave itself?"

"Yes, I believe so, you little vixen! Great idea to use the wave to strengthen our shield! Raise your hands to mine and then help me form a sphere around us," he instructed.

⥲⥲⥲

Conall checked their handiwork thoroughly. Once he was satisfied that they were adequately isolated inside their protective orb, he pulled Ki'ara back into his arms and began kissing her in earnest. Neither was holding back any longer.

The passion between them ignited full force. The StCloud's hands started to roam down Ki'ara's back and over her arms, leaving such a fiery sensation in their wake that it was driving her wild. He undid her dress and slid it off her shoulders to give himself better access to her bare skin.

Now that her gown was out of the way, the StCloud trailed hot kisses down Ki'ara's neck to her small, firm breasts. This left her gasping for air and arching against him. With each touch, the desire and need kept growing between them. Before long, it had reached a level neither could have ever imagined.

Releasing the ties to his trousers with one hand, the StCloud pulled his wife closer with the other for yet another feverish kiss. Ki'ara was returning it with a fierceness equal to his own. Feeling her response, his need for her grew so great that all coherent thought stopped. All he wanted was to make love to this beautiful woman once more, to bury himself inside her.

Pushing the skirt up to her waist, his hand found its way between her legs. Conall spread them apart gently, and Ki'ara obliged him by opening herself up even wider. With a moan, he started to explore the gift being offered, impatiently tearing the underwear when it got in his way. One of his fingers found their way inside her and plunged deep. The StCloud relished the wetness he found there, a testimony to his wife's reaction to him.

As he continued to stroke her, thrust inside her, he stretched her gently by adding more fingers. Ki'ara began to move with his hand. She had completely given herself over to the sensation, and her head was thrown back in ecstasy.

Here was a woman not afraid to take her own pleasure! This thought pleased Conall immensely. Never in his life had he been so turned on by a lady! They would have to bring this to a conclusion soon; the throbbing of his member was growing painful.

Being inside a carriage, the room was just a bit limited, and the benches were relatively narrow. This conveyance was definitely not designed with what they had in mind! How could they accomplish what they both hungered for with a modicum of comfort? The StCloud so wanted her, needed to bury himself deep inside her, wished to please her, to give and take release!

Moving forward to the edge of the seat, Conall reached with his free hand for a couple of the cushions. He evaluated them for a minute, then dropped them on the floor between Ki'ara's wide-open legs. That should give him just about the right height!

Just the look of her offering herself to him like that, freely and without any embarrassment, almost wantonly, sent a shiver of intense desire through his groin. His balls were starting to ache from craving her so badly. He could not wait to drive into that delicious wetness, to give her his seed, to claim her again as his wife.

ᕀᒼᐧ᙭ᕀᐧᐧᐧ᙭ᕀᐧ

The StCloud had continued moving his fingers inside Ki'ara. His thumb was stroking her sweet spot, stimulating her further, driving her to the brink of insanity. Her motions had taken on even more of an urgency, and she was moaning loudly and calling his name.

Her abandon destroyed the last of Conall's self-control. Getting down on his knees, he prepared to enter her as slowly as he could in the state he was in. Instead, Ki'ara moved forward on the bench. Using a hand to guide him, she thrust her hips towards him and slid him inside. Her action of taking him turned the StCloud on to the point he cried out and exploded as he dove deep inside her.

Ki'ara threw her arms around his shoulders and held him against her. She allowed him a moment before starting to slowly and carefully move her hips back and forth. She had every intention of keeping him inside her, to use him to pleasure herself, to find her own release. Her brazenness made him hard as a rock once again.

Conall had intended to pick up the rhythm and to take her gently, but instead, she had met his thrust. He had ended up pushing inside her much harder than he had planned. She was so tight around him that all thought went out the window. Her moans drove him on, and he forgot everything else except becoming one with his wife.

⁖⸙⸙⸙⸙⁖

The carriage was bumping along the uneven road, hiding some of the rocking motion within. Ki'ara's hands tightly gripped Conall's shoulders, and her head was thrown back as she moved against him in an ever-increasing frenzy. All she could think of was getting and giving release from this continuously heightening pressure inside her. It was threatening to become almost more than she could bear.

The StCloud obliged her by increasing the rhythm. Faster and faster, harder and harder, and more urgently, they moved until he was virtually pounding into her. Conall had intended to go very slow and be gentle with Ki'ara the first few times, but his wife and the craving they had for each other would allow none of that.

Ki'ara had shifted her hands down to his waist and was pulling him deep inside her with each thrust. She wanted him, all of him, and was taking him just as much as he was taking her. Even here, making love, she was his equal, no soft little flower submitting to her mate! The StCloud absolutely loved it.

They both cried out when their ardor finally carried them over the brink, and they found blessed release. Panting, hot, and sweating from the exertion, the newlyweds collapsed into each other's arms.

⁖⸙⸙⸙⸙⁖

Conall and Ki'ara stayed there, holding each other for some time. Finally, their heartbeats started to slow. The young wife breathed in her husband's beloved scent. It triggered a flood of happy memories from her childhood. He smelled so right, so appealing to her. How lucky she was to be sharing her life with this wonderful man from this day forward!

When they finally moved apart and Conall withdrew from inside her, he gently tugged down her long skirt. Ki'ara watched him unashamedly as he pulled up and retied his trousers. She loved the look of those long legs, that flat stomach, the well-muscled chest, not to speak of what was protruding from the nest of dark hair. To her own disbelief, just eyeing him such brought on a stirring inside her. Should she tell him that she wanted him yet again?

When the StCloud slid on the seat beside her, the heat in her groin further intensified. If this was what it was like to be married, to truly love and want someone, and to be loved and wanted in return, it was just plain heaven! Getting herself under control, Ki'ara picked up the cushions and placed them next to her.

She spotted her underpants where they were lying on the floor. They were beyond repair. Ki'ara picked them up and started twirling the ripped, lacey garment around her finger, all the while giving Conall a saucy look. With a laugh, he snatched them away from her and let the evidence of their encounter disappear into his pocket.

❦

The StCloud pulled his new wife next to him and got them as comfortable as possible. He could still smell a faint odor of smoke in Ki'ara's hair. When she had arrived at the meeting, he had instantly known that she was very upset. Conall had not been surprised that her brother had something to do with that. As it turned out, she had been in grave danger.

"Ki'ara, my love, I hate to disrupt this pleasant moment, but would you please tell me again what happened at Seamuir Castle today? If I am to help you, I really need to know, including those facts or suspicions that you did not share with the council!" he asked her gently.

His new wife raised her head from his shoulder and looked up at him. There was a sea of sadness in her luminous eyes.

"The fire in the courtyard was the result of those two spells I mentioned. My brother used his mistress, the riverboat captain he had grown tired of, to start the fire. Through no fault of her own, Gina was extremely accident-prone until I healed her," Ki'ara began.

"When I was almost half-way to the carriage, the woman managed to set the straw on fire by dropping an enchanted lamp Ragnald had handed her. I had realized that I was walking into a trap and that the especially thick cover of hay in the courtyard had been bespelled," she continued, her voice devoid of emotions.

"The magic and I had dampened down the straw at the edges already. It and the power I was granted by the gods of old helped me slow down the speed of the blaze. This allowed me and others in danger to get to safety. I pretended that I had to run back to the stairs since I did not want to get into a magical duel with Ragnald," Ki'ara continued in a matter of fact manner.

"Gods of old? You did not mention them during the council! What powers have you been granted, and how did this happen?" Conall immediately questioned. Leave it to him to home in on the one part she had purposely left out in her account! With her husband, however, Ki'ara would have no secrets.

"This morning, I was drawn to the stone circle by the castle. There, I met the gods who were in the Highlands long before the Zidhe came. They decided to make me their High Priestess, and they have charged me with teaching people more about them and the magic of the land. I am to begin once the whole thing with Ragnald is over with. These gods are lonely and wish to be known once again," Ki'ara explained.

The StCloud looked at her in awe. He was stunned. There was much more to his new wife than even he had suspected!

"I would really love to hear more about this, Ki'ara, but right now, we have more pressing things to discuss. When we have time, will you share more details of that encounter with me?"

Ki'ara smiled and nodded. "I would love to! It was amazing!"

"Sounds like a deal but now back to the incident. You said that your brothers did not assist you?" Conall asked pointedly. "Ragnald should have been able to put that fire out with a wave of his hand!"

"No, he just stood there and did nothing but laugh," Ki'ara told him sadly. Tears started to fill her eyes. "Lyall was trying to get him to help, but he was so focused on watching me that he forgot all else. Had it not been for the magic, many more would have been hurt!"

Conall's jaw clenched as he tried to get the fury that had risen up inside him under control. He loved Ki'ara. Had he even suspected that she could end up in such danger, he would have removed her from Ragnald's guardianship long ago, with or without the council's approval.

"So you did not openly use your full powers to prevent Ragnald from knowing how strong you had become? To avoid him challenging you?" the StCloud inquired.

"The fire was fueled by potent magic. Had I used my own powers to put it out, Ragnald would have known that he was no longer the MacClair. I did not want to start my time as the ruler by killing my own brother," his wife told him. Her voice was tinged with sorrow.

Conall hated to have to ask the visibly upset Ki'ara more questions, but he needed all the facts to be able to best help her. The more he learned, however, the angrier he got. The desire to punch Ragnald, to utterly destroy him, became almost overwhelming.

⁕

Ki'ara could clearly sense her husband's feelings but held nothing back, not even her brother's furious rant her new senses had made her privy to. The StCloud could only shake his head in disbelief when he heard of Ragnald's intent to do away with all his siblings.

"I hope that I get a chance to make him pay for this!" Conall muttered through clenched teeth.

"We will deal with him, my love, but together with the council and all above board. I do not want my husband to be taken by the Zidhe!" Ki'ara reminded him gently but firmly.

She trusted Conall to keep his temper under control. Her husband was too smart and levelheaded to do something as stupid as risking the wrath of the Zidhe when there were better ways of dealing with the situation.

"If my uncle is right, the wave might have affected Ragnald rather badly. Let's wait and see until we know more. I am just glad that Gawain and Lyall are alright!"

Completely switching the subject, Ki'ara asked calmly, "What do you think of me making Gawain my steward? Since I don't think you want to live at Seamuir all the time, I will need someone to represent me while I am staying with you or when we are off traveling!"

The StCloud could only stare at her. It took him a moment to switch gears, but then he started smiling. Leave it to Ki'ara to so effectively draw his mind away from such a disagreeable topic!

"He would be well suited for the position if you can get him to accept it. He does love his freedom, but he is well-liked by the clan. And the ladies just adore him," Conall replied, giving Ki'ara a playful wink. Both started laughing.

It felt good to release some of the tension the unpleasant but necessary discussion of the day's events had produced.

The StCloud felt like the luckiest man alive. This beautiful woman before him never ceased to amaze him. Even as a young girl, her mind had been incredibly fast in assessing a situation and finding the best solution. Life with her would most certainly never be boring!

Kissing her forehead, Conall pulled his wife closer. He tucked her head under his chin. To soothe her after their talk, he began to gently rub Ki'ara's back. It was not long before her rhythmic breathing told him that she had fallen soundly asleep.

Chapter 17

A Warm Welcome

Cloudshire Hall was a beautiful place, well cared for, and very efficiently run. Many of the local seabirds liked to roost in the elaborate spires of the stronghold, which had been built on a sheer rock pillar hundreds of feet high. The fortress was separated from the rest of the hill by a wide gulch, and the churning sea tossed restlessly far below. This made access from that angle almost impossible.

Its placement made Cloudshire highly defensible. A long, slender draw bridge was the only way to gain entry to this magnificent abode. The walls seemed to shimmer with an intrinsic light that contributed to its overall splendor. Ki'ara could still hardly believe that from now on, this delightful building would be her home for a good part of the year.

The servants had been informed to expect their lord home. Therefore, lanterns had been lit from the start of the bridge all the way to the front door. This gave the graceful span an enchanted air. When the guards saw the lights of the carriage appear in the distance, they alerted the watchman who gave the alarm.

All was ready for their lord and his new wife by the time the coach arrived in the courtyard. The tired footman opened the door for the StCloud and assisted him and his lady to disembark. Conall took Ki'ara's hand, and solemnly led her to the half-moon shaped stone stairs.

⚜

The servants at the castle had felt the wave and were more than a little curious. Therefore, they had assembled on the steps just outside of the large doors. The butler and housekeeper stood on the bottom stair, ready to greet the couple. Many could not hide their expressions of anticipation and wonder, for all were aware that something momentous had occurred.

"Ki'ara, you do remember Robert, my faithful Butler, and Lady Annabelle, my ever so efficient housekeeper?" the StCloud asked her with a smile. Ki'ara happily greeted the pair and then moved back to her husband's side.

"My friends, may I present to you Lady Ki'ara Marie StCloud?" he introduced his new wife formally to the staff. Smiles broke out all around and then clapping. Once it subsided, the housekeeper stepped forward.

"Welcome, Lady StCloud, to your new home. May life bring you nothing but blessings!" she stated with a huge smile.

The rest of the retainers greeted her words with renewed applause. Then, they all spoke in semi-unison. "Welcome, Lady! May you always be happy at Cloudshire Hall!"

"Thank you! I am so pleased to be here! It has been such a long time, but I remember some of you! It is wonderful to see all of you again!" Ki'ara responded joyfully.

⋅⋅⋗⋖⋅⋅

With the introductions to the other inhabitants of Cloudshire Hall out of the way, the lord of the manor was ready to get down to business. He carefully picked up his new bride and prepared to carry her over the threshold.

Realizing what their lord was about to do, the staff rushed inside. They lined up on both sides of the entry hall all the way to the stairs. This created an aisle for their lord to carry his new bride through.

The housekeeper made sure that everything was going just as they had planned it. Then, she and a couple of the maids hurried upstairs to turn down the bed. Everything else had been seen to hours ago.

Ki'ara felt so touched by their gesture of welcome that tears began to shimmer in her luminous eyes. This was so very different from the reception she had received just a few days ago by her own family!

When everyone was in place, Conall gently carried his beautiful bride across the threshold and towards the stairs. The servants' broad smiles and happy faces clearly showed their pleasure at finally having a mistress in the castle. That it was the Lady Ki'ara, the love of their lord, was best of all.

⋅⋅⋗⋖⋅⋅

Many of the older retainers still remembered the precocious and active little girl who had come visiting with her family so many years ago. Mikael, Ali'ana, and she had usually stayed for several days. Ki'ara had been all over the castle, and one had never known where one would meet her.

The StCloud had encouraged his staff to treat her special. They had orders to always be kind and helpful to the child. It had not taken Ki'ara long, however, to win their hearts. The servants had gladly allowed her to tag along and watch them while they worked or sometimes help, even if things had taken a bit longer that way.

Soon, the staff had started to look forward to the girl's visits almost as much as their master. They had gone to great lengths to make her time among them as pleasurable as they could and had delighted in her joy at their kind gestures.

Ki'ara had always been thankful for even the slightest of favors. Her gratefulness had made it so much fun for the servants. Since they had the full support of their master, they had gone out of their way to bring some additional amusement and excitement into the little one's life.

The StCloud and his people had all worked together to make her birthdays as memorable as possible. Somehow, they had managed to surpass themselves every year. The last one had been a true extravaganza, and Ki'ara had absolutely loved it. She had made sure to thank each and every one of them.

Had they known that this was to be the last birthday she would spend amongst them for many years to come, the servants would have gone even more over the top. They would have made sure that the little girl had an absolutely unforgettable memory to hold on to.

⚜

The staff of Cloudshire Hall was comprised of human or mostly human clan members. Many came from families that had served the StClouds for generations. Therefore, they were familiar with the ways of the immortals. Conall had seen no reason to guard his feelings in front of them, and the kinfolk had come to regard the child as their future mistress early on.

Great sadness had reigned in the castle when their lord had informed the staff that Ragnald had forbidden him any contact with Ki'ara. The clan had been told to be very careful around the MacClairs' from then on since the new lord was unearthing old grievances.

Conall had not been the only one who had mourned Ki'ara's absence. To see her now, all grown up and so beautiful, filled the retainers' hearts with boundless joy and gladness for their lord, whom they deeply revered.

The StCloud carried his new wife up the stairs with long strides. It seemed that her weight did not even faze him. Soon enough, they reached the bedroom, which was pleasantly warm. A fire had been lit, and candles placed around the chamber to give the room a welcoming and festive atmosphere.

Conall gently placed Ki'ara on her feet and stepped back. He had a good idea of what was planned next. As much as he wanted to undress his lady himself, he also understood how special it was for his people to prepare his bride for the wedding night.

"My lord, please allow us to get her ladyship ready for you," the housekeeper addressed the StCloud reverently. Conall was amazed to see a lacy nightgown laid out on the bed as well as brushes and other feminine items on an ornate dresser. Those things had been conspicuously absent in his room until this day.

Seeing his quizzical look, Lady Annabelle smiled. "We raided your mother's chambers!" she explained with a laugh. "Since this was so sudden, we were not sure if her ladyship would have any luggage!"

"Ki'ara does have a couple of bags in the back of the carriage. I would appreciate it if someone could bring them up here!" the StCloud replied.

Lord Iain, always thoughtful, had sent one of his men to fetch the luggage from the MacClair family's quarters right after Lyall had set off for Seamuir Castle.

The housekeeper immediately shouted an order, and one of the maids rushed off to get her new mistress's things. In the meantime, Conall was being shooed out the door so that Lady Annabelle and the maids could start getting Ki'ara ready for bed.

The preparations turned out to be a festive affair. Much laughter could be heard emanating from the suite. There was a lot of rushing in and out of the room. It seemed that every few moments, something else was needed to make the newlyweds first night together as special as it could possibly be.

Still, it did not take that long before the young bride was ready for her new husband. When Lady Annabelle was finally satisfied, one of the maids was sent to retrieve the StCloud. He stopped dumbfounded when he entered the room. All he could do was stare at Ki'ara in awe.

"By the gods, you are beautiful!" was the only thing Conall finally managed to get out as he walked towards his wife like a moth drawn to the flame. All he was aware of was she.

Lady Annabelle gave a satisfied smile and waved the maids out the door. She firmly closed it behind herself and her helpers.

⚜

Ki'ara's hair had been brushed and shone in the candlelight like spun copper. The pure white of the lacy nightgown set off the vibrant red of her hair and her creamy complexion to perfection. Her eyes were filled with love. They were very dark green from the sense of anticipation that was filling her from head to toe.

Conall pulled Ki'ara towards him and kissed her like a man who was about to drown. How long had he waited for this moment! Gently lifting her up, he placed her on the bed. After kicking off his boots, untying, and dropping his pants, the StCloud slid under the sheets beside the lady who was the love of his life.

Laying on their sides facing each other, they regarded each other solemnly. After all of these years, they were finally husband and wife. Conall stretched out his hand and gently stroked his bride's soft cheek. He felt so lucky to have won this gorgeous woman's heart. Ki'ara's eyes darkened even further at his touch and locked with his.

Reaching out, the StCloud slowly pulled his wife towards him, never taking his gaze from hers. When their bodies touched, he could hear her sharp intake of breath. Conall once again claimed her lips. Passion resurged between them, and their kisses became more demanding as his hands stroked down her lean body.

His breathing was getting faster and harder, and the room seemed to grow inordinately hot. The StCloud could feel the need ignite between them once again. He finally had Ki'ara all to himself and in the comfort of his own bed!

Life did not get much better than this!

⸙

Conall intended to go slow and give Ki'ara all the pleasure he could. He felt that it was high time that she received a proper introduction to what this part of being married was all about. And, he wanted to make sure that she would genuinely enjoy it.

All this went out the window when Ki'ara divested him of the rest of his clothes and then stripped off her nightgown. Setting eyes on all of her shapely body, lit up perfectly by the light of the numerous candles, kicked the StCloud's desire into high gear yet once again.

Ki'ara's mischievous smile as she gently prodded him onto his back and positioned herself above him did the rest. He rose up to meet her as she lowered herself to receive him. This time he managed to delay his own gratification until he gave her release.

After resting for a few minutes, the StCloud gently lifted his bride off him and placed her on her back. Ki'ara gave him an inquisitive look, and he smiled at her as he began to trail kisses all over her small, firm breasts. Next, he used his tongue to explore her perfectly flat stomach and then continued to work his way down first one leg then the other. By now, they were both highly aroused yet once more.

Conall could not help himself; he wanted her time after time. His wife was eager and willing. Ki'ara experimented and soon found clever ways to pleasure him and increase his desire as well as her own.

It took a good while before the newlyweds were ready to fall peacefully and contentedly asleep in each other's arms. Both were well sated and glowed with happiness as well as perspiration.

Conall pulled Ki'ara tightly against him and gently covered her up. He was determined to hold onto her even in his sleep. After losing her once, he had no intention of ever letting her go again.

Chapter 18

A Rude Awakening

Conall and Ki'ara felt like they had just gone to sleep when an insistent knocking on their door awoke them. To their surprise, it was already light outside. Here and there, sunbeams were finding their way around the thick velvet curtains and were leaving bright patterns on the stone floor.

Covering up his wife, the StCloud gave permission for whoever was so determinedly demanding entry to do so. It turned out to be Robert. The butler gave his lord and lady an apologetic smile.

"What is it?" the StCloud enquired sleepily.

This had to be some sort of an emergency. Otherwise, the levelheaded and always considerate butler would not have awoken them this early. Especially not on their first day as a married couple!

"I am so sorry to wake you, sir and milady, but a messenger from Sir Iain just arrived. He says that he needs to speak to the both of you immediately and that it is extremely urgent. Judging from his poor horse, it must be," Robert responded.

"Please make him and the animal comfortable and inform him that we will be right down," Conall ordered. "Oh, and Robert? Please see to it that our breakfast is ready! We are both in need of coffee and food!"

"Yes, sir, immediately!" the butler retorted, smiling. After bowing to the couple, he rushed out of the room to see to their morning meal as well as the messenger.

⟡

As soon as the door was closed, the StCloud turned to his wife. Her bright eyes had grown dark with concern. This had to be about Ragnald! Her oldest brother had not been very nice to her, but they were still family.

What had happened to her brother to warrant a messenger? Why had her uncle not used the magic mirror to contact them? That would have been a much more expedient way! Could they have overheard its chime?

"Good morning, love!" Conall greeted her, gently placing a soft kiss on her lips. "I had imagined our first morning together a bit different, but it seems duty calls. Do you need a maid to help you with your gown?"

"Could you please assist me? It would take extra time to call for someone to dress me," she responded with a brief smile. "Let us get ready and find out what this is all about. My instincts tell me it has to do with Ragnald and that it is not good."

Pouncing out of bed, Ki'ara unabashedly walked naked over to the closet where the few clothes she had brought with her had been hung up. The StCloud could feel the instant reaction this produced in his body and deeply regretted that further explorations of his lovely wife would have to wait.

⟡

Ki'ara quickly slipped into her underclothes and then into a dress. In the last years, the only times she had been privileged to the services of a maid had been when she had been allowed to visit Seamuir Castle. Therefore, most of her gowns did not require assistance. The dress she picked out laced up in the front.

For expediency, Conall, who had gotten into his own clothes, helped Ki'ara pull the cords tight. Just this small gesture made him want her again, and he pulled her close and kissed her passionately. His vixen of a wife responded instantly by wrapping her arms around his neck and moving closer to him.

Did Ki'ara have any idea what an effect even this small gesture had on him? The growing bulge in his pants should have definitely been a clue. He had always loved her, but this sensual, sexy side she was now displaying was the biggest turn-on of all. Who would have thought that his virgin wife could make love to him with such abandon?

After a few delicious moments, the StCloud ended the kiss. He felt a distinct sense of regret for not being able to indulge in the pleasure of their lovemaking at this moment. However, the smile they exchanged spoke volumes. They both hoped that they could return to the bedroom in just a few minutes, but first, they had to deal with whatever emergency was waiting for them downstairs.

After brushing a gentle kiss across Ki'ara's rosy lips, Conall released his now panting wife. He felt incredibly blessed to have married a woman who desired him as much as he did her! Not all men were that lucky!

✦✦✦

Ki'ara put some distance between them. They would never leave this room if she stayed close to him! Feeling his hardness against her had been so very tempting! For a moment, it had crossed her mind to lift up her skirt and let him have his way with her. Only the knowledge that the messenger was waiting downstairs had kept her from acting on this enticing impulse.

Slowly, her breathing returned to normal, and she finished getting ready. Ki'ara straightened up her clothes and quickly ran a brush over her unruly hair. It seemed especially obstinate this morning. Finally, she had to use her magic to give it a semblance of order.

⋯⋰⋰⋱⋱⋯

The StCloud watched her, entranced. Here she was using all those womanly articles that had been placed on his dresser. Looking around, he noticed that the atmosphere of the entire chamber had changed. It was much more feminine now. With amusement, he realized that his housekeeper had most certainly been busy!

Conall could still barely believe that this was real, that Ki'ara was actually here in his very own bedroom! In his home, as his wife! How many years had he longed for this moment! Had anticipated it, dreamt of this very instant!

The day he had laid eyes on Ki'ara, he had been smitten. It had been as if his soul recognized hers and formed an instant bond. Mikael had been only too happy to agree to a tentative engagement. Since then, no other lady had ever set foot in these chambers, had shared this bed. To him, doing so would have felt like a betrayal, a sacrilege.

⋯⋰⋰⋱⋱⋯

Being a virile male, however, he had needs. Those, he had taken care of elsewhere. The StCloud had met enough willing women, but most of them had held little to no appeal for him. His heart had been taken, and his interest in other women minimal. He also did not want to take a chance at fathering a child.

Past experience and watching his friends had taught him that a quick dalliance could turn into a nightmare. Some women would use any and all tricks to land themselves a well-to-do lord!

Conall had wanted to save himself such drama and avoid the strings that often came with bedding a lady. He had ended up making a mutually beneficial agreement with Willa, the widow of one of his kinsmen.

⁕⁕⁕

When her husband had died suddenly, the young woman had found herself out on the streets. The man's son from his first marriage had kicked Willa out. He had taken over her home before his father had even been in the ground!

This had left her in dire need of a way to support herself as well as a place to live. Therefore, Willa had asked for an audience with the lord of her clan. Conall StCloud had been the one to see her. Keeping it brief, she had explained her plight and had asked for a position at Cloudshire Hall. The young woman had been willing to do just about anything to build a new life for herself.

Conall had volunteered to evict the son, but the widow had declined. Her marriage had turned into a nightmare when she had been unable to conceive a child. Finally, her husband had called in a midwife to examine her. At the tender age of 17, she had been declared barren.

Willa really had no desire to return to the place that held so many terrible memories for her. She also had not wanted another husband. In her opinion, one had been more than enough. She would bear the scars of his abuse for the rest of her life.

Most of the kinfolk, including herself, had been aware of the arrangement between the StCloud and Ki'ara's father. Seeing this young, virile lord before her had suddenly given the clever Willa an opportune idea. The more she had thought about it, the more she had liked it.

The lord was engaged, but his bride was an infant. He had many, many years to wait before making her his wife. In the meantime, what was he to do? He was a man and, therefore, obviously had certain needs. What if she volunteered to meet those? It could be a win-win for them both!

Brazenly, Willa had made Conall the proposal. He had looked stunned for a moment. Taking a mistress had not even occurred to him, but he had been able to see the benefits of the young widow's suggestion. She had been right, he had needs, and he had not wanted children with anyone but Ki'ara. Nor had he looked-for an attachment.

Willa had been a virgin when she had gotten married, and she had an upstanding reputation. The StCloud would be the second man to take her. To sweeten the deal, the young woman had sworn to be available only to him, anytime, any place.

To the widow, this had been a business arrangement. She had gladly promised no drama, no jealousy, no possessiveness over the young lord. Knowing how some of the fine ladies behaved and how clingy they could get once bedded, Willa had known that this would be very enticing. She had surmised that Conall had started considering it by his reaction.

For a life in relative comfort, the widow had been more than willing to sell the only thing she had left, herself. It would give her protection from other men as well, and to Willa, that had been huge. She had found the young lord rather attractive and had thought that she might actually even enjoy being his mistress.

When the StCloud had still hesitated, Willa had decided to get drastic. Can't expect him to buy the cat in the bag! With a coy look, she had slipped out of her dress and dropped it to the floor. With him watching, she had stripped off her underclothing. Seductively, she had stepped towards the young lord, had moved around him to come up behind him. Willa had eagerly pushed her naked body up against him.

At this point, the young woman had been totally enamored with her idea. She had been prepared to do anything to get her way. Therefore, she had used all her charm to turn on the young lord. Willa had placed her arms around Conall's slender waist, all the while rubbing up against his rear like a cat.

Boldly, she had run her hands over his crotch, had touched him, squeezed him. Once she had felt his reaction, she had slid her left hand inside his trousers and had started to fondle him, first softly, then harder. With her other hand, she had loosened the strings to his pants, working them down his slim hips.

Conall had been trying to object, but Willa's dexterous fingers had done the trick. In a way, her future had depended on this performance. Being this wealthy man's mistress had appealed to her much more than most other jobs she might have been able to get. Therefore, she had been willing to employ any and all tricks in the book.

For the very first time, the young widow had been thankful that her depraved husband had made her watch when he brought home the whores. Whenever she had tried to look away, he had slapped her. Later, he had forced her to behave just like them. On the first few of these occasions, Willa had gotten violently ill.

Knowing what was at stake, she had pulled out all stops. Before long, her ministrations had the StCloud moaning. She had smiled to herself; she had the young lord just where she wanted him. Now it was time to clinch the deal.

Looking around for the best place to pleasure Conall, her eyes had settled on the thick rug in front of the fireplace. The couch was too narrow and would hamper her motions. Guiding him from behind while keeping her fingers occupied with his throbbing member, she had steered him to the desired location.

Willa had moved around him and had let her mouth do some of the work. Using both hands, she had encouraged Conall to get down and lay on his back, all the while sucking and licking him. Once she had him reclining comfortably, she had positioned herself above him and had slid him inside her.

The StCloud had given in to her insistence and had taken her right then and there. To her surprise, Willa had actually enjoyed the act for the very first time. So much, as a matter of fact, that she had encouraged Conall to do it again a few minutes later.

By that time, however, he had assigned her a small but beautifully decorated bedroom close to his own. Willa had instantly fallen in love with the chamber. This was so much nicer than any place she had ever called her own!

Conall had satisfied his needs with her, but he had also made sure to give her pleasure in return. This had been beyond unexpected, and Willa had thanked her lucky stars for giving her such a splendid idea!

The 18year old widow had wanted the StCloud to know what he was getting and that she could please him, better than most fine ladies or even a whore. Her talents had left quite an impression. Papers had been drawn up, and her life of leisure had begun.

⋆｡˚⚘˚｡⋆

Whenever the StCloud had been home and had wanted her, Willa had taken up residence at the castle. With his permission, she had made the lovely room close to his entirely her own. The imaginative young woman had turned it into quite the lovenest for the two of them since his bedroom had always been off-limits.

When Conall had gone traveling, Willa had packed up, collected the guards he had assigned to her, and returned to her small house out in the woods. She had loved the peacefulness and isolation of the location and had always been thrilled to return to her home.

Willa had been attractive, intelligent, and discreet. She had gladly given him her body in return for her independence and never having to marry again. Her price had been a secluded cottage close to the castle and a monthly stipend for life. The arrangement had suited them both, and they had become friends.

On one of her visits, Ki'ara had figured out that Willa was the one who took care of the StCloud's needs. Displaying a rare maturity for one of her tender age, she had befriended the woman. The girl had thanked her instead of getting jealous.

Ki'ara, to both Conall's and Willa's surprise, had let them know that she approved of their deal. In her mind, it had been much safer for her future husband to associate with such a nice woman. It had kept him from falling prey to one of the ladies who wanted him for her own. The StCloud, however, had never visited his mistress whenever Ki'ara was at Cloudshire Hall.

Then, everything had changed. Willa had been the one he had shared the actual depth of his grief with when Ragnald had broken Conall's engagement to Ki'ara and had forbidden him to speak to the girl. Never before that day had the young widow seen him cry and never since.

A few days later, Willa had a dream. She had seen Conall and a grownup Ki'ara happily laughing together, walking hand in hand. She had known in her gut that this had been a foretelling and had shared it with him.

Genuinely caring for the young lord, Willa had always encouraged the StCloud not to give up hope. She had reassured him, time after time, that love would find a way. She had kept telling him that Ki'ara would come back into his life and that he would win in the end.

Conall was grateful to Willa. Her support had kept him strong through the years and made this miracle in front of him possible.

The newlywed's eyes met in the mirror above the dresser. Desire sparked instantaneously only to be replaced a moment later with weariness. With a sigh, Ki'ara turned to the StCloud, and he rushed to embrace her. His wife laid her head on his well-muscled chest, seeking comfort. Conall protectively tightened his arms around her.

After enjoying his embrace for a few moments, Ki'ara nodded. She was ready to face whatever was coming. Staying in their room any longer would not make it go away.

Their pleasure would have to wait until later. Being as presentable as they were going to be, the couple headed out the door.

Chapter 19

Seamuir Castle

In the meantime, chaos reigned at Seamuir Castle. The wave had hit there especially hard. Some people were milling about in confusion, while others were still unconscious. Not all had been accounted for, and the injured had not been seen to. Since no one dared to take charge for fear of reprisal, disorder ruled. As usual, the MacClair was nowhere in sight.

Lord Iain had finally managed to reach Seamuir by the magic mirror. The attendant had passed the message on to James, the castle's butler. Being an old and rather prudent person, the man had decided to find out what information he could before checking on Ragnald.

James was only too aware of his lord's dreadful temper. If he disturbed his master without an acceptable explanation, Ragnald would make him pay. No one at the castle cared to be subjected to that!

The butler, therefore, had immediately searched out the most senior inhabitant of the fortress. The ancient crone was well versed in herbs, the lore of the land, and she was a seeress. She would know what was going on and what had caused all that commotion!

Ragnald had been furious that his father had granted this useless, feeble old woman lifetime residency of the castle. Since he could not evict her totally, he had banned Zertra to the stables.

⚘⚘

Before the butler even entered the building, he could hear the witch cackling with glee. He immediately realized that this did not bode well for his lord. The old woman hated Ragnald since he had treated her abysmally after his father departed. If she was this merry, then things did indeed look bleak for the master.

James reached the stall that Zertra had been forced to make her home. It was located right next to the pigs, and the smell was plain awful. To his surprise, he saw her stretched out on the cold floor. He knew she was old and frail and immediately rushed to assist her.

"Old Mother, are you alright?" the butler inquired.

Zertra nodded and gave him a toothless grin. She did, however, seem weak and maybe a little confused. James gently lifted the still chuckling woman up and placed her back on her bed. It saddened him when he noticed how light she had become; her body had been reduced to nothing but skin and bones.

This woman had been much beloved, and her wisdom honored by Lord Mikael. The butler had been horrified to see the new lord treat her so cruelly. He had covertly done what he could to ensure that Zertra had some comforts and was not abused by the stable hands, but it seemed that this had not been enough. It was evident that she was starving.

Ragnald would punish anyone who showed kindness to those who could no longer pull their weight. Zertra, he had hated even more because he could not throw her out of the keep and because his father had valued her. It seemed that little food had been sneaked to the stables to this helpless old woman.

"Please, can you tell me what has happened? Why were you on the floor?" James asked her with concern once he had made Zertra comfortable on the rickety cot that served as her bed. The crone finally desisted in her cackling and regarded him with bright eyes.

"Much has happened! Did you feel that wave? It knocked me out! The prophecy has come to pass, and change has arrived at this old castle!" Zertra told him excitedly. "All the evil one's attempts to prevent this have come to naught!" The laughter that followed that proclamation shook the seeress's entire body.

⋆⁂⋆

The butler gave her a puzzled look. He could make no sense of her cryptic explanation. Seeing his confusion, the old woman began to cackle even louder. James did all he could to stay patient, but he needed to check on Ragnald. The message from Lord Iain had said that it was urgent.

"I have no idea what you are talking about and need to get back to the castle. Zertra, please, if you help me out, I will have the cook send out a big bowl of food and some bread for you," James promised. The least he could do is see to it that she was fed. Who knew when the old woman had last enjoyed a decent meal!

"I have been asked to check on the MacClair, and if I burst into his office and he is just fine, he will have my hide! You know what he is like! I am scared! Could you please explain to me what has happened?" he requested urgently, now that he had her attention.

The laughter subsided into mirthful chuckles. "She has done it! Married the StCloud!" the crone finally squeezed out between giggles. Seeing James' look of complete incomprehension, she went on.

"It was their joining that caused the wave of power we all felt! It raced across all of the Highlands! Our magic is free, has chosen a new ruler, and had its revenge! You don't have to fear that brute ever again!" she stated with an expression of ultimate glee.

"Thank you, Old Mother! I will have a really nice meal sent out to you! You deserve it!" he told the old crone with a huge smile before rushing off towards the castle.

⋄

Hope had risen up in James at her words. Could their cruel lord's rule truly have come to an end? Nothing would have pleased him or the majority of the clan more! Something had to happen sooner or later! Their lives had been abject misery for too long!

That the magic, however, had bonded with another already, without the ceremony, that was a huge surprise. Who was the new ruler? Lyall, who was next in line, was weak and under his brother's control. Gawain was well-liked but had no interest in taking over, and the Lady Ki'ara had not been home much.

None of them were perfect and might turn out to be little better than Ragnald, but at least, they were not as cruel and could, therefore, not be worse.

⋄

The kitchen door was closest, and James figured that he could take care of his promise to Zertra on his way to check on Ragnald. Not that he actually felt any great desire to go to his lord's aid, but appearances had to be kept up! Especially with Lyall and Lord Iain's guards riding towards the castle.

Also, there could be others in need of assistance. With their master out of commission and his siblings absent, it fell to James to look after them. Racing through the cavernous kitchen, the butler shouted commands to the confused cook and her helpers. The urgency in his voice had them jump to the task with alacrity. The disoriented staff was relieved that someone was taking control.

If the magic had affected others in the same manner as the crone, they would need food and hot tea. James continued yelling orders at the bewildered servants as he was rushing up the stairs to check on Ragnald.

The butler enjoyed the feeling of being in charge. He had a mission, had to make sure that all were taken care of the way they deserved. There was no telling what kind of damage that beautiful, life-changing wave had caused! Or, what the magic had done to Ragnald if it truly had taken revenge!

People needed to be checked on and order restored, and he, James, as the representative of their new ruler, would see to it that this was accomplished quickly and efficiently.

The MacClair Clan would be cared for and the injured seen to. The butler was determined to do this properly this time, and not in the heartless manner of their once lord!

Chapter 20

A Dire Discovery

In Deansport, the MacClair family had a suite reserved just for them. This was where Lyall had been hiding out. He had been unaware that not far from him, an unexpected marriage was taking place. The pensive man had much to think about. He had barely paid attention to the comfortable and richly furnished rooms that were exclusively for the ruler of the clan and his relatives.

Having the place all to himself for the moment, Lyall had decided to make himself at home in the living area. He was still on the fence about breaking with Ragnald since he loved his brother dearly. Turning his back on the oldest was such a drastic step, one that Lyall feared. Also, it felt like he was abandoning his sibling in his time of need.

How drastically things had changed in one day! That morning, Lyall had been sure of his place in the world and in his family. But not anymore! After the incident in the courtyard, his gut had told him that he needed to leave Seamuir Castle and quickly! He had decided to heed the warning.

Hope, however, is hard to kill, and it still lived in Lyall's heart. Maybe Ragnald would see reason, and things could go back to the way they had been? Could there be a chance for a reconciliation? Not if the news that he had been seen with his other siblings would reach his brother's ears. Therefore, Lyall had decided to wait for Gawain and Ki'ara in the suite.

It was still hard to believe that the day had started out so well! He and Ragnald had a pleasant breakfast together, and all had been good between them. There had been no indications of Ragnald's insane plan, of things to come.

Just a few hours later, the whole world had been turned upside down. How could he have missed that the one person he had respected and loved so completely had such hatred in his soul?

In a way, Lyall had not only lost the connection with his brother but also his best friend. He had been deeply hurt by the realization that he really did not know Ragnald at all. The cruelty he had seen in his brother's face, as well as in his actions, had stunned him.

It seemed that Ragnald had lost all perspective. He had become downright dangerous. As unhinged as he was, he had probably seen Lyall's concern for Ki'ara as a huge betrayal that he most likely would never forgive. Would it ever be safe for any of them to go back to Seamuir Castle?

～✿⚘✿～

The MacClairs' suite was not far from the hall where the wedding festivities were taking place. When the wave reached Lyall, it knocked him out cold. He came to on the floor a short while later. The magic had moved on to spread out across the land.

It took Lyall a moment to clear his mind. What had just happened? He had been peacefully sitting there having a drink. Then, all of a sudden, he had gone flying. What had caused this? Fear stabbed through his heart. Did Ragnald have anything to do with that surge of power? Did his brother know where he was? Was this an act of revenge? Was he now trying to kill him too?

Raising up on his elbows, he started shaking his head in an attempt to regain his wits. That did not help; if anything, it made matters worse. Lyall got violently sick right there on the floor. Groaning, he laid back down and curled into a ball. It took several more minutes before he started feeling somewhat better and decided to try sitting up.

Lyall's whole body was still ringing like a bell, and coherent thought was not yet possible. His brain was positively pounding, and he was starting to feel nauseous again! Moaning, he supported his head between his hands before letting it sink down upon his knees. He could not remember ever being this miserable!

By the time Lord Iain's messenger came to check on him, Lyall had somewhat recovered. Still, it took him a couple of tries to make it out of the chair he had crawled to and collapsed into. Eventually, he had managed to get on his feet. On still rather wobbly legs, he had made it across the room to open the door and let the man in.

Once the guard had told him the actual cause of that incredibly powerful wave, however, Lyall forgot all about his own misery. He turned white as a sheet and, for a moment, concern for Ragnald drowned out all other thoughts. Then apprehension and caution set in.

Should he go to Seamuir Castle to check on his brother? Was it safe to do so? He had fled their home and, after the incident in the courtyard, had been afraid of

Ragnald. Then again, the magic had affected a Zidarian like him, who had no powers, this strongly. What had it done to someone like the MacClair?

Fear battled with deeply entrenched feelings of loyalty and concern for Ragnald. Finally, the love he had once felt for his older sibling won out. Together with the messenger, Lyall immediately rushed to the stables. There, he found two horses and a number of already mounted guards waiting for him.

Each soldier had a spare horse. This would allow them to switch mounts frequently and to ride faster and harder. His uncle, that wonderful, thoughtful man, had understood Lyall's need to get to Seamuir as quickly as possible but also his fear.

Having a good grasp of human nature, Lord Iain had anticipated his nephew's desire to check on his older brother. How well that kind lord knew them all! Lyall felt immensely grateful to his uncle, especially for sending the extra guards.

Lyall could not help being afraid of Ragnald. He had a lot of trepidations about returning to Seamuir Castle. Having some backup along was going to be a great comfort. It made him feel much more secure just in case his brother was fine and decided to see this as a chance to make his younger sibling pay for showing concern for Ki'ara.

All was in readiness. Lyall asked the messenger to convey his thanks to his uncle. Since time was of the essence, the young Zidarian saddled up. He was still a little unstable but resolute to go along.

Soon, he and his companions headed out of Deansport. They had a hard ride ahead of them. The young lord wished, not for the first time, that the gate could be located closer to the castle.

It was already getting towards dusk and would be sundown before too much longer. Therefore, the group carried lamps and were accompanied by a Zidarian wizard. They were well equipped to ride in the dark but would have to slow down a bit or risk injuring the horses. Consequently, they intended to get as far as they could while it was still light.

Now that he had made the decision to head to Seamuir, Lyall was determined that nothing would stop them from reaching the castle as soon as they possibly could.

Having verified that it would be safe to enter the study and that Ragnald was really in trouble, the castle's butler, James, went charging into the room. He did not notice the crumbled form of the MacClair. The lord had been flung to the floor close to the fireplace.

James kept looking around the office. At a glance, it appeared that there was no one in the chamber. It was not until the butler walked around the loveseat that he saw the motionless form of the lord of the manor. From the door, Ragnald had been perfectly hidden by the furniture placed in front of the hearth.

One glimpse told the experienced man that his master was not in good shape. He had come to rest on his side close to the bricks of the fireplace and was deeply unconscious. Somehow, Ragnald appeared to have been mangled by some unknown force. Had the wave done all that?

Rushing to the door, James called for help. Before long, a couple of servants arrived. The butler ordered one to find the lord's manservant and a healer, and the other, a rather stout chap, to stay and aid him in moving Ragnald to a more comfortable place.

Carefully, they straightened out the contorted form of Ragnald. Then, they lifted up their lord and placed him on the couch.

⚬⚬⚬

When he got his first good look at his master's face, it shocked James. His lord's eyes were sunk into his skull, and his lips bluish. He seemed to have aged decades in just these few minutes. Even though he did not much care for Ragnald, the butler could not help but feel compassion for him now.

A short while later, the lord's manservant arrived. He had no idea what to do for Ragnald and just stood there wringing his hands. Then, the second servant entered with the disoriented healer in tow. Having more Zidarian blood than many others at the castle, the effects of the wave had hit Kendrick much harder than most.

The usually extremely competent healer tried to look at his lord but kept seeing double. He finally gave up attempting to do so with both eyes open and closed one. James eyed him concernedly. "Are you ok?"

"I think so, but I am still not sure what happened," Kendrick responded weakly.

"It seems we were hit by a wave of magic," James replied cautiously.

"A wave of magic? I don't understand! Why?" The healer felt even more confused now. How could a wave of magic knock him out like this? Where had it come from, and what had caused it? And, why was their lord so deeply unconscious? The magic of the realm should have protected him!

⚬⚬⚬

James sent one of the men to fetch a drink for the healer. After a few more long minutes, Kendrick finally managed to get himself back into functional shape. His examination of Ragnald brought up more questions than it answered. The lord appeared to be aging, but this was impossible! He was an immortal Zidarian!

What had happened to the MacClair? Nothing Kendrick observed made any sense until James divulged that the magic had chosen another lord. Then the healer began to suspect that it had taken more than just the lord's powers.

Kendrick came to the conclusion that all he could do for Ragnald was to attempt to stabilize him. Healing the lord and reversing the damage that had been done by the sudden onset of rapid aging was beyond his or anyone else's abilities. He was not a god after all who could pass out immortal life.

Some of the more curious servants were hanging around the entrance to Ragnald's office under the guise of waiting for further instructions from James. Most kept shooting surreptitious glances at their lord. Seeing how badly he had fared, hope shone in their eyes, and many did not succeed in hiding their feelings of glee. One question was clearly written on their faces. Was this the end of their cruel oppressor?

Kendrick decided that they would serve his purpose perfectly. But, because most of them hated their master, he feared that they would rather let Ragnald die than help him. The other siblings and the new lord, however, would most likely want their brother alive. Maybe he could use that to gain this lot's willing cooperation!

"Listen up! I need a few things!" Kendrick began. Immediately, several of the servants began edging their way towards the door. James, however, would have none of that.

"Stop right there! Don't you dare leave this room until I say so! You will listen to what the man has to say!"

he bellowed. Cowed, the retainers scooted back to their previous spots.

"Thank you, James! Look, let's be honest! None of us liked him! Let me assure you that he is done for! I am just trying to keep him alive until our new lord gets here! How would it look if we just let him die?" he began.

"We don't know who the new MacClair is, but all the other siblings are much more compassionate! They are not like him; they would want to say goodbye to their brother! Can you help me make this possible? Please, for our new lord? Let's behave better than him!" Kendrick pleaded.

First one 'aye' then another resounded around the room. People started to line up to get their orders. The healer's words had touched them deeply. He had reminded them that they were still Highlanders and that they could show kindness and compassion even to one they hated as much as they did Ragnald.

✦❦✦

Kendrick needed herbs and items from his rooms and from the gardens, and he needed them quickly. He, therefore, took full advantage of his eager helpers. One after another was sent off to retrieve much-needed items. A flurry of activities ensued.

Before long, a cauldron was bubbling on the hearth, and space had been cleared on Ragnald's desk so that Kendrick could work. He needed room for all the things required to prepare the elixir. Mumbling spell after spell to add extra strength to the brew, the healer made the concoction.

Ragnald's color did get a little better once Kendrick managed to administer a bit of the tonic to the unconscious man. He had to do this one spoonful at a time and massage the lord's throat after each to get him to swallow. It took a long time to even get some of it in him, and after a while, James took over under the healer's supervision.

Even after the speech he had given and the help he had gotten from the castle's servants, Kendrick did not feel very comfortable leaving anyone else in charge of Ragnald's care except himself and James. The hatred for their once lord just ran too deep.

⁜

James greeted him at the door when Lyall and his contingent of guards arrived sometime later. The butler immediately escorted him to the office where the still unconscious Ragnald was being cared for. Kendrick had been unwilling to move him until the elixir had a chance to do its job.

Despite the healer's best efforts, Ragnald had continued to age. He looked like a corpse, just barely alive. Lyall was deeply shocked and rushed to his brother's side. Tears started to run down his cheeks, and all the evil and hurt his sibling had done were instantly forgotten.

Sobbing, Lyall sank into the chair Kendrick quickly pushed his way. With ultimate care, he picked up his beloved brother's hand and held it ever so gently. He did not have to be told that Ragnald was on death's door; he could see it and sense it.

⁜

The butler watched Lyall carefully. Something was different about him. The mousy man seemed to have a little more color to him than before; his hair was darker, his eyes clearer, and his pasty complexion more rosy. This was more than just appearing flushed due to the long ride and being so upset.

There was a slight air of power about Lyall that had never been there before. James noted this with great interest. Could it be that as Ragnald was declining, his shadow was coming into his own?

The butler was sure of one thing. If the magic had passed to the second MacClair, it would not have been to the benefit of the clan. He was too weak, too easily influenced. Lyall did not have a strong enough personality to govern the high-spirited Highlanders. Also, his close association with Ragnald would have caused doubt and resentment from the start.

As long as Ragnald was alive and conscious, even as feeble as he was now, his wishes would have influenced Lyall's decisions. If the cruel lord ever woke up, he would have ruled through his weakling brother. In both cases, not much would have changed for the clan.

Chapter 21

James In Charge

Over the head of the sobbing Lyall, James exchanged a concerned look with Ragnald's manservant. Their once lord looked barely alive. All the elixir the healer had administered had achieved little. It had been unable to stop the ongoing aging process.

Once Kendrick had taken over Ragnald's care and had gotten the helpers somewhat under control, James had slipped away. He had used the magic mirror to contact Lord Iain to make his report. The Lord of Ravenshire had been greatly upset by the news of his nephew's condition. He had not expected it to be this bad.

Lord Iain firmly believed that there was only one person who could help Ragnald, and that was Ki'ara. She was the new ruler and had the full power of the magic of the land behind her. The lord thought that she might be able to keep him alive and possibly even undo some of the damage. He had told the butler that he would immediately send a messenger after the lady and inform Gawain.

˙˙⸳ꞏ⸙ꞏ⸳˙˙

James had been very surprised to hear that the Lady Ki'ara was the new lord. Being the youngest and having been absent so much, this was rather unexpected. He did mention to Lord Iain how very impressed he had been with her conduct after the fire. Unlike Ragnald, she had taken care of the clan's people.

The Lord of Ravenshire had smiled sadly. Ki'ara's nature was far different than Ragnald's, almost opposite. He had told James as much before asking to be kept informed of his nephew's condition and breaking off the contact.

James had considered the news carefully. Even if the lady could save her brother, she had to be a saint to do so after the way Ki'ara had been treated by her oldest sibling. No one would blame her if she refused, and deep down, the butler wished that she would. In his opinion, Ragnald was getting what was coming to him.

˙˙⸳ꞏ⸙ꞏ⸳˙˙

When the riders had been reported, the butler had hoped that it would be someone who would take over the responsibility for the dying Zidarian as well as the castle. One look at Lyall disabused him of that notion. The young man was still not fully recovered and a picture of abject misery, especially after the fast, hard ride. James realized that not much help could be expected from that quarter.

Lyall was so distraught after seeing his brother that he was shaking like a leaf. When asked if he had any idea how to help Ragnald, he sadly shook his head. Since it appeared that all the responsibility was falling on him, James concluded that he better do everything he possibly could. It would not look good to have Ragnald die on his watch.

The butler, therefore, decided that since Kendrick had been unable to help Ragnald, the witch should give it a try. At the very least, she might have mercy on Lyall and provide him with something to settle his nerves. The healer had his hands full making more of the elixir and did not have the time to deal with yet another patient.

Even though Lyall was clearly leaving James in charge, proprieties had to be observed. "Sir, what would you like me to do for your brother? He looks like he is in desperate need of more help than Kendrick can offer. May I send for the Old Mother? Your father trusted her implicitly," he asked respectfully.

"James, do whatever you think is necessary. I can sense that his life is slipping away, but I have no clue how to help him. I'm not feeling so well myself; my head is killing me," Lyall responded weakly. He scooted closer to his brother, laid his head on the armrest, and closed his eyes. This was all the butler needed to hear.

"Go get the Old Mother! Carry her here if you must!" he commanded a couple of the servants lingering in the room. Hearing the ring of urgency in James' voice sent his underlings scrambling. The lord must be in really bad shape for the butler to send for the witch. Everyone knew that she hated Ragnald!

James thought that the fragile lord would be much more comfortable in his own bed than on that hard sofa. The healer had objected so far, but the butler felt that it was time to override him.

"Kendrick, I am having his lordship moved to the bedroom. He will be much better off there than scrunched up on that sofa!" James informed him. His tone conveyed that he was committed to this course of action.

When the healer was going to object, the butler gave him a look that made him bite back his remark. In the end, Kendrick nodded his acquiescence.

James ordered his men to find a stretcher. They gently maneuvered Ragnald onto the soft blanket covering the rough canvas. Very, very cautiously, they carried him up the stairs and into his bedroom. It had been challenging to keep the contraption level and to prevent the dying man from being jostled, but they had done their best.

At this point, Ragnald was so fragile that they were all afraid to touch him. His body was skeletal, and the skin stretched taut and waxy looking. Kendrick had feared that picking him up would break his bones. Therefore, they carefully lifted the invalid up with the blanket to place him on the bed.

By the time the manservant had removed his master's boots and tie, Zertra was brought in. When they had been unable to convince the old witch to come with them peacefully, one of the servants had just picked her up. Her cussing him out could be heard long before the group ever reached the chamber.

On James' orders, lights had been lit all around the room. The butler got a really good look at Ragnald. The Zidarian was deathly pale, and his breathing was shallow. He looked like a cadaver. The grey streak that had started at his temples had spread. Most of the hair was grey now and falling out in clumps. The lord seemed to have aged even further in the last few minutes.

It took several tense minutes, but finally, James managed to calm down the irate Zertra. However, she still refused to help and loudly complained about the treatment she had received since Lord Mikael's departure. Lyall, who had been sitting beside the bed holding his brother's fragile hand, decided that is was time for him to step in.

"Old Mother," he began deferentially, "please forgive us for the way we have treated you. I am truly sorry that you have suffered so. I will give you whatever you want to make up for this, just please, help my brother!"

Zertra saw the tears in Lyall's eyes. She was touched by his devotion to a brother who had manipulated and used him for years. Her heart softened, and she made up her mind to start negotiations. After all, what did she have to lose?

Once Lyall promised her a warm bed in the castle, three meals a day, and an occasional tankard of beer, she agreed to take a look at the dying man.

The wise woman gently lifted up the lord's eyelids and carefully examined his hair and face. She gingerly placed her head on his chest and listened to his heart and breathing. Mumbling and clucking to herself, she opened his mouth and checked his teeth and gums.

Finally, Zertra seemed to be satisfied. She started walking up and down in front of the fireplace, deep in thought. "Lord Lyall, I could use your help!" she finally addressed Lyall in her creaky, high voice.

"Yes, Old Mother, what can I do to assist you?" came the immediate response.

"For one, you might want to send for his uncle and your siblings if you have not already done so!" Zertra continued.

"James, would you please see to it that my siblings and uncle are informed? I am not up to talking to any of them at the moment," Lyall requested.

Getting up from his place close to his brother, Lyall made his way to the Old Mother's side. His face looked positively green like he was going to throw up at any moment. The old woman waved him back towards the bed.

Obeying her without giving it a second thought, Lyall stumbled over his own feet. He was exhausted and sick from his personal experience with the wave and from the emotional drain of seeing his beloved sibling in such terrible shape. James rushed to push a chair under the lord's rear.

"I know you feel terrible, but I cannot do this without you," Zertra informed Lyall.

"Your brother is aging at a rapid rate. If we can't stop it, he will die. I need your connection to the land to help slow it until your sister arrives," she told him quietly.

"Why my sister?" Lyall asked perplexedly.

"Because she is the new lord and the only one who has the power to help him," the old crone explained patiently.

Lyall was utterly stunned for a brief moment. Then, understanding of his brother's condition began to dawn. The wave had brought about changes, huge changes! There had been some truth to that prophecy, after all!

A voice startled Lyall out of his reverie. "With your permission, Lord, I will send a message to Lord Iain to come just as quickly as he can and to bring Lord Gawain. He should still be in the town where the wedding took place," James addressed the faint looking man.

Lyall gave him a weak wave. "By all means, do what you think is best. Please, James, take charge of this entire situation. You have my permission to order anything you deem necessary. I will assist Zertra and do what I can for my brother," came his tired reply.

As James rushed off to contact Lord Iain, the ancient woman took Lyall's left hand in her own. "I need a much stronger connection to the land. You can help me with that. Don't think about it or worry about it, I will do all the work. Just let it all go and relax. Close your eyes and take some deep breaths," she instructed the exhausted lord.

For once, this was easy for Lyall. He was tired beyond caring. Soon he could sense himself touching the ancient power. He could barely believe it, for he had resigned himself to never feeling this connection that was the birthright of every Zidarian child. He experienced such a sensation of homecoming that it brought tears to Lyall's eyes.

"Open yourself fully to the magic," the wise woman commanded. Lyall gladly obeyed and could feel the welcoming warmth of the land's magic spread through his entire being.

⚜

By the time Ragnald was marginally stabilized, both Lyall and the old woman were exhausted. James was the only one still awake and had made himself comfortable in a chair by the fire. He had been watching the pair with concern for some time. If they extended themselves any further, they might both collapse! It would not do to have two more invalids to care for!

The butler was greatly relieved when Zertra finally raised her head. Lyall was partially resting on the bed and immediately fell sound asleep. The witch limped over towards James and looked at him with blurry eyes. It was evident that she was beyond tired.

James immediately jumped up and helped her into the other chair. After using that much magic, they would both need to eat. Therefore, the butler had broth, thick sandwiches, and tea waiting for them.

At his questioning gaze, Zertra shrugged her shoulders. She was old and much weaker than she used to be, especially since meals had been few and far between these last few years. But, even in her prime, the task of saving this lord would have been beyond her.

"I hope his sister arrives in time. Only she can help him, but I don't think that he will live long even then. The magic has taken revenge. It has made him mortal for all the crimes he has committed against it and the clan," she explained.

"Can't say that he doesn't deserve it," she mumbled under her breath just loud enough for James to hear but too faint to wake up the sleeping Lyall. The butler could only agree but felt that it was best not to voice his opinion.

His first priority now was to get nourishment into these two. Carefully, James held a cup of broth for Zertra to sip from. When she felt strong enough, she took it from him and proceeded to empty it rather quickly before asking for more.

After refilling the old woman's mug, the butler prepared another. He gently woke the sleeping Lyall and handed him the hot soup. James stayed close by just in case the fatigued lord needed him. After the broth was all gone, he fetched one of the thick sandwiches.

Only after Lyall had eaten all the food James felt was necessary to restore him, did he allow the young man to put his head back down and go back to sleep. Zertra, in the meantime, had eaten her fair share and had fallen asleep in the chair.

※

Since someone needed to keep watch over Ragnald, James pulled up a chair close to the bed. Here he sat for a couple more hours before sending for Kendrick to relieve him. He desperately needed some sleep. He was in charge of the castle and its people and not the youngest anymore. A clear head was essential in making the right decisions!

As much as the butler had disliked his master, he could not help but feel pity for Ragnald. What must it be like to go from being a virile, healthy man to an almost corpse in just a few short hours? It had to be beyond devastating! How could one possibly adjust to that, deal with that?

Not that James would say so to Lyall, but maybe it was best if Ragnald never woke up!

Chapter 22

Immortal No More

When Ragnald came to, it was late in the morning of the next day. He looked around, disoriented. The last thing he remembered was sitting in his study, taking a drink. He had no idea what had happened to him after that, but it must not have been good. He felt worse than he ever had in his entire life, and his whole body ached.

His eyes were open, but everything was blurry. Ragnald decided that he was probably just hungover from all the alcohol he had consumed. That might also explain why he felt so awful. Well, the clan and the realm did not run itself. It was time to get up and make sure everyone was sufficiently intimidated, especially after the debacle of the day before.

When Ragnald tried to move, his body would not cooperate. He tried to speak, but all that came out was a barely audible moan. Still, Lyall, who was sitting near the window reading, heard the sound. He realized that his sibling was finally awake.

Lyall immediately jumped up and rushed over to the bed. Bending over Ragnald, he anxiously studied his brother's withered face. He could not hide his concern. Even with all the magic he and Zertra had used to try to arrest the rapid aging, it was still proceeding. At least they had managed to slow it down significantly.

"How are you? How do you feel?" came the younger lord's worried questions. Ragnald tried to answer, but his mouth was too dry to do so. Funny, even his teeth felt loose. That must be some hangover! How much did he drink anyhow? After a brief moment, Lyall realized the problem and carefully dripped some water into his brother's parched mouth.

"I feel terrible, my whole body hurts! Why are you treating me like an invalid? Why can't I move? What happened to me?" Ragnald finally managed to squeeze out feebly. Lyall had to bend close and put his ear right up to his brother's mouth to be able to hear him.

"You are suffering from the effect of a wave of magic. It seems that you went flying across the room. I came to after a bit with a headache from hell, but you did not stir until now! When we could not wake you up, we carried you up here to your bed," Lyall explained. He decided not to mention that he had been in Deansport when the magic struck. Now was not the time to bring that up!

Ragnald tried to move again and groaned when the pain that seemed to be afflicting his entire body became unbearable. He hated feeling helpless. Why did things always happen to him? Life was so unfair! It should be his brother lying in this bed right now and not he!

⁕

To make matters worse, it was a bright and beautiful morning. Sunlight was happily pouring into the room, and dust motes were dancing in the sunbeams. How dare the weather be so pleasant when he, the MacClair, the ultimate ruler of the realm, felt so lousy?

It should be raining or, even better, there should be a storm! A bad one with lots of strong winds and driving rain! With frequent lightning and deafening thunder! Where was that magic? Maybe he could coerce it to bring in some clouds!

When Ragnald reached out to force the power of the land into compliance, there was nothing. No connection, no magic singing in his blood, just a yawning emptiness where his bond had once been. How could this be? He was still the lord, wasn't he?

It took him a few moments. Then Ragnald started to remember some of the events from the previous day or at least the version that had been implanted in his mind by the magic. He recalled the strange tearing feeling as the wave washed through him. Horror set in, and self-pity overwhelmed him. How could the world be this gay, this cheerful, when his life had changed forever?

Lyall was still bent over him, and he could see the worry in his eyes. Fear rose up inside Ragnald and almost swallowed him whole. Did his brother know? It did not seem so. He most certainly would not be here if he was aware that he was watching over a has-been lord!

What would Lyall do once he realized that his once so mighty sibling was as weak as a baby? That he had no way of defending himself? Would his brother kill him or denounce him? That was surely something he, Ragnald, would have done if roles were reversed!

꧁꧂

As the eldest, he had terrorized all his siblings, and they had been scared of him. Ragnald knew that the youngest two intensely disliked him and that many of the clan members despised him. Loyalty had never been that important to him; he had preferred intimidation. He had wanted everyone to fear him to the point that no one would dare cross him.

"What was that wave? What triggered it? Was it her fault? Did she marry the StCloud?" Ragnald whispered. He figured that, as always, if something was wrong in his life, it had to be Ki'ara's or Conall's fault. They had caused this somehow, just like all the other calamities that had made his life hell over the years!

Lyall hesitated for a moment and then nodded weakly. He did not trust himself to speak. Leave it to Ragnald to immediately point the finger at their sister and the StCloud, as always. He was right, this time, but still! Could his brother not see that his own actions had caused the magic to take such severe revenge?

Ragnald had blanched even further. He firmly believed that if Ki'ara was married to that brute, life as they had known it was over. The Highlands were doomed. How long would it take his brother to figure this out? And, was he even smart enough to understand the severity of the situation?

"It seems we are all still alive, and not much has changed. Can I get you anything? Would you like some broth?" Lyall inquired, searching his brother's face. What he did see made him take a step back. His newfound senses did not allow him to ignore the truth any longer.

⊱✿⊰

Leave it to Lyall to be totally clueless! And why was he hovering like that? With tremendous effort, Ragnald raised his arm to push a strand of hair out of his face. He stopped in mid-motion.

His hand! Ragnald looked at it in horror. His vision had not improved, but he could still make out some of the changes in his once strong and healthy appendage. It was gaunt and covered in age spots and looked more like something belonging to a fleshed skeleton and not a man!

"Bring me a mirror!" Ragnald tried to scream at his brother, but his voice, which had once been vibrant and deep, came out more like a weak, whispering croak. His agitation was clearly visible to his concerned sibling. "Mirror!" he demanded once more.

"Calm yourself, please! If you insist, I will get you a mirror in a few minutes! Why don't you eat some broth first? It will help you feel better!" Lyall tried to distract his brother. He really did not want Ragnald to get a glimpse at himself. The shock might be too much and kill him right then and there!

Ragnald was furious. If that little twerp was not going to do his bidding, he would just get up and fetch it himself! He tried desperately to make his body obey him, but his aching bones and arthritic joints would not cooperate. And, he was incredibly weak! How could he not even have the strength to get out of this bed?

⚘

Lyall realized that Ragnald would not relent until he had what he wanted. Being so fragile, his sibling might actually hurt himself if he kept trying to move. Therefore, the resigned man went to the bathroom and brought back a mirror. Hesitantly, he held it so that his brother was able to get a look at himself.

It took him a moment to focus, but once he did, Ragnald stared as his reflection in pure horror. "I look like a bog mummy, a corpse, and I am old! How can that be? I am immortal! What has she done to me?" he muttered in his weak old man voice.

Suddenly, he recalled the tearing sensation when the wave had hit him. That must have been when his link to the magic was severed! It must have taken his immortality as well! Was this the power of the land's way to get even with him for all the years he had oppressed it?

The arrogant man quickly decided against that possibility. That surge of raw energy spawned by Ki'ara and the StCloud must have done this, taken his power, and with it, his rule and immortality! Only something created by the abomination was cruel enough to punish him such! The magic, after all, had been firmly under his control and would have never dared to harm its master!

"It's all her fault! She did this to me on purpose! Had to marry that man just to get even with me, to harm me! She has brought disaster to us all! I should have killed her! Should have killed them both that day, her and Gawain, when he burst in and stopped me!" Ragnald muttered feebly.

Lyall looked at his brother as if he had never seen him before. How could he have missed that his best friend and constant companion was this thoroughly evil and completely deluded? Had he always been like this, or had he gotten worse recently?

✦⁓✦⁓✦

Ragnald became increasingly angrier and more agitated the longer he thought about the abomination and that she had gotten the better of him instead of him managing to destroy her. His eyes began rolling in his head. Spasms started to shake his entire body, and bloody foam appeared on his lips, which had turned bluish again.

Lyall was terrified. He rushed to the bell pull. Help arrived quickly, but none of them knew what to do for the convulsing Ragnald. No one dared even touch him for fear of breaking his bones. The manservant rushed off in search of the wise woman.

Just as the witch walked in the door, Ragnald suddenly sat up in the bed like a stiff marionette. His eyes were rolled up in his head and appeared pure white. His wrinkled face was contorted with hatred.

".... Kill her! Should have killed her when ..!" he coughed. Bubbles of blood were flecking his lips, and droplets were splattering all over the dark green covers. Ragnald jerked like he had been hit by lightning and then collapsed back on the mattress. There, he lay as still as the dead.

✦✦✧✦✦

At his words, every person in the room had frozen in place. They stared at the unconscious Ragnald, and their feelings of revulsion showed plainly on their faces. Not a one of them felt pity for him any longer, and no one wanted to go near him, not even his very own brother.

In response to Lyall's pleading looks, the wise woman finally did. She checked Ragnald's breathing and heartbeat before pulling the covers up to his chin.

"Is he dead?" Lyall's shaking voice broke the silence in the room. "No, but not far from it either. Do you think your brother would want some form of absolution?" the witch inquired.

"No, I don't think so. Ragnald hated the priests and the druids as well. He only believed in the vicious old gods of our grandfather, and to them, what he has done was no sin," Lyall replied sadly.

"I realize now that he is truly evil, but he is still my brother, and I love him. Is there anything else that you can do for him, Old Mother?" he pleaded.

"No, my lord, I have done all I could. The only chance he has is the Lady Ki'ara arriving in time," Zertra replied.

The old woman stood there for a moment and regarded Lyall with compassion and understanding. Overcoming his revulsion, he had returned to the bed and was sitting beside his deeply unconscious brother, quietly sobbing. She realized that he was grieving for Ragnald as well as himself.

With a wave, Zertra commanded everyone out of the room. There was nothing any of them could do. She silently closed the door behind herself. Only a miracle could save Ragnald now.

⁘⁘⁘

Not long after, Lord Iain and Gawain arrived. They had left immediately after receiving the request to come to Seamuir and had ridden hard. The butler escorted them straight up to the chamber. Neither was prepared for the state Ragnald was in. Both were shocked when they first laid eyes on him.

They had known that his condition was dire, but this, they had not expected. The body in the bed resembled more a corpse than a living, breathing man. If Ragnald continued to deteriorate, Ki'ara would be too late to save him.

One standing on each side of the bed, Gawain and his uncle raised their power until it crackled between their outstretched hands. Bit by bit, and with the utmost care, they funneled their magic into the barely alive Ragnald. The lord of Ravenshire and Gawain hoped to buy Ki'ara just a little more time.

When they had done all they were able to, they released their hold on the magic. Lord Iain pulled a chair over towards the bed. Exhaustion was written all over his face. After sending a servant for a bite to eat and something to drink, Gawain joined him.

The two had decided that they would stay by the bedside and keep the vigil together with Lyall. All three were aware that the situation was desperate. Ragnald's only hope was that Ki'ara would arrive before too much longer.

⁘⁘⁘

Lord Iain had not liked his oldest nephew very much, but to see him in such awful shape was heartbreaking.

He and Gawain tried to comfort the distraught Lyall, who was not just upset over his brother dying.

The second MacClair's heart was also filled with remorse that he had been so compliant and supportive of his favorite sibling without ever questioning Ragnald's motives. Lyall now understood that he had condoned all kinds of ugly acts by keeping silent. By giving his brother his unconditional adoration and approval, he had given him the license to commit all sorts of atrocities.

With great sadness, Lyall faced the fact that he had allowed himself and his view of the world to be poisoned by Ragnald. Due to his extreme love of his brother, he had refused to see what kind of a despicable person his adored sibling actually was.

Lyall realized that by not speaking up, by not taking a stand, by turning a blind eye, he had been complicit in all the crimes Ragnald had committed over the years. This filled him with immeasurable grief and regret.

Chapter 23

Dreadful News

Earlier that day at Cloudshire Hall, Conall StCloud and his wife received the messenger in the breakfast room. Ki'ara saw how tired the man looked. He must have ridden really hard to get here this soon. She offered him a cup of tea, but he declined. His message came first; everything else could wait.

"Lady, Lord, my master, Lord Iain, asks that you hurry back to Seamuir Castle. Lords Gawain and Lyall are alright, but your oldest brother is in desperate need of your help. My lord bids you to get to the castle just as fast as you can!" he told them.

The StCloud rushed to the door and began shouting orders. He wanted the carriage out front now. Robert, his capable butler, had already figured as much and assured his master that it would be there momentarily.

Ki'ara thought of all her new abilities and wondered if it was possible for her mind to travel across the miles to Seamuir. She wanted to get a better estimate of the situation. She was still standing there starring at the messenger, but she was not really seeing him.

Centering herself, Ki'ara tapped into her powers. She thought of where she wanted to go. In a flash, her mind traveled the distance to her family's home. That it was that easy surprised even her! Now, this had definite possibilities for keeping abreast of things!

The magic entity of Eastmuir started to sing just as soon as it felt her presence, and Ki'ara greeted it like an old friend. Part of it was always with her, even here at Cloudshire Hall, but the rest kept watch over the realm. It seemed it had missed her!

Ki'ara turned her attention to the castle. She could sense her Uncle Iain and her two other brothers, but not Ragnald. How could this be? Was he dead? Sending her mind to his chambers in Seamuir, Ki'ara let out a horrified gasp. Her hands flew to her face, and she started to cry.

❦

Conall had heard her sharp intake of breath and instantly turned to his wife with concern. Tears were slowly rolling down her pale face, and her eyes were large and full of sorrow as she turned to him.

"We do not have time for the carriage, my love. We have to go over the moors, the shortest way possible! I need pants or a riding dress! We have to get there as fast as we can!" she told him. Her agitation was evident to all those in the room.

The StCloud gave her one more searching gaze and then began to shout more commands. Ki'ara raced upstairs to their suite with the housekeeper and several of the maids hot on her heels. Time was of the essence!

With their help, Ki'ara was quickly dressed in a dark green velvet riding dress that she thought might have once belonged to Conall's mother. She did wonder, somewhat preoccupiedly, when she noticed that the gown fit rather well. It molded itself to her body in all the right places.

As far as the young woman remembered, the lady was a little shorter than her. She could be wrong since the last time she had seen the StCloud's mom, she had just been a child.

Now, however, was not the time to worry about any of that. She needed to go!

Chapter 24

A Long, Fast Ride

By the time Ki'ara came down the stairs, their horses, spare mounts, and a group of guards were waiting by the front door. The magic mirror had been used to send communications to Seamuir Castle and to let the family know that they were on the way. Lord Iain's tired messenger would stay at Cloudshire Hall. He had been assigned quarters and would rest for the day.

Everyone present was aware of the urgency of their mission. Ragnald might have mistreated his sister severely, but he was still her brother. His life depended on her getting there as fast as she possibly could. From what Ki'ara had sensed, time was rapidly running out for him. She had, however, been able to convince the reluctant magic to keep him alive until she arrived.

Conall helped Ki'ara into the saddle and mounted up himself. The lord was barely seated when his impatient wife spurred her horse on towards the drawbridge. He quickly followed, as did the guards.

The group would be able to take the road for a bit before cutting overland. Taking this route would shave off almost an hour on their way to the gate. They intended to do the same once they reached Eastmuir.

⁘⁙⁘

The young couple and the soldiers with them started out at a breakneck pace. The StCloud pulled up even with his wife, and they exchanged a long glance. They did not need words to agree on what had to be done. Conall nodded, and together, they began to work the land's magic.

The effect was almost instantaneous. The horses seemed to pick up more speed and ran easier than just a moment before. Their hoves appeared to no longer touch the ground, and they galloped effortlessly faster and faster along the highway.

After a little more than half an hour of heading straight north, the road began to turn towards the west. The path leading across the moor was cleverly hidden, but Conall knew precisely where to find it. He took the lead and guided the group down the barely visible trail between bubbling bogs and shallow ponds.

As lord of this land, the path was evident to the StCloud but invisible to all others except Ki'ara. As the High Priestess of the Old Gods, she was privileged to all the Highlands secrets and not just those of Eastmuir. She was also able to draw on the magic of all the realms.

To avoid accidents, they did have to slow down a little. Still, the distance was much shorter heading this way. More dangerous, but definitely faster. Traveling across the moors saved them close to an hour to the gate even if it was hard riding overland like this.

⁘⁙⁘

Once they were through the portal, Ki'ara took over. Due to her gifts from the Old Gods, she knew her territory on a level that no other lord was privileged to. Her connection to the realm went deeper than any of them could have imagined.

Ki'ara led them on the straightest course possible towards the castle. It seemed that the very land was smoothing and straightening the path for her. Until that moment, not even Conall had an inkling how powerful Ki'ara had become.

The improved conditions allowed the group to ride faster despite the uneven and unsafe terrain. They fairly flew along the trail bordered by the dark brown waters of the perilous moors and through the occasional stand of stunted trees. If they could maintain their momentum, they would reach their destination more quickly than they had expected.

The StCloud figured that this had to be a record of sorts. No one had ever traveled between the two castles in this brief a time!

⁘⊱⊰⁘

To be able to keep up the pace, Conall called for a brief halt about every half hour or so. Quickly, everyone would dismount and switch to their second horse. Then, they were off again. This tactic allowed them to keep up their incredible pace since time was of the essence. It was also less straining and exhausting on the valiant animals.

Still, by the time the group saw Seamuir Castle in the distance, all the horses were starting to look rather exhausted. They were covered in lather, and steam was pouring off them in waves in the frigid air. They would have to be walked and cooled off slowly, given just a little water at a time.

Their brave mounts had done their best, had willingly and courageously given all that they had. They deserved a good rubdown, some oats, and a long rest. Ki'ara knew that they could rely on Conall's men to see to their comforts.

Had it not been for the magic imbuing the horses, they would have most likely collapsed. They had run faster than their riders had ever expected, had shown more endurance than any of them would have thought possible.

For the entire journey, Ki'ara and Conall had continued to reinforce their mounts with the land's magic. She had called on the Old Gods for help, and they had willingly granted it. Still, the exertion of this fast-paced ride had taken its toll.

Chapter 25

Worse Than Expected

It was early afternoon by the time the tired group finally reached the castle. To Ki'ara's surprise, her reception was very different this time. It was evident that the guards had kept an eye out for them and that their imminent arrival had been anticipated. The butler, as well as the housekeeper, were waiting by the front stairs. Several grooms were also standing by, ready to take charge of the horses.

"Welcome, Milady! Welcome, Lord StCloud!" James and the housekeeper greeted them with respectful bows. Upon the butler's command, the stablehands immediately jumped into action and helped with the mounts.

'Now this is different,' Ki'ara thought to herself. She exchanged a surprised glance with Conall. It seemed that the staff of the castle had suddenly remembered their manners! Maybe there was hope for them yet!

"I know you have ridden a long way and very fast. You would probably prefer to rest for a while, but could you please follow me?" the butler requested politely, bowing once again.

"Time is of the essence! Lord Iain and your brothers are waiting for you," James informed them. "We will see to the comforts of your guards and the horses!"

Motioning Ki'ara to go ahead of him, Conall and she followed the butler up the stairs. James took them straight to Ragnald's chambers.

⋆⋅☆⋅⋆

As they neared the rooms, the butler turned to Ki'ara. He had seen how much Ragnald's condition had affected his uncle and brothers and wanted to warn the young lady what to expect.

"It is not good, Lady Ki'ara, please prepare yourself. I have never seen anything like this! I don't think anyone has. As far as your uncle knows, something like this has happened only a few times before!" James told her concernedly as they reached the doors.

Ki'ara took a moment to take a deep breath and to exchange a worried glance with her husband. She had expected things to be dire, but this warning still took her aback. Ragnald was a Zidarian, after all! He should have been immortal and not on death's door!

She had felt just a flicker of life from her oldest brother when she had sent her mind out exploring earlier that day. What exactly had happened to him, Ki'ara did not know. None of this made any sense!

"Are you ready?" James asked, and when she nodded, knocked on the door. "Enter!" commanded the strong voice of her uncle from within. The butler opened the doors for the couple. Ki'ara entered quickly and then came to a stop.

She had just realized that Ragnald would be furious when he saw that she had brought Conall with her. He hated her husband and saw him as the one person, besides his sister, responsible for all the misery in his life. Good thing that her love was such an understanding person and adept at smoothing the waters!

Ki'ara had no clue if Ragnald still believed that he was the lord of the realm and in charge of the castle. All she knew was that he was in terrible shape. The last thing she wanted to do was upset him. She just hoped that the situation would not get too unpleasant. What a blessing that their uncle was here!

⁂

From where she was standing, the figure of Ragnald was hidden. The elaborate board at the bottom of the bed blocked the view. Lyall was sitting on one side, as close to his brother as he could get, Gawain and Lord Iain had pulled up chairs on the other. Her uncle greeted her with a sad smile, and her brothers with a brief nod. No one spoke a word. Instead, they waved her forward.

Seeing them all this quiet and somber further increased Ki'ara's apprehensions. Her family and the staff were acting as if Ragnald was dying! As if all hope was lost! That was impossible! He had hundreds of years left to live!

It was not until she was right next to the bed that Ki'ara got her first glimpse of her oldest brother. She let out a horrified gasp. How could this be? What had happened to Ragnald?

Back at Cloudshire Hall, Ki'ara had sensed that something was very wrong with him but had assumed it to be an injury that could be healed, especially with all her new powers. This, however, she had not anticipated. How could Ragnald have gotten so ancient in just a few hours?

Chapter 26

An Extreme Healing

Once the first shock of seeing her oldest brother and the condition he was in had passed, Ki'ara became all business and immediately took charge of the situation. She rushed to the side of the bed and began to examine the invalid more closely.

"Lyall, do you any idea what has happened to him?" she asked as she was checking Ragnald's heartbeat and breathing.

Lyall despondently told her what he knew of the events of the night before. Ki'ara was stunned and could not help feeling guilty. The magic wave of hers and Conall's joining had done this! How was this possible? How could an act of love cause such havoc?

When Lyall was finished, her uncle spoke up. "It is almost unheard of for one of us to lose our immortality. It only happened a few times in the very distant past. Usually, when a lord abused his powers to harm or allow harm to those of his clan."

"Like yesterday, you mean? The fire in the courtyard? Several people did get injured, some serious, but I did heal them all!" Ki'ara exclaimed.

"Ragnald started the fire with foreign spells, didn't he? And then he would not help. He has been punished by the magic in the ways of old." stated her uncle.

"But the wave of magic of Conall's and mine joining did this! This is terrible! I cannot help but feel responsible for what has happened to him!" his niece uttered unhappily. Tears were rolling down her cheeks.

"I don't think so! No one else was harmed like this! It did knock a few people off their feet, but that was the extent of it! I think you need to check with the magic of the realm. I have the suspicion that it saw an opportunity and took its revenge!" Lord Iain suggested.

<hr/>

Ki'ara went within and reached out to the magical being. It came to her willingly and happily but grew very cagey when she asked it straight out about Ragnald. She explained how terrible she would feel if the power of her and her husband's first joining had caused her brother such grave injury. All of a sudden, she could detect a profound sense of guilt.

This had not occurred to the entity at the time. It had just felt too irate and vengeful to think things through clearly. Ki'ara sent it compassion and let it sense that she understood. She was not angry, but she did need to know the facts so that she could get an idea of what to do.

At this point, Ki'ara could feel the magical spirit weakening. She assured it again that she would not punish it for this act of revenge. She could not even blame it for taking action. This being was like a small child, after all. It had experienced such abuse from the one person who was supposed to be its champion that it had snapped.

Suddenly, the pictures of what had taken place flooded into her mind. Ki'ara thanked the entity for telling her the truth. Then, she asked it to please cooperate with her to undo what they could of the damage. It took a few minutes, but the power finally reluctantly agreed.

✦҉⳾✦

"You were right, Uncle Iain. It was not the wave," Ki'ara informed them.

"Just as I thought!" came their uncle's thoughtful response. "Ragnald abused the magic, and it judged him cruelly. The wave gave it just the opportunity it had been waiting for," he continued after a moment.

Looking at his nephews, he asked each in turn. "The magic has chosen Ki'ara, but I would still like to know. Lyall, do you want the rule?"

"No, sir, I do not! I have watched what the craving for power did to Ragnald, and I want no part of that!" came the young lord's vehement response.

"Gawain, what about you?" "No, sir, not me either!" the youngest brother answered with a grin.

"Well, Ki'ara StCloud, there is part of your answer to why you were chosen! Now, what have you learned? What can we do for Ragnald?"

Ki'ara briefly shared with them what she had been shown. While she was talking, she kept drawing more and more magic into her system. The way Ragnald looked, she figured that she would need every ounce of it just to be able to keep him alive a while longer. She was not sure yet if more could be done. The damage to his body was too extensive.

Finally, Ki'ara felt that she was ready. "May I please have some more space? I am not yet used to all that magic, and I do not want to hurt anyone else accidentally!"

Hurriedly, Lyall, Gawain, their uncle, and the StCloud retreated to the fireplace. Conall had been silent during the entire interchange and had kept his distance. Now, he warmly greeted Lord Iain and the brothers.

The small group made themselves comfortable near the hearth. They figured that this was a safe distance away from the bed and that the healing would take time. Therefore, they settled in for a lengthy wait. With all the magic Ki'ara would be working, it was best if they were close by just in case they were needed.

⟡

Conall had been talking with Lord Iain when he suddenly paused and turned towards his wife.

"If I can be of any assistance, my love, please, do not hesitate to call on me," he told Ki'ara. Lyall looked at him in complete surprise.

"You would help our brother after everything he has done to you?" he asked nonplussed.

"Yes, I would. Ki'ara is my wife. That makes all of us family! But even without that, I would never turn my back on anyone or any being in need," came the StCloud's calm answer.

Lyall could only stare at Conall. He felt a sense of respect for this man that astounded him. Much had changed in his world in the last couple of days. He felt like he was waking up to a whole new reality, one that was far more pleasant than the one Ragnald had painted.

⟡

Ki'ara calmly stood beside her brother's bed. He was so pale, his lips were blue, and deep wrinkles covered his aged face. His hair had lost all its vibrant color overnight and was falling out in bunches. Ragnald looked like an ancient, shrunken, skeletal version of himself. His face looked tight and pinched, the skin mottled and thin, and he was deeply unconscious.

If she did not find a way to stop and reverse his aging, he would be gone soon. Ki'ara realized that even though she had not been able to sense Ragnald, her instincts had been right. A couple more hours would have been too long.

It was time to begin. Ki'ara grounded herself by sending imaginary roots deep into the earth. Then, she opened herself fully to not just Eastmuir's but all the Highlands' magic. It came to her willingly and easily, like an old friend, and she welcomed it with pleasure.

Using the sight her powers gave her, she carefully scanned her brother's motionless body. The magic entity had done terrible harm when it took its revenge and tore itself free. Ki'ara hoped that she could repair some of it before it was too late.

Firmly, she set her intention to heal her brother's wasted form. Next, she attempted to supply the power to Ragnald's body and soul to reknit itself. Carefully, she tried to begin work on the worst of the damage. Even for her and with all the power at her disposal, this would be no easy task.

Before long, Ki'ara was covered in sweat. Ragnald's own body and mind were fighting her all the way. Even deeply unconscious, his hatred for her was still present. It was preventing the healing! Without any higher brain functions, his instincts were rejecting her while she was trying to save him!

✦⋆⸙❀⸙⋆✦

Ki'ara realized that she needed help. Opening her eyes, she looked at her husband. The StCloud had sensed that something was wrong and had been watching her with concern. Every eye in the room had turned to her.

"He is fighting the healing because it is coming from me!" she explained. "Conall, could you please add your magic to mine?"

The StCloud immediately rushed across the room. Once he placed his hands over hers, she could feel the increase in power. But still, Ragnald fought them.

The couple realized that they could not force this healing, but maybe, just maybe, they could sneak it in!

"Lyall, would you please come here and assist us?" Ki'ara finally asked, turning towards her brothers. Lyall was more than prepared to do whatever he could and quickly moved to her side.

"He is not letting us help him. I believe that there is a possibility that if we channeled our power through you, we could trick him into accepting the healing," the young lady explained.

"What do I need to do?" Lyall asked instantly.

"Place your hands on his chest, I will put mine over yours, and Conall his on top," Ki'ara directed.

Immediately, Lyall gingerly put his shaking hands on Ragnald's chest. He could feel the power buzzing through him as Ki'ara placed hers on top and could sense it amplify even further when Conall added his.

'If this is what it is like to be connected to the land, it is pretty amazing!' popped into Lyall's mind unbidden.

The thought was accompanied by a wave of sadness. For some reason, Lyall had never developed the bond that should have been his birthright.

✦

At first, nothing happened. Ragnald's unconscious form was still fighting them. They had just about given up when all of a sudden, the resistance vanished. A wave of healing swept through their brother's body, leaving restored tissue in its wake.

Ragnald's breathing deepened, and his face relaxed. The deep wrinkles carved into his features began to smooth out. Time seemed to reverse as his body regained some of its health and youth. He would never be the same, but at least he had a chance now.

All went well until Ki'ara tried to reknit Ragnald's connection to the land. To make the healing permanent, he needed his immortality back. Without it, his years would be numbered.

Healing Ragnald had been one thing, but giving him back the connection to the realm was a totally different story. The entities did not want him to regain the ability to hurt others. They felt that he had done enough damage already!

No pleading on Ki'ara's part had any effect. What had been granted up to this point was all that her brother was going to get! He would spend the rest of his life as a mortal, without even the slightest hint of power.

The beings felt that her brother had actually already been given far more than he deserved. They had reluctantly agreed to allow Ragnald to live but had decided that he would age like a human. That was his punishment for trying to kill Ki'ara, for abusing his power, for harming his own people.

According to the magical entities, her brother had forfeited his right to be an immortal lord. They had no intention of budging on this verdict.

Chapter 27

Unexpected Revelations

When Ki'ara and Conall had done all that they could for Ragnald, he looked more like his former self, just much, much older. It had been impossible to reverse all the effects of the rapid aging. At least, the couple had bought the once immortal lord some time. He was peacefully asleep now with his breathing even and regular.

Ki'ara and Conall were exhausted, and so was Lyall. Incredible amounts of raw power had been channeled through him. If he was honest, he had really enjoyed the feeling. Never before in his entire life had he felt so vibrant, so alive!

No Zidarian possessing magic abilities would have been able to act as a conduit like this. To have so much energy fed through them would have destroyed their connection to the magic forever. Unbeknownst to all, the opposite had taken place in Lyall.

Even long after the flow of power that Ki'ara and Conall had been sending through him ceased, Lyall still felt it buzzing in his blood. At first, he was too tired and dazed to notice. It was not until much later that day, when he was lying in bed that night, that he became aware of the phenomenon.

Lyall dismissed it as a possible byproduct of his assistance to Ki'ara and her husband. He figured that it was temporary and would go away.

⚜

Once they stopped working on Ragnald, the StCloud gently assisted his wife while Gawain helped Lyall. Soon, they were all comfortably seated in chairs by the fire. It was now time to get some nourishment and drink into the three. Lord Iain had ordered several plates with food a while ago in anticipation of this necessity.

Using magic, especially to such an extent, burned up incredible amounts of energy that needed to be replenished. After taking a bite, Ki'ara gratefully let herself sink down into the soft cushions. She closed her eyes for a moment.

"Sweetheart, I know that you are exhausted, but you need to eat!" Conall gently admonished her.

Opening her tired eyes, Ki'ara determinedly began devouring the homemade bread thickly layered with meat and cheese. It was really quite delicious, and she ended up reaching for another.

This one, she ended up consuming much slower. She could feel the energy restoring itself in her body. She was not as exhausted as she had been a few minutes ago.

Conall had wolfed down four of the delicious snacks to her two, and he was looking better as well. To channel so much power had taken a lot out of them. Especially, since the magic would have preferred to let Ragnald die and not help at all. Having to send it all through Lyall had also created a slight resistance, but at least it had made the healing possible.

"How is he?" Lord Ian asked anxiously when Ki'ara had finished her second sandwich. His niece regarded him sadly and sighed.

"He will live, but we do not know for how long. The magic refused to restore his immortality, and we were barely able to heal him. His soul is so poisoned that it wanted nothing to do with us at first. I am sorry we could not do more," Ki'ara responded unhappily.

The death of a member of an immortal family was always tragic. To lose one this way, however, even more so. It saddened them all that one of their own had slipped into such darkness that the magic of the land saw no alternative but to reject him.

"Child! You and Conall have done more than most would have! Especially after the way he has treated you! Yes, his fate fills me with sadness, but he has brought this upon himself!" Lord Iain assured her gently.

Looking around at his assembled family, the Lord of Ravenshire came to a decision. "James, please summon the healer to stay with Ragnald and watch over him for a while," he requested.

Then, turning to his niece and nephews, he continued, "Once Ragnald is taken care of, let us go down into the breakfast room! I have things to discuss with all of you in private!"

The siblings exchanged surprised glances. This sounded serious! What was it that their uncle wanted to address that was so urgent that they needed to do this right now?

Not long after, Lord Iain, Lyall, Gawain, and Ki'ara were comfortably seated around the table in the small dining room. Conall had been asked to be present as well. Each had refreshments and a small plate of snacks sitting by their side. On the table were several dishes heaped high with rolls, fresh-baked scones, and cookies.

Their uncle had ordered it all and had also made sure that James knew that they were not to be disturbed. Lord Iain had then placed a cone of silence around the room. This would prevent anyone from making out what was spoken within.

To Ki'ara, this looked like it might turn out to be a lengthy meeting. What could be so important that her uncle wanted none of the servants to overhear their conversation?

❦

Conall did not want to intrude on the family's affairs. He knew that Lyall had not cared much for him in the past. Therefore, he volunteered to wait in the library. Lord Iain, however, felt that it was important that he attend. He regarded the StCloud as a friend and wanted him there to back him up. What the lord had to say would not be easy for his niece and nephews.

"You are part of this family, now and for always, and this does concern you! I, for one, would appreciate your presence," he declared, looking at Lyall and Gawain. Neither objected.

The Lord of Ravenshire waited until everyone was seated and had served themselves from the delicacies on the table. After locking eyes for a moment with each one of the people present, he finally began to speak.

"You are all familiar with the Highland's history, so I do not have to go into that again," he began.

"You also know that no marriage outside the immortal families is acceptable for any of us Zidarians. What you do not know, however, is that some of us have continued to interbreed with the Zidhe. All the families have done so at one point or another but some more than others."

Here, Lord Iain paused for a moment. "Most of us Zidarians are at least half Zidhe, but your family, as well as the StClouds, are even more so. Your father, for example, is more than three-quarter Zidhe, as is Conall."

Looking at his nephews, the Lord of Ravenshire continued. "Your mother was more than half, as am I, so that makes all of you almost three-quarter Zidhe. After Morena's death, Mikael was inconsolable. Your mother had been the love of his life. He had intended to spend the rest of his years with her." Lord Iain paused to let his words sink in.

"It took a long time before your father began to take an interest in the world around him again. His sorrow was so profound that for many years he focused solely on the day to day governing of the realm. Then, when the clan was doing well, and everything was under control, he decided that he needed to start living once more."

Gawain nodded. He remembered those days only too well. He had been relieved when Mikael's grief seemed to finally lessen, and he started to pick up some of his hobbies again.

"He had not traveled, nor had he been hunting for years. Mikael decided to head inland because as long as he stayed near the coast, he would run into people. It was solitude that his heart and soul craved," the Lord of Ravenshire continued.

"Most of the area inland belongs to the Zidhe. Some Zidarians, as well as a few humans, however, are allowed to go there. We are welcome as long as we abide by the elves' rules. And, we have to ask for permission before entering their lands."

Lord Iain now had everybody's undivided attention. None of them had been aware where their father had gone and where exactly he had met Ali'ana.

"High up in the hills, Mikael found a beautiful, secluded valley with a gorgeous view of the mountains. He could even see the distant sea. A waterfall had carved out a good-sized swimming hole nearby, and the whole place was lush and green. He was so enchanted with the spot that he decided to stay and set up his tent."

"The atmosphere of the valley seemed to soothe him, and your father slept peacefully for the first time in a very long time. His soul began to heal. He stayed there for five days and then made his way back home much refreshed," Lord Iain told his rapt audience.

"Every year after that, he headed for his hidden retreat, sometimes even twice a year. One year, on his last night there, he had a dream. He saw a beautiful red-haired woman swimming in the water close to the falls. He watched her entranced. She was Zidhe. He could tell by her ears which were much more pointed than his own."

Every person around the table was now hanging on Lord Iain's words. None of them had any knowledge of this. Mikael had never shared with any of them, not even his daughter, how he came to court Ali'ana.

"Mikael returned home, but every night after that, he dreamed of her. At first, she acted as if she did not see him at all. One day, however, she turned around and looked straight at him. She waved him closer and, as if drawn by unseen strings, he walked down to the water's edge."

At this point, you could have heard a pin drop in the breakfast room. Ki'ara and her brothers barely dared to breathe. They could not wait to find out what had happened next.

"Over the next few nights, in each following dream, she swam closer and closer. Mikael was stunned by her beauty. He had never seen anyone more gorgeous than her. When she locked eyes with him and waved for him to join her, a deep longing grew in his heart. He now believed that she was waiting for him. He decided that he would answer her call.”

“The very next morning, Mikael rode out towards the valley. It took him all day to reach it, and it was getting dark by the time he arrived. He immediately rushed to the waterfall, but no one was there. Bitterly disappointed, he set up his tent. He was so heartbroken he did not even bother to eat but went straight to bed.”

“Before he knew it, he had fallen asleep and was dreaming of her. She was once again in the pond, waiting for him. If he could not have her in life, he at least wanted to touch her just once in his dreams. Using all his considerable magic, he jumped into the water beside her.”

Lord Iain paused for a moment and took a drink. The expectancy on the faces of his niece and nephews had him continue after just a brief moment.

“Her joyous laughter awoke him. To his surprise, it was early morning! The dream had ended, but he could swear that he could still hear her laughing!”

“Mikael rushed out of the tent and down to the pond. There she was, waiting for him, naked as the day she was born. He jumped into the water and joined her. Your father never even thought twice. He took Ali’ana up on her invitation and made her his wife right then and there.”

⚘

This was a whole new side to their father that none of his children had ever seen. The Mikael they knew was usually very deliberate and thought everything through before acting, weighing all the pros and cons before coming to a decision.

"As so many of the full elves have done for generations, Ali'ana put a glamour on her face and ears. This made her appear more human and allowed her to join her new husband at his home. Twenty-five years later, little Ki'ara was born," Lord Iain went on. The eyes of those present were glued to him.

"All went well for many years, but when her daughter turned thirteen, Ali'ana discovered that she was very ill. She needed to return to her people and quickly."

Ki'ara was stunned by her uncle's words! There had been a reason for her parents departing so suddenly and for leaving her behind! Tears filled her eyes.

"Mikael could not bear to be separated from her, to lose yet another wife. He knew that if Ali'ana stayed, she would die. Time was of the essence, so making Ragnald the new lord, he went with her to her people," Lord Iain concluded.

The siblings gasped. So that was how Ki'ara's parents had met! And why their father had left in such a hurry! For the first time, it all made sense!

"Will they ever return?" Lyall asked Lord Iain. He had gained a whole new understanding of his father and his new wife during the story. Especially since Ragnald was not around to taint his view!

"I am not sure, and neither was Mikael when they left. His first priority at the time was Ali'ana's health. He was so worried; I don't believe that he was thinking too clearly. He felt he had done his duty to the clan and that it was his right to take some time for himself and stay with his wife." The lord answered.

"As far as I know, they have been in the Zidhe's lands ever since. Before Ali'ana got sick, they had intended to explore places few ever get to see. I have no idea where they are, but they left a message with me for you. I will give it to you once we have addressed some other formalities," Lord Iain informed them.

Ki'ara looked disappointed but knew her uncle well enough that she respected his judgment. She had waited this long to hear from her parents. What were a few more minutes?

✦⁖⟡⟐⟡⁖✦

"In any case, the MacClair Clan needs to know that it has a new ruler. But, before that, there is something we need to take care of. Would you all please stand?" Lord Iain continued.

Turning to Ki'ara, he regarded her solemnly. "It is rather unusual for a ruler to belong to two clans, let alone three, but you are the MacClair. You will need someone you trust to see to things here whenever you are away," he began.

"I do not believe ruling the realm is much to Lyall's taste, so that leaves Gawain. Are you comfortable with him looking after the clan and the land for you?" Lord Elvinstone asked her.

"Yes, Uncle, I am, if he is willing," Ki'ara answered instantly. She implicitly trusted Gawain to do right by her people. Looking at her brother, she bowed to him formally.

"Lord Gawain MacClair, would you consent to be regent in my place whenever I am away at Cloudshire Hall or Fairholme Castle?" Kiara asked formally. Then, she paused for a moment. Suddenly, she felt strongly that she needed to add something more. "Or otherwise absent due to duties that need my attention?"

Gawain looked at his sister and uncle in surprise. He was too stunned to speak. That they would entrust him, the youngest brother, the realm had never even occurred to him. He had to think about Ki'ara's request for a moment.

Accepting the stewardship would most certainly be the end of his carefree lifestyle, of days spent down at the pub, or just playing around. But, if Gawain was really honest with himself, he had grown bored with that long ago and had just kept it up because it had annoyed Ragnald and Lyall.

Since his sister was married to the StCloud, Gawain assumed that she would be spending a fair amount of her time at her husband's home. Ruling for Ki'ara whenever she was absent would still give him occasional holidays and was far better than being the lord all the time.

Then, it suddenly occurred to Gawain that being in charge might actually turn out to be fun! With her approval, he could finally institute all those ideas for improvements Ragnald had shot down for all those years! Therefore, he returned his sister's bow equally as ceremoniously.

"Lady Ki'ara MacClair StCloud and Lord Iain Elvinstone, I am beyond honored! I gladly accept this great privilege you both have bestowed upon me. I swear to carry out this office to the best of my abilities and to care for the clan with compassion and love. I will always keep their best interest at heart!" he promised in a deep, clear voice.

Ki'ara smiled at Gawain and reached out her hand to his. Just then, a knock on the door interrupted the solemn moment.

Chapter 28

The Message

When the knock resounded on the door, Lord Iain looked annoyed for a moment. The ceremony taking place was important for the clan and would firmly establish Gawain's position as the steward. Then, the irritated gent realized that the butler would have made sure that they were not disturbed unless it was vitally important.

"Enter!" he shouted. James opened the door and, with a most rueful expression, stepped within. "My apologies, Lords and Lady, but I thought you would want this dispatch immediately," he stated. He waved a man inside who was carefully herding a large animal ahead of him.

"It will not let us remove the message! I do believe this is a bird bred specifically by the elves. Maybe it will allow one of you to retrieve the note," the butler finished before shooing the other man out the door ahead of him and closing it firmly behind them.

The assembled family regarded the large creature with great interest. It was definitely some form of a bird but much more colorful than most. "I believe this is a Rainbow Kayrex!" Gawain muttered in awe.

When the animal moved, or whenever the light hit its feathers, its plumage shimmered in all the colors of the rainbow. The creature's beak was bright red, and its eyes a vibrant turquoise blue. The intelligence in those intense orbs was far beyond that of a regular bird.

The Kayrex was eyeing each of them with a keen interest in return. Finally, it seemed to decide on Ki'ara and made its way towards her. Without any fear, the young lady stood very still and let it approach. She was enthralled by this beautiful being and smiled at it encouragingly.

When the bird got to Ki'ara, it raised its leg with the note tied around it towards her and chirped invitingly. The young woman gently reached out and removed the message. She gazed at it in wonder. Could this be from her parents? What a miracle to hear from them after all this time and then in this manner!

꧁꧂

After an instant's hesitation, Ki'ara handed the note to her uncle. Her hands were shaking so badly that she almost dropped it. She had realized that she was not steady enough to untie the bands holding the little capsule surrounding the paper!

Having been relieved of its responsibility, the bird chirped again. It looked around for a moment. Then, it scooted closer to Ki'ara. She absentmindedly began to stroke its soft head. This put the large creature into a state of pure bliss.

꧁꧂

Lord Iain quickly had the paper unrolled and began to read the message out loud. The siblings and the StCloud were all leaning towards him eagerly.

"My beloved children and brother of my heart,
I was horrified to hear what has happened in my absence.
I had no idea that Ragnald would mistreat his power the
way he did. He had a terrible cruel streak when he was
young but seemed to have mended his ways.
When I put him in charge, I truly believed that he was
the best qualified and would make a good lord. I am
heartbroken over the punishment he has suffered. My
apologies to all of you for putting you in this situation,
especially you, Ki'ara. We should not have left you in his
care.

If the wave was as strong as you describe and affected
Ragnald this badly, then Ki'ara is the rightful MacClair
and needs to be established as such. I am sure you will
see to that, Iain.

That being said, I need both Ki'ara and the StCloud
to travel to Elvenhorst. Their presence is being requested
by Lord Syl'vian himself, and no one says 'No' to one of
the rulers of the Zidhe. If Ragnald is still alive when this
note finds you and if at all possible, please send him
along so that we can help him adjust.

I would ask you, Iain, to support Ki'ara in putting
Gawain in charge during her absence. Could you please
remain at the castle for a time until he becomes familiar
with his new duties?

Lyall, I would have suggested making you the
temporary steward, but it seems that you have some soul-
searching to do. Also, I am not sure you really like being
in charge. Ragnald has influenced you for so many years,
and you need to reevaluate all that you have been told. It
is time to shake off the influence of your older brother,
my beloved son. I do hope that you will assist Gawain
and advise him whenever he needs it.

Knowing Ki'ara, I am confident that you, Ragnald,
have survived. But, I suspect that not even she and Conall

together have been able to make you immortal once more. I feel very responsible for your fate since I was the one who put you in charge. I believe that we can help you adjust, dear boy, but in any case, now that you are entirely powerless, you are not safe among the clan. I hope that you will be happy here.

My dear Iain, I thank you for all you have done and for looking out for my family. I promise, I will find a way to repay you.

Ali'ana and I are doing well. She has recovered from her illness. At present, we are out exploring the Zidhe realm, but we will be returning to Elvenhorst to be there when Conall, Ki'ara, and Ragnald arrive.

Maybe in a few months, once Gawain is more comfortable with his new position, Lyall can come and visit us as well. We would truly enjoy that. I have missed you, my children.

With much love,

Lord Mikael MacClair
P.S. The messenger bird is a Rainbow Kayrex. His name is 'Shimmer.' He is free to stay or return and will carry a note if asked nicely.

He prefers to eat nuts and fruit and is very good at letting you know if there is something else that he wants. He does love wine, but I would suggest keeping him away from it. He gets very exuberant if given too much.

⁂

For a moment, there was complete and utter silence in the room, only interrupted occasionally by the ecstatic chirping of the large bird. Ki'ara was still petting its soft feathers, and it had moved even closer. It was now firmly pressed up against her.

"Well, it seems that your father had the same idea for the steward of the clan," Lord Iain finally commented dryly.

"And, it appears that the honeymoon must wait. Your father is right about one thing, children. Ragnald needs to be out of here as quickly as possible. He is too hated to be safe here. Do you all agree?"

"Aye!" one after the other of the assembled family members stated. They looked at each other sadly, but they all understood the necessity for this course of action, even Lyall.

At this point, neither Ki'ara nor her brothers were in the mood to continue the ceremony they had previously started. After a brief discussion, it was agreed that they would hold a public ritual along with a celebration. They would invite the clan members as well as all the lords and ladies.

In all the excitement, the previous message from Mikael and Ali'ana was utterly forgotten. It remained in Lord Iain's pocket for the moment.

By this time, the castle was rife with rumors, but it was too late in the day to call the residents together. Therefore, James was called in, as well as the housekeeper. As the senior staff, they had the right to be informed first.

Seeing how tired Ki'ara and Conall were from the exertion of helping Ragnald and as the oldest ruler present, Lord Iain took charge. He caught the butler and Berta up on the state of affairs. He also gave orders for a gathering in the castle yard after breakfast the next morning.

A date was set nine days hence for the official celebration, and messages would be sent out with invitations. Usually, something like this would be done at the biannual council meeting, but time was of the essence. No one kept the elves waiting, and every day Ragnald remained at Seamuir Castle, his life was in peril.

⚜

Night had fallen, and it was time for the evening meal. The butler knocked respectfully and informed the group that their dinner was ready to be served. Ki'ara suddenly realized how hungry she was but also how tired. Conall offered her his arm, and together they walked to the dining room.

The cook had gone out of her way to make this meal special. The oxtail soup was delicious, and the salmon of the main course juicy and tender. Potatoes with parsley, fresh vegetables, and a heady red wine completed the meal. For dessert was a plum pudding made just the way Ki'ara liked it.

On purpose, the conversation during dinner was kept superficial. It would not do to discuss clan business with this many ears listening intently. Somehow, there seemed to be a lot more servants around than usual. No glass was allowed to remain empty for more than a moment.

Ki'ara quickly switched to water during the feast. She enjoyed wine and relished the taste but usually stopped at one glass. She allowed herself another small goblet of the sweet blueberry wine served with dessert but refused all attempts to refill her glass.

As it was, the dinner turned into somewhat of an impromptu celebration. Ragnald's life had been saved, Ki'ara and Conall were finally married, Gawain would never suffer under his brothers again, and Lyall was free of all the manipulations he had been subjected to for so many years!

To top it all off, they had finally had word from their absent father and knew that Mikael and Ali'ana were doing well. Ki'ara was so grateful to hear that her mother had recovered from her severe illness. What an eventful couple of days it had been!

Ki'ara was excited about going to see her parents and the elves but also about her new friend. Shimmer had refused to leave her side. He insisted on sitting close to her. Cuddled up right next to her, he enjoyed his small bowl of blueberry wine and plum pudding.

The colorful bird seemed to have quite a sweet tooth. Its happy chirpings assured Shimmer plenty of attention from the serving staff. Ki'ara finally had to put her foot down. She insisted that the Kayrex ate some more species-appropriate foods besides dessert and the tasty little cakes it was begging for.

To the amusement of all, the creature promptly put its head in Ki'ara's lap and started pouting. She had just enough time to save her dress by placing a napkin under its beak that was brightly streaked with blueberry wine.

When Ki'ara started to yawn more and more often, Lord Iain called the meal to a close. His niece had a hard ride behind her and then had performed a lengthy and exhausting healing. She needed to rest.

The siblings and Conall agreed that it was time to go to bed. It had been a long and emotionally exhausting day. The group climbed up the stairs together and parted on the landing to head off to their separate rooms. The goodnights that were exchanged were full of love and tenderness.

This had been the warmest her brothers had ever been to Ki'ara. Both had insisted on giving her a big hug, and Lyall had even whispered, "Thank you! I love you!" in her ear. She had never heard those words from him before!

Without Ragnald around, everyone was much happier and kinder. This made Ki'ara sad for her oldest brother. All this warmth and love could have been his. Instead, he had chosen to fill his heart and life with envy, hate, and bitterness.

Chapter 29

A Morning's Interlude

The next morning dawned, brilliant and clear. When a persistent sunbeam tickled her nose, Ki'ara awoke with a sneeze. Despite the thick curtains, an inquisitive ray had somehow managed to sneak into the room and roust her out of her dreams. Sighing contently, she relished the warmth of the blankets and the sleeping man next to her.

Who would have thought just a few days ago that this would ever happen? It still seemed like a miracle to Ki'ara. She stretched luxuriously before scooting over to be closer to her husband. The StCloud sleepily wrapped his arms around her and pulled her tight against him.

Ki'ara could feel the response her nearness was having on him. As if out of their own accord, his hands started roaming over her body. First, he explored her perky breasts, then her flat abdomen, and up and down her slender legs. His teasing touches, sometimes light, at others firmer, were having quite the effect. She was starting to feel rather hot all of a sudden.

From her quickened breathing, the StCloud could tell that his endeavor was a rousing success. He had awoken Ki'ara's desire with a vengeance. Upping the ante, he made his way to her most sensitive place. The moistness he found there further increased as he started stroking her gently.

His dexterous fingers soon found her sweet spot, and she began to moan from the pleasure her husband was providing. Ki'ara was relishing every single caress. She began to realize that the StCloud was an expert at pleasing a woman, at heightening the blaze building inside her. Willa had trained him well!

Having been a virgin until that day in the chapel, all this was new to Ki'ara. She found it incredibly thrilling and exciting. From the first moment on, she had decided to freely embrace her own sensuality and sexuality. Her husband's reaction had shown her how much he approved.

Even right there, during the consummation ceremony, with all those people present, Ki'ara had realized that being totally in the moment amplified her enjoyment immensely. Therefore, consciously putting all thoughts and concerns aside, she gave herself over fully to his delicious ministrations.

Conall, wide awake now, started kissing her neck. This additional stimulation added fuel to the fire, and she could feel the fervor inside her grow to almost unbearable proportions. Her body shuddered, and her hips raised up involuntarily when the sensations became too much. She cried out as it ended in a rather spectacular release.

As Ki'ara lay there panting, she heard her husband's soft chuckle. He had genuinely enjoyed this little diversion. The StCloud gave her just a minute before touching her even more intimately. He teasingly slipped a couple of his fingers inside her, relishing the wetness he found there. Her response was almost instantaneous. With her ardor renewed, she craved for more.

Giving her a playful smile, Conall slid down under the covers. The next thing Ki'ara knew, it was his tongue making its way inside her, licking her, driving her wild. At first, this gave her pause but only for a moment. She had not even had an inkling how much one could be turned on by such an act! Her head thrown back, and her fingers clenched into the sheets, she moved with the rhythm of his pleasuring her.

Soon, her husband's insistent attention pushed her over the top yet once again. He waited a couple of seconds and then gave her one last, hard lick. This just about drove her crazy and had her hips come up almost a foot off the bed! She could feel her insides contracting and another gush of moisture temporarily relieving all that built-up heat.

Conall's ability to stimulate her body, to give her pleasure, was more than she had ever expected. Ki'ara had overheard some of the women talking about making love to their husbands. None of them had ever described it like this! This was incredible, and had her wanting more!

The StCloud made his way up her body, leaving a trail of kisses in his wake. When he looked into her eyes, she could see her own passion reflected in his. Conall's hard member was throbbing against her as he gently nudged her legs further apart. Ki'ara arched up to meet him, and he drove deep inside her.

At first, he wanted to go slow, but Ki'ara would not have it. She could tell that he was holding himself back, and she wanted, needed to please him just as much as he had pleasured her. With her driving hard against him, it did not take long. He violently exploded inside her when she clenched around him with yet another climax.

Conall collapsed on top of her, his breathing hard, and his pulse racing. Ki'ara wrapped her arms around him and let him rest for a few minutes. Then, she gently prodded her husband onto his back. He gave her a quizzical look, which she answered with a mischievous smile.

It was her turn to explore his magnificent body! First, she let her hands play over his tight abdomen, then she moved lower. When she touched him gently, she could hear his sharp intake of breath. Making her way under the covers, she slid alongside him. Her tongue left a wet trail as it made its way across his well-muscled chest, and then progressively lower.

Her husband just about came off the bed when she moved lower and lower. Positioning herself between his long, powerful legs, her eager hands and mouth started to explore his intimate region. Using her imagination and gaging by his reaction what felt good, she licked, sucked, and squeezed him. Before long, she had him moaning, and he was hard as a rock yet once again.

Pushing the blankets aside, Ki'ara sat up and shifted until she was straddling him. With one quick move, she slid him inside and started riding him hard. Conall's hands grabbed her hips, and he met her thrust for thrust. Placing her hands on his chest gave her just the leverage she needed to glide up and down him in such a fashion that it gave them both maximum pleasure.

Their movements got faster and faster, more urgent with every second. Ki'ara's eyes closed as she gave herself over to their lovemaking with wild abandon. Her head was thrown back, and she moaned loudly every time he drove deep inside her. Her entire body spasmed when Conall came, triggering her own release.

Opening her eyes, Ki'ara looked at her husband in wonder. She had never even imagined that being with a man could feel like this! Good thing that Conall was so virile because she wanted more of this! Just not this morning, or at least not right then! She could feel that they were both spent!

'ᵕᐧᵗᵎᵎᐧᵕᵎᵎᐧᵗ'

Exhausted, the couple fell back asleep in each other's arms. Ki'ara drifted back up from her deep slumber a while later. She just laid there, enjoying the moment and being grateful for all the blessings in her life. What bliss it was to wake up with Conall next to her!

The Rainbow Kayrex, noticing that his favorite person was stirring, got out of the nest Ki'ara had made for him. He came over to the bed for a quick pat. Then, he curled up contently once more in the soft, warm blankets just a few feet away.

The remnants of fruit scattered around the bedroom were evidence of his early morning snack. Someone had silently slipped a bowl full of goodies into the chamber without disturbing Ki'ara or Conall. The beautiful bird was fast becoming a favorite here in the castle!

The StCloud was coming awake as well and reached for Ki'ara. She slid closer. Happily, she buried her face into her husband's chest. How safe and secure she felt with his arms around her! How nice would it be if they could stay here all morning!

Unfortunately, there was much to do this day. To start with, there was the introduction of herself as the new lord of the MacClair Clan. Also, she needed to present her choice of a regent. Then, they all wanted to take a close look at the books and examine some of the archaic rules Ragnald had instituted.

Ki'ara feared that she and Gawain had a lot to undo. She wanted the clan to be content and happy and the laws to be fair, just like they had been under her father. Much had been changed in the last eleven years, and not for the better.

Conall's soft chuckle drew her out of her contemplations. When he began to nuzzle her neck, the room suddenly seemed to become way too hot. Laughing, she pushed off the blankets. Regrettably, it was time to get up. Further sexual exploration of each other would have to wait.

⁘⁘⊱⊰⁘⁘

A while later, the couple was dressed and ready for the day. Before going downstairs, they went down the hall to check in on Ragnald. The oldest MacClair was still deeply asleep. His valet was sitting beside him, keeping a silent watch. The man looked incredibly tired despite the cup of fresh coffee next to him.

Ki'ara checked her brother's pulse and breathing. Both were strong and even but a little too fast for her liking. Ragnald somewhat looked like himself again, just 40 human years older. The much healthier color of his skin pleased her but not the tension she noticed all over his body. What could possibly cause this?

There was only one way to find out. When Ki'ara checked Ragnald's sleeping mind, she was repulsed by the seething anger, boiling hatred, and abject despair pervading his dreams. Would his waking mind be any different? She feared that her brother was a danger to himself as well as to others. For a moment, she even considered putting him in restraints.

Calling the butler, Ki'ara ordered two guards to be placed in the room and two more in front of the doors at all times. If anyone asked, they were to be told that this was for the lord's protection. He was hated by most people, after all, especially in this castle.

In addition, to make sure that he would not be all alone when he woke up, either the valet or one of the more trusted servants was to sit with Ragnald 24 hours a day. Ki'ara told James to advise them that if any harm came to her brother, they would be answering to her. But, just in case, she wove a spell of protection around his defenseless form.

Having done all that she could to ensure everyone's safety, Ki'ara turned back to her brother. She sent love, acceptance, and forgiveness to his sleeping mind in the hope of steering his dreams into a more peaceful and healthy direction.

Conall, picking up on his wife's concern, suggested that maybe it would be best for her brother to remain asleep for a while longer. After a brief discussion, Ki'ara agreed that having him wake up in a rage without one of them near to subdue him could turn out catastrophic.

The couple discussed several options. Finally, they settled on a spell that would not only keep Ragnald from awakening; it would also steer his thoughts into a more peaceful direction. They would rouse Ragnald once the morning's activities were done, and they had the time to talk to him at length.

Together they placed a sleeping compulsion on her brother and watched him visibly relax. Ki'ara breathed a sigh of relief. Maybe now Ragnald would find some peace in his slumber.

After taking care of her problematic sibling, the couple made their way down to breakfast. Shimmer was waddling along behind them. He loved being petted and would make a detour every time they passed one of the servants. Most were only too happy to oblige.

Ki'ara quickly realized that a person's reaction to the big bird was a dead giveaway of their personality. She decided that it would be wise to keep track of those who avoided or pushed away the sweet animal. She would advise Gawain to find them jobs outside the castle.

Chapter 30

The Hidden Agenda

Overnight, the news of their wedding had spread throughout Seamuir Castle. Therefore, people kept stopping the newlyweds to congratulate them. It took much longer than usual for the couple, with their feathered friend in tow, to reach the breakfast room.

Ki'ara saw with pleasure how bright and cheery the chamber was in the sunlight. Much of the dark aura pervading the building seemed to have evaporated. Her uncle was already there, waiting for them. He was enjoying a cup of tea with cream and one of the delicious scones the cook had baked early that morning. Lord Iain quickly rose from his chair to greet them.

"Good morning, you two! Did you sleep well?" he asked with a broad smile.

Reaching out to shake the lord's hand, Conall replied. "Yes, we did! It was nice to get a full night's rest after that ride and the healing we did on Ragnald yesterday!"

Ki'ara gave her uncle a hug before taking her place next to him. For now, Lord Iain still occupied the head of the table. After today's announcement, however, that position would be legally hers, or then Gawain's in her absence.

"Have you checked on Ragnald?" Lord Iain asked. His brow wrinkled with concern.

"Yes, and physically he is as good as can be expected, but I am not so sure about his mind. I fear he might harm himself or others. I have ordered guards to be placed in and in front of the room just in case. I hope our father can help him," Ki'ara replied.

"Losing one's immortality has to be a dreadful blow, but I believe being stripped of one's connection to the land's magic has to be even worse. Sort of like being deaf, dumb, and blind. It was a terrible punishment, and death might have been kinder," Conall added.

⚜

The three had just started their breakfast when Gawain entered the room. The usually so energetic man was still tired and yawning. Given a choice, he did not get up this early. This day, however, was special. It was the beginning of great changes in his life as well as for the clan.

Gawain was much more formally dressed than usual. For once, he had made an effort to comb his often scruffy hair neatly into place. Even though he was still a bit sleepy, his eyes were clear and bright. They had lost some of their guarded looks. Ki'ara noticed with pleasure that he seemed considerably more the young lord this morning than he ever had.

"Good morning!" he greeted them cheerfully before coming over to hug his sister. Ki'ara could tell that with the end of Ragnald's tyranny, a huge weight had been lifted off her easy-going brother's shoulders. Not even having to step up at times and govern the clan could take away from that!

Once Gawain had seated himself, he paused and eyed Ki'ara questioningly. "You are having Ragnald guarded?" he finally asked. "For his protection or all of ours?"

Once again, this astute young man had managed to get straight to the heart of the matter. He had always been quiet and pretended to have little interest in the goings-on around him. In reality, he missed little. Ki'ara felt very reassured. Gawain would make a very good regent!

"A bit of both, actually," she answered with a smile. "As you well know, there are some in this castle who would like nothing better than to get even with Ragnald for all the things he has done. He is still our brother, and I do not want to see him harmed!"

Lyall had come in just as Ki'ara was giving her explanation. The angry frown on his face smoothed out. He had been furious when he saw the guards at his brother's door. Old habits were hard to break. Instantly assuming the worst and becoming protective, he had felt that Ragnald was being treated more like a prisoner than the former lord.

Rage was quickly replaced by gratefulness. Lyall would never trust his older brother again, nor would he help him in any of his schemes, but he still loved him. For most of his life, he had been closest to Ragnald. Until these last few days, he had actually never had a connection to his other siblings.

"Good morning!" Lyall greeted the group. After giving Ki'ara a warm hug and shaking hands with the men, he took a seat next to Gawain.

Lyall felt relieved, as well as a bit remorseful. Once again, he had allowed Ragnald's view of the world to color his own. The oldest's victim mentality was still affecting him. Feeling that he needed to make amends, he looked straight at his sister and smiled at her.

"Thank you, Ki'ara, for looking out for Ragnald. It never occurred to me that people might actually still consider doing him harm! Right here in this castle! I appreciate that you are doing everything in your power to protect him! Just knowing that makes me feel so much better!"

Ki'ara smiled back at this sibling of hers whom she really knew least of all. "You are most welcome, Lyall. He is my brother too. We are family and need to stick together no matter what has happened in the past!"

Regarding Lyall solemnly for a moment, she continued: "I propose that we too, you and I, start over and leave all past hurts behind. Great change has come to this family, and we all need to find our place within the new order of things." Ki'ara paused for a moment, looking thoughtful.

"How do you feel about all this, Lyall? Are you good with the way we have planned the running of the clan?" the young lady asked him sincerely.

Lyall looked at her in surprise. No one in years had asked him how he felt about anything. Ragnald had just dictated. He had never cared about anyone else's feelings or opinions. He would have never even considered posing such a question.

Something inside the young man shifted, and for the first time that he could remember, Lyall felt truly free and light. His life was his own, and suddenly, he was a valued member of what was rapidly becoming a real family instead of the lackey to a tyrannical lord. What a remarkable transformation!

After considering Ki'ara's query for a moment, Lyall realized that he was actually really good with the way life had developed. He started to feel happy, an emotion that was almost alien to him. A laugh bubbled up inside him.

"Sister dear, I could not be happier with the way things are. I am finally free to get to know myself. If you will allow it, I can be of great assistance to you and Gawain. Of all the people in this keep, I am most familiar with the way Ragnald ran the realm," he began.

Lyall stopped and looked contemplative for a moment. "Ragnald changed so many things! Anything father instituted, he set out to undo. If you would like to hear them, I actually have some suggestions about what we should reverse as quickly as possible," he stated.

⚜

Lord Iain regarded Lyall with surprise. This was a whole new side of his nephew that he had never seen before. None of them had! Here was a depth of character and self-assurance that had been sorely missing until this very moment!

With Ki'ara's encouragement, Lyall started sharing some of his ideas. Once he realized that they were taken seriously, even his appearance began to change! He seemed to gain more color by the minute! It was astonishing to literally watch him blossom and come into his own.

The family began a lively but very productive discussion about what could be done and what needed to be remedied first. Ki'ara liked many of the ideas Lyall and Gawain came up with and finally asked James to send for Ragnald's secretary.

⚜

The man entered rather pensively. He was used to his lord's vile temper, and being called for had never been a good thing. It had only happened whenever something had been wrong, and Ragnald had wanted it fixed right then and there.

For a moment, Ki'ara watched the secretary in silence. She intended to get a sense of what kind of person she was dealing with before addressing him. He was very nervous but did not seem to be a bad sort, just scared. The longer she waited, the more fidgety the man was becoming.

"I am Lady Ki'ara, the new lord of the clan. Are you willing to work for me, or do I need to look for someone else?" she finally asked.

"No, please, Lady Ki'ara, I would be honored to work for you! How can I be of assistance?" came the immediate and heartfelt reply.

"Will you assist my brothers and me to bring a new, more progressive, and kinder era to our realm?" Ki'ara asked the clerk, point-blank.

She had detected no deceit coming from him of any kind, only apprehension and anxiousness. The poor guy had been severely frightened. Going on past experiences, he had assumed the worst. Her words finally put him at ease, and he visibly brightened.

The extremely relieved man had not expected to be treated this cordially. That he would be given a chance to work for the next lord left him almost dumbfounded. He was only too happy to help undo some of the damage Ragnald had done.

⸙

Gawain, to Ki'ara's delight, turned out to be amazingly adept, as well as fast, at assessing a situation. She was confident that he would take excellent care of the clan in her absence. Conall's and Lord Iain's input, as well as Lyall's knowledge of many of Ragnald's secrets, were also going to be invaluable in restoring fairness and just laws to her people.

Ki'ara had the secretary take notes of several issues that had to be dealt with later that day. After a while, when he started to feel more comfortable, the man began to share his own knowledge of his master's hidden agenda.

Some of the edicts in place at this time were beyond cruel, unfair, and arbitrary. They needed to be reversed immediately. As they delved deeper into the rules that had been instituted for the realm, more and more of their brother's atrocities came to light.

The sheer depth and magnitude of Ragnald's betrayal of their people left the family stunned. Until the pieces started coming together, no one had been aware of the true extent of evil their sibling had caused and intended to bring down on the Highlands. Ki'ara could not help but shudder at the thought.

Not even Lyall had known that Ragnald still served his grandfather's depraved and bloodthirsty gods and had intended to reinstate them. That religion had always been practiced in secret and for a good reason. No sane person would worship such beings! Because of their perversion, these deities had been outlawed by the Zidhe long ago!

Ragnald, not Ki'ara, had been the menace and danger to them all. The new lord ended up having to swear the secretary to silence until they had a chance to remove his previous master from Seamuir Castle.

It would be almost impossible to keep their brother from being harmed if this information was disseminated among the clan.

Chapter 31

An Important Announcement

The assembled MacClair family members, including Lord Iain and Conall, were extremely pleased with how well things were coming along. They felt that they had made great strides already when James came to inform the group that it was time to brief Seamuir Castle's residents.

The fortress had been buzzing with all kinds of rumors since Ragnald had been found unconscious in his study. Ki'ara hoped that by revealing most of the facts, she might be able to put at least a few of these to sleep.

Ragnald's loss of immortality and powers, however, was another matter. If at all possible, the family wanted to keep that to themselves for the time being.

Those who worked in and around the castle and in the immediate area had gathered to hear the news. Lord Iain was the first to step out on the balcony overlooking the courtyard. As the acting ruler since Ragnald's collapse, it was his privilege to address the members of the clan first.

"Good morning to all of you! We have much to do in the next few days, and I know that you are dying to find out who the new lord is. Therefore, I will keep my speech brief. I am sure you all know by now that Lord Ragnald MacClair is desperately ill. You all felt the wave of magic, and it affected some of you more than others. For him, being tied to the land, it was almost deadly," he explained.

Lord Iain was sharing the version of events that the family had agreed on. They had initially intended to divulge the whole truth, but to their surprise, James and Berta had advised against it. As the senior staff, the pair had felt strongly that it would only cause more fear and anxiety among their people.

Once he had given it some thought, Lord Iain had agreed with the butler's and housekeeper's reasoning. Much had happened in Eastmuir since Ragnald took over and in the last few days. The kinfolk were already unsettled and could do without having their view of the world turned upside down!

The power of the realm was seen as beneficial, as kind. Its purpose was to look after the people and to protect them. The clan did not need to know that the magic of the land had intended to murder its oppressor!

"Lord Ragnald is doing better, but due to his illness, he will be unable to continue as the ruler of this clan." Loud whispering broke out and interrupted Lord Iain. It took a moment before he was able to continue.

"The wave was caused by the union of the MacClair family with the Clan StCloud. I am sure that many of you have already figured out that Lady Ki'ara and Lord Conall are now husband and wife," he went on when silence descended once more.

At this pronouncement, loud cheers broke out in the courtyard. Once again, the Lord of Ravenshire had to pause.

"This marriage was something your previous ruler, Lord Mikael, had approved years ago! Two days ago, it finally came to be!" More clapping erupted. It was evident that the clan soundly approved.

"When Lord Ragnald fell ill and became incapacitated, the magic of the land passed on to one of his siblings. I know that you are all wondering and can't wait for me to tell you which one!" he teased, drawing out the moment. At this point, you could have heard a pin drop so quiet had it become!

"Your new ruler is, Ki'ara MacClair StCloud, Lord of Eastmuir and Fairholme!" Lord Iain pronounced. The surprise of the kinfolk was evident, and loud whispering broke out only to be replaced by an exuberant display of approval.

"Please welcome your new lord!" he went on once he could be heard once more.

Lord Iain waved Ki'ara out on the balcony. As soon as she could be seen from below, the courtyard erupted into deafening applause. When the new ruler held out her hand to her husband and had him join her, the roar of appreciation got even louder. It was evident that her clan did not share Ragnald's dislike of the StClouds!

Many of the kinsmen had been tempted to clap, dance, and shout when Lord Iain shared the welcome news that their cruel lord had been replaced. One glance at the butler, however, who was standing on the front stairs, had dissuaded them. James had been insistently signaling them to keep quiet by waving his arms and shaking his head.

Now, finally, the assembled folk could show their happiness over this change in rule and their previous lord's misfortune. Things were bound to get better; it would have been hard for them to get much worse! Loud shouts and impromptu dancing broke out all over the courtyard.

The kinsmen and women figured that anyone was better than Ragnald! Ki'ara had won many a heart with the healings she had done after the fire. She had also gained their admiration with her show of mercy for the hapless riverboat captain.

None of them, however, really knew the lady. She had been absent so much these last few years. What alleviated many of their apprehensions was that Ki'ara's husband, the StCloud, was known to be a fair and caring lord. He was sure to keep his wife in line!

Ki'ara smiled at the noisy reception and waved to the crowd congregated below. When the noise finally quieted down, she addressed the people who had become her responsibility for the very first time.

"Thank you for this warm welcome! Being your new lord is an honor that I do not take lightly. I promise you that I will do my very best to make life better again for all of you! I know how much you have suffered these last few years! My family and I are working together already to change all that." she began.

"I want to hear laughter in this castle once again! Many of the rules you have had to live under will be repealed. Life will become easier and more pleasant once more! You have my word on that!" Ki'ara went on.

The new lord had said all the right things, and the clan was ecstatic. People were crying, laughing, and hugging each other. Hope, which had been absent for so long, had been reborn. Finally, there were better times on the horizon!

Ki'ara waited for her kinfolk to compose themselves a little before she continued.

"I will do my utmost to bring happiness back to this clan! I am, however, married to this wonderful man right here, and I am also the Lord of Fairholme," she paused to let her words sink in for a moment.

"This means that, at times, I have responsibilities elsewhere. Therefore, to serve you best, I have decided to enlist my brothers Gawain and Lyall to help me govern you!" Ki'ara announced, waving for her surprised brothers to join them.

Gawain had anticipated being the steward of the clan, but no more than that. Lyall had expected no consideration or position at all. Both were too stunned to be able to speak. They felt incredibly honored by the trust their sister was placing in them.

◦⊹⊱✦⊰⊹◦

The new lord's announcement was greeted with more cheers. Gawain was very popular and well-liked by all. He had always treated them with kindness and consideration. Their feelings about Lyall were more reserved. He had been too close to Ragnald, but if the lady believed in him enough to involve him, they were willing to give him a chance.

When the happy shouts ceased, Ki'ara continued. "Any time I need to be absent, Lord Gawain will be in charge with Lord Lyall acting as his second-in-command and adviser. Unfortunately, the first time for my brothers to govern you will be very soon. I have an important errand that requires me to be away from you for a while. As per Lord Mikael's request, my husband and I are taking Lord Ragnald to a place of healing."

Loud clapping showed her people's approval of this course of action. Most assumed that things could only get better with that evil man removed from the castle, even if this took their new lord away from home for several months! The kinsmen felt that this was a small price to pay for peace and contentment returning to Eastmuir!

Ki'ara patiently waited for the courtyard to grow quiet once more. Being able to pick up emotions so easily and strongly, she was only too aware of their feelings towards Ragnald. She could sense their relief at the welcome news of his imminent departure.

"We will hold an official swearing-in ceremony eight days from now. The rest of the clan has been invited as well as the other rulers. There is much to do to get things ready in such a short time, but I am sure that we can pull this off if we all work together! Let's show them a true MacClair welcome when they arrive and make this the best celebration ever!" Ki'ara shouted while raising one fist into the air. Somehow, this had just felt appropriate and seemed to set just the right tone.

A roar of approval went through the courtyard below. Being Highlanders, they loved a good party. It had been many years since there had been any kind of event at the castle. The kinsmen were all looking forward to this welcome opportunity to have some lighthearted fun.

Most agreed that this was already turning out to be one of the best days they had seen in the last few years. And, the new lord had just begun! Hope and renewed optimism were spreading through the keep at lightning speed.

If anyone had been outside to watch, they would have observed Seamuir Castle visibly brighten. The dark miasma caused by Ragnald's evil ways was lifting further!

Taking their cue from their sister, Lyall and Gawain retreated back into the room with Lord Iain right behind them. Waving to her people one last time, Ki'ara and Conall joined them shortly after.

"That went well! Thank you all for your help and support! I need to go make sure that the housekeeper has the preparations firmly in hand," Ki'ara informed her siblings, husband, and uncle. She had a huge smile on her face. At the door, she turned around suddenly.

"We do not have much time, and there is so much to do! If you don't mind, could we retreat to the office to deal with some of the things we discussed earlier?" she requested, giving each an imploring look. "I will meet you there!"

Her brothers groaned good-naturedly but agreed to the meeting. Ki'ara invited her husband and Lord Iain to attend as well, then set off to find Berta. Not only did the festivities need to be planned and arrangements made, but the lady wanted lunch to be ready around noon.

Before long, the family was assembled in the study to work out the new laws for the clan. Much that had been instituted by Ragnald was malicious, archaic, and made little sense. No one could possibly thrive under these rules.

They had to be undone, and the sooner, the better!

Chapter 32

A Busy Few Days

While the MacClair siblings, Lord Iain, and the StCloud, were sequestered in the study diligently working on better and much more humane rules for the clan, the housekeeper was busily shouting orders. She had begun some of the preparations on the previous night, but now things were moving along full force.

The resolute woman had not forgotten her first encounter with the new lord, and how rude she had acted towards the young lady. Her behavior had been very unbecoming of a competent housekeeper! Actually, she had been lucky not to have been fired right there on the spot!

Now that the Lady Ki'ara was in charge, Berta feared that she may not have a job much longer unless she managed to impress the new ruler. The lady had treated her nice enough when she had come downstairs to discuss the arrangements, but one never knew!

To Berta's immense surprise, the new lord had even asked for suggestions from her, a lowly servant. Now, this was something that the housekeeper was not used to anymore. Therefore, she had rather timidly presented her first few ideas. She had, however, gained confidence when these had been well received.

Eight days was not very long to prepare a great feast, but Berta's pride would not allow her to fail in this momentous task. She was determined to make this the best party Seamuir Castle had seen in many, many years.

Showing Berta respect and taking her seriously had made the woman feel like she was once again part of a team and not just a lowly servant. Without knowing or even intending it, Ki'ara had gained a staunch supporter in the once so rude housekeeper.

❧

Work on the revised laws was proceeding slowly but steadily. Some decisions were easy, and many of the rules Lord Mikael had introduced were reinstated. For other issues, Gawain had suggestions for improvements. These needed to be discussed, and the pros and cons considered carefully.

To everyone's amazement, Lyall was displaying all kinds of talents none of them had been aware of, not even himself! For one, he had an incredible memory for details and conversations.

He had actually kept track of most of the changes his brother had set into motion. This made him invaluable and made it much easier to undo some of the damage the cruel lord had done.

When Ki'ara's stomach kept growling, she finally called for a break. She rang for James, who arrived promptly to inform her that the meal was ready and could be served in the dining room at their convenience.

To everyone's amusement, Gawain immediately got up and headed for the door. The others followed him down the stairs, and just as soon as they were seated, servants brought in a delicious smelling soup followed by fish, potatoes, and vegetables.

Eating in the office would have been more expedient, but the group had been hard at work for a couple of hours and needed a break. After finishing their food and relaxing around the table for a few extra minutes, the family decided to return to the study. It was time to get back to discussing the clan business.

***

Before returning to the office, the siblings and Lord Iain went by Ragnald's chambers. He was still in the main suite of the castle that was actually now rightfully Ki'ara's. She, however, had decided that she really did not like those rooms. Also, she figured that the less change went on while their brother was in such a critical condition, the better. He had enough adjustments to make already.

After asking the guards to wait outside, she placed a hand on Ragnald's forehead. Her spell gently awoke the now mortal lord. As soon as his eyes opened and he realized where he was and who was touching him, he immediately slapped Ki'ara's hand away as one would something disgusting and unclean.

He may now be mortal, but her brother's nasty disposition had definitely not improved!

***

Ragnald would have much preferred not seeing any of them. Therefore, he furiously glared at his assembled family. He wanted them to leave, especially since he had been asleep for a very long time. His bodily needs were asserting themselves.

With his manservant's help, Ragnald headed for the adjoining bathroom. It would have been prudent to have someone support his other side, but, rather rudely, he refused any aid from his brothers. When he reemerged, he was more composed but no less cold or angry.

"What do you want, you bunch of traitors? Come to gloat over my misfortune, have you? Don't you have anything better to do, anyone else to stab in the back?" Ragnald snarled at them.

"I don't want your company, especially not yours, you bitch! This is all your fault! All of you, get out of my room!" he ended shouting, spraying spittle all over his robe.

At this point, Lord Iain had enough. "You ungrateful wretch! If not for Ki'ara, you would be dead by now! It is not her fault that the magic found you wanting but your own! Did you really think you could get away with abusing the power like that?" he finished, eyeing Ragnald with disgust.

"Guards! Watch the lord. He is not to leave his rooms, nor is he allowed visitors or special favors," he ordered with a look at Ki'ara, who nodded her approval. Being mortal and almost dying seemed to have not changed this evil man.

"Come, children, let's leave this mutt to stew in his own misery and bitterness. I, for one, have had enough of him and his poison!" Lord Iain continued.

The furious Lord of Ravenshire stormed out of the suite with Gawain on his heels. Had there not been others behind him, he would have loudly slammed the door. After giving Ragnald a last look, one after the other, his remaining siblings left the room.

Lyall stayed the longest, still hoping for some sign of the brother he had so adored and loved. But, there was nothing, only anger and contempt. This man before him was a complete stranger, one he did not like at all.

He ended up locking eyes with Ragnald for several minutes. Defiantly, he returned his sibling's hate-filled glare. Lyall was greatly saddened, but it felt good not to be afraid any longer, to be his own man.

Finally, Ragnald was the one to glance down. Now that was a first! Feeling like he had won a major victory, Lyall turned on his heel and followed the others from the chamber.

The rest of the family was waiting on the landing in front of the suite. Ki'ara was visibly upset, and the StCloud had placed a comforting arm around her shoulders. Lyall could not blame her for being distressed. She had kept Ragnald alive, and all she had gotten in return had been him hitting her! Not even a thank you for the major healing she had done!

Lyall exchanged a stunned glance with Gawain. He was not sure what he had expected or hoped for, but not this! None of them deserved to be treated such after they had worked so hard to preserve Ragnald's life!

⁂

Since more business needed their attention, the group once again met up in the study. Each had taken a few minutes in their rooms to compose and refresh themselves after this unpleasant encounter.

It was Lyall who brought up his brother once they were all comfortably seated. "Ki'ara, I know you want to leave Ragnald where he is until you leave with him to take him to father," he began.

"To care for his comfort so much is very commendable and sweet of you, but I do not believe that he should be here for the celebration or, for that matter, a day longer than necessary. Conall, I believe you are returning to Cloudshire Hall tomorrow?" he addressed his brother-in-law.

"Yes, that is my intention. I have things to take care of before we set out," the StCloud answered. "Ki'ara has to remain here, as much as that grieves me. But, there is much left to be done before we depart."

"To be honest, I want Ragnald as far away from my sister as possible, especially for the next few days when you are not here. Do you have a place where you could stash him?" Lyall queried. Conall eyed him with surprise then nodded.

"Also, I believe he might be safer among your people than ours. Throw him in a jail somewhere for all I care! Actually, that might be best for everyone involved, including him," Lyall continued.

Ki'ara looked at her brother in surprise. One of the reasons she had taken it easy on Ragnald had been for Lyall's sake. She had felt that her second sibling had been hurt enough and had not wanted to add grief over the unfair treatment of a man he had idolized to the list.

Conall was visibly relieved. It would take some time to deal with all his obligations, and he needed to be gone for at least five days. The StCloud had not liked the idea of that vicious man anywhere in the vicinity of his wife. Especially without himself around to protect her!

Also, none of them wanted the upcoming celebration interrupted by one of this cad's wicked schemes! It was quickly agreed that Conall would take Ragnald with him to Cloudshire Hall to start with. He had the perfect place to stash the unpleasant man when he got ready to come back to Eastmuir.

The StCloud would leave him in the capable hands of one of his friends. He would make sure that Ragnald was kept under heavy guard. The estate would be a little out of his way on the return trip to Seamuir Castle, but it was well worth it. The small detour would save him and Ki'ara several hours on their journey to Elvenhorst, the city of the Zidhe.

After the hostile reception the family had received just a few minutes earlier, all were in agreement. The sooner Ragnald was handed over to the elves, the better. Maybe their father could do something with his wayward son.

It was early evening, and Ki'ara felt that she and her family had done all they could for the day. They had achieved so much! A timetable for the implementation of the new rules had been developed, and the old ones had been examined carefully.

Some of the laws Ragnald had put into place would just be repealed outright, some replaced by those their father had introduced, others with new and kinder edicts. Ki'ara wanted her people to be happy and prosper and quickly so. They had been through so much!

Ki'ara had been impressed by the competence both of her brothers had displayed during the sessions. It lightened her worry and confirmed her choice of involving her siblings in the governing of the realm. Gawain was rapidly growing into his position as regent and Lyall as a valuable adviser and second in command.

Thanking her brothers, her husband, and Lord Iain for all their valuable input and assistance, Ki'ara called the meeting to a close. She was pleased with the progress but had noticed that all of them were starting to get fatigued.

Also, the evening meal would be served soon. Ki'ara wanted everyone present to have a chance to return to their rooms for a few minutes and get freshened up before going downstairs.

Not much later, James rang the gong to announce that it was time for dinner. Ragnald had been invited to join them but had rather rudely refused. His meal was being served in his rooms. This was not unexpected but had still put a temporary damper on the family's enjoyment. As usual, Gawain went out of his way to lighten the mood and soon had them laughing again.

Once again, the cook had outdone herself. The steaks were tender, the potatoes perfectly cooked, and the vegetables seasoned to perfection. Dessert was the most delightful chocolate mousse covered in vanilla-flavored whipped cream.

Ki'ara declined all refills of the delicious red wine offered with dinner. Fearing that she would fall asleep at the table, she took just a few sips from her glass. She had noticed the servers eyeing it longingly and was confident that the lovely drink would not go to waste.

After all the excitement and working all day, Ki'ara was not the only one who was tired in the little group. When Lyall could not stop yawning, and Lord Iain fell asleep at the table, they decided to head off to bed.

Conall and Ki'ara were the first to leave with the others following quickly behind. The newlyweds wanted to spend at least a few hours alone together before the StCloud set out the next morning.

⚜

It was very peculiar, but the attitude in the entire castle seemed to lighten even further when the carriage with their once lord pulled out of the gates. Even the ancient building itself felt suddenly less oppressive. The dark aura that had surrounded it for so long was starting to dissipate more and more.

Ki'ara had not intended to begin her reign by having to punish one of her people for attacking her much-hated brother. Therefore, she had the courtyard cleared as much as possible before having him brought out. Still, several people had managed to be around and spit in Ragnald's direction when he walked out to the coach under heavy guard.

Her own goodbye to Conall had been sweet and tender. They would miss each other much and regretted to be parted so soon after their wedding. At least they had woken up early enough to make exquisite love one more time.

Ki'ara was still glowing from her husband's expert attention. He had driven her completely wild yet once again! She was looking forward to his return and all the things he had promised to introduce her to!

⋆⋅☆⋅⋆

The next few days went by, as if in a dream. Everyone was busy from morning until night, and the entire castle was abuzz with activity. The great hall and the courtyard were being decorated, and the smell of cooking and baking permeated the air.

Ki'ara, her two brothers, and their uncle spent most of their time working on a new constitution for the realm. It would be presented after the swearing-in ceremony. The siblings wanted the changes to go into effect as quickly as possible to ease the burden Ragnald had placed onto their people.

⋆⋅☆⋅⋆

Two days before the ceremony, Conall returned. Ki'ara, who had been very lady-like the last few days, flew into her husband's arms and kissed him soundly, right there before the front doors of Seamuir Castle, in plain sight of all. After a moment of surprise, the StCloud returned his wife's kiss with equal ardor.

No one present really seemed to mind. If anything, it endeared Ki'ara more to her people. Young love they understood, and it made the couple more human and approachable to them. A few good-natured snickers were all that resulted from the newlywed's open display of affection.

Then, the day before the ceremony, the guests began to arrive. The housekeeper and her staff were all over the place, getting everybody settled in comfortably. Ki'ara, Conall, and her siblings were busy dealing with the last-minute problems cropping up before the big event.

It had been decided that the lords and their spouses would reside in the manor. The majority of the clan, however, would be housed in tents. Rows upon rows of these were being erected in the field in front of the castle.

With Conall's help, Lord Iain and the siblings finally managed to get the first of the new rules and regulations hammered out enough to be put on paper. There was much left to do, but this was at least a beginning. Gawain and Lyall would continue working on this and put new temporary laws in place until Ki'ara could approve them.

That night, dinner took place in the great hall, the only room in the castle large enough to hold all the people. The fireplaces on each end were roaring, keeping the large stone room pleasantly warm.

Ki'ara, her husband, and her family entered last. A high table had been set up for them and the attending lords and ladies. Once everyone was seated, Lord Iain extended a welcome and greetings to all the guests.

Along with a wonderful meal, mead, wine, and beer were offered to those who cared to indulge. All knew that this was just the prelude for the next day's festivities, and most did not overdo it too badly. As usual, there are always exceptions.

Highlanders love a good party. For the MacClair kinsmen and women, it had been a long time since they had been invited to join the family at Seamuir Castle for any kind of event. They were therefore really looking forward to the celebration, especially if the bounty of this evening was any indication of things to come!

It was very late before the castle, and the camp grew quiet. Around midnight, the exhausted staff finally fell into their beds. It had been a long few days, but each and every one of them was looking forward to the morrow.

The housekeeper took one last check of all the preparations before heading to her own room. She was well satisfied. She and her people had done it! Tomorrow would be the party of the decade, of that Berta had made sure.

Chapter 33

A Festive Event

The day of the big ceremony dawned bright and clear. The castle was and had been abuzz with a flurry of activities since long before sunup. The camp outside its walls, on the other hand, was just slowly waking up. This was a holiday for the clan, after all, and sleeping in was part of the treat. Besides, one had to be ready and in good shape for the festivities to come! Being tired would just not do!

Long tables had been set up in the courtyard, and a sumptuous breakfast was being served. To the great appreciation of the hungry and thirsty Highlanders, a constant supply of delicious smelling food and drink was being carried out from the kitchen.

When the cook poked her head out, she was rewarded with a raucous round of applause. Unused to such praise, the rotund woman smiled shyly and made a somewhat clumsy curtsy. When renewed clapping from all around followed, she started grinning from ear to ear.

She was absolutely delighted. Even the noble lords and their ladies liked her offerings! Who would have thought! This truly made her day!

⚜

Once everyone was finally sated, it was time for the ceremony to begin. Instead of holding it in the great hall, Ki'ara had chosen to follow tradition and conduct it out in an open field close to Seamuir Castle. The small tent city had been set up on the other side of the keep for just that reason.

Strict rules governed such events, and a certain decorum and pomp were expected. Therefore, a formal procession formed by the front stairs with Lord Iain leading the way. Next came Ki'ara with Conall by her side, followed by Lyall and Gawain. The Zidarian lords and ladies fell in behind them, and the rest of the clan got into their proper places after that.

Once everyone was lined up, the entire affair took on a very officious air. The stately and ceremonious parade slowly made its way out of the gate. The seriousness of the moment was lost on none. The often so boisterous Highlanders were for once respectfully calm and kept their talk to a minimum.

An arch, decorated richly with white roses, had been erected in the field. Lord Iain stepped through it and then turned. Ki'ara and Conall stopped just in front, and the other rulers and their spouses ritually fanned out to the sides behind them in the shape of a half-moon circle. Gawain and Lyall remained standing behind the couple.

As directed by James, the rest of the clan arranged themselves in a wide circle. In days of old, everyone would have been armed and ready for anything. Enclosing their new lord in such a manner had helped protect her or him from possible attacks by enemies of the clan. Now, it served to ensure that all had a good view of the activities to come.

The Lord of Ravenshire waited until all had reached their places, and quiet had descended upon the area. Each person knew just what to do since this ceremony had been conducted in a similar manner, with only very minor variations at best, for many generations.

Magically enhancing his voice, Lord Iain began to speak the age-old words of the ritual.

"We are all present here to confirm the new ruler of your clan, the MacClairs. Are you ready to bear witness?" he called out.

The customary answer of "Aye" was shouted by every person assembled and rang loudly across the sunlit fields, startling some peacefully grazing sheep in the distance.

"Then let the ceremony commence!" Lord Iain continued. Facing Ki'ara, he motioned her to step forward under the arch and then began.

"The land is our life. The magic binds us as much as we bind it. We are the instruments of its will as much as it is the instrument of ours. It is our sworn and solemn duty to use the power granted to us for the benefit of all. The care of the clan is our greatest responsibility and also our greatest gift." he shouted.

"I, Lord Iain of the Clan of Ravenshire, having been given the authority by Lord Mikael MacClair to oversee this realm in case of an emergency or event such as this, am here to conduct this swearing-in," Lord Iain went on.

"Is this acceptable to all?" came his question. Once again, a thunderous 'Aye' roared across the clearing.

"Then, with the power invested in me, let us begin!" the lord stated solemnly.

"Do you, Ki'ara MacClair StCloud swear to respect the magic of the land and to use it only for the good of the clan?" he addressed her.

"Aye!" Ki'ara responded loud and clear.

"And do you, Ki'ara MacClair StCloud, swear to never use the magic to maliciously harm one of the clan but to protect your kin against all enemies or dangers?"

"I do," came the firm answer.

"Do you, Ki'ara MacClair StCloud, promise to be a fair and good lord who will rule with the best interest of all at heart?"

"I promise!"

"Then, by the power invested in me, I now declare you, Ki'ara MacClair StCloud, to be the Lord of the great clan of the MacClairs! May you reign in peace and with wisdom and fairness!" Lord Iain concluded the ancient ceremony.

The Lord of Ravenshire turned Ki'ara to face her peers and raised up her hand in the age-old show of victory.

"I now give you - The MacClair!"

The sound of the cheers was so loud this time that it sent many of the poor sheep in the nearby field fleeing to the far end of the pasture. Bewildered, they looked around for the source of this rude interruption to their otherwise peaceful day.

⁂

Being magically amplified, a faint echo of the clan's approval of their new lord could be heard for miles around. The kinfolk had suffered much under Ragnald, and all were looking forward to better times. To an ever-increasing degree, hope was growing in their hearts.

Once the tumult died down, Lord Iain stepped back, leaving Ki'ara to stand alone under the fragrant flower gate. It was time for her to address the assembled crowd.

"Thank you for your heartfelt welcome! I greatly appreciate that you approve of me as your new lord! Usually, this would conclude the ritual, but before we return to the castle, we have some important business to discuss. My apologies for keeping you from the feast a little while longer!" she began.

"Just don't make it too long!" shouted one of the Highlanders in a good-natured, teasing fashion. His outburst was followed by much laughter. Hearts were light, and the clan members were happy.

Ki'ara laughed right along with her people then signaled for silence. She was obeyed almost immediately. The new lord was impressed with this show of respect.

"First, let me introduce you to my husband, whom most of you already know! Conall StCloud!" she shouted, using the magic of the land to project her voice. Conall stepped up beside her to deafening applause.

"Next, let's address some of the laws of the realm. We all suffered under the previous lord. Many of the rules that he instituted were unfair and arbitrary. I, therefore, give you Lord Gawain MacClair and Lord Lyall MacClair, who will now read you part of the new constitution of the MacClair clan!"

Good-natured groans followed her pronouncement, but once the brothers stepped up to join her and Conall, they were greeted with enthusiastic clapping. Her people were well pleased that the reign this time was to be a family affair.

※※※

Gawain bowed to the assembled guests and then began to read. Several times he was interrupted by the sound of enthusiastic applause. When he finished with another bow, shouts of approval and thunderous clapping were the clan's response. It seemed that the family had done well in working out the new laws!

"Thank you, Lord Gawain!" Ki'ara said, stepping forward. It was then, at that very moment, that the glamour her mother Ali'ana had placed on her at birth was suddenly broken.

Until then, the spell had covered most of the elven traits Ki'ara possessed, but not all. Her irises had resisted any attempt of disguise and had, at times, unnerved some of the folk. Now, she stood in front of them in all her glory.

The young lady was completely unaware that anything had changed. Her bright green eyes regarded the gathered people with affection and kindness. A wave of love emanating from Ki'ara washed over the assembly. She smiled at her clan and the attending lords.

"As you just heard, a new age has begun! Let us live and work together in harmony with nature as well as our neighbors!" the newest MacClair Lord shouted.

Her words were greeted with loud cheering and exuberant clapping initially. But then, as more and more people were starting to notice the subtle changes in Ki'ara's appearance, a sudden hush fell over the crowd. Their respect for their new leader went up a fair notch. How lucky were they to have an almost pure Zidhe for their very own lord?

Ki'ara was more than a little honored and surprised when first one, than another, of her kin went down on one knee in a show homage. This was something they had not done for Ragnald. Him, they had mistrusted from the very start.

༺⚜༻

The Rainbow Kayrex had been convinced to stay in the castle and allow Ki'ara to go somewhere unescorted for once. It had taken copious amounts of some extra special treats to achieve this and to keep him distracted for at least a little while.

Now, the beautiful, iridescent bird took this very moment to appear. Shimmer swooped in and gracefully landed in front of Ki'ara, who regarded him with amusement. Some of his snacks were still stuck to his beak, distracting just a little from the regal air the avian was trying to put on as, with all the flair he could muster, he bowed to his lady.

That even this messenger of the Zidhe would honor their lord in this manner filled the clan with immense pleasure. The kinsmen, their women, and children looked upon their new lord with great pride as she stood there illuminated by the rays of the sun. She was beyond just beautiful.

A sense of awe spread through the crowd. How many other clans had a ruler who was almost full Zidhe? And, how many of the lords were willing to share the limelight of their swearing-in ceremony with her siblings? Not one! They had been truly blessed by this fortunate turn of events!

Ki'ara's red hair shone like spun copper in the brilliant sunlight. Her delicate facial features and vivid green eyes made her look very elven and exotic. At that moment, she looked more like a goddess of nature than a part-human.

The pure white gown Ki'ara was wearing, together with the crown of twigs and flowers that had been placed on her head, gave her the appearance of innocence and renewal. They heightened the air of divinity surrounding her. The clan looked upon their new ruler with admiration.

They could still barely believe it. In just a few days, she had managed to change their life for the better! The new rules Ki'ara and her brothers had put into place undid much of the injustice and damage the cruel Ragnald had done.

When the kneeling clan, almost as one, lowered their heads to Ki'ara as an additional show of respect, she bowed to them in turn. Tears had gathered in her eyes, and her throat was choked with emotions. When she could finally manage to speak, she asked her kinfolk to please rise.

"I think we have spent enough time in this field! Let's go feast!" her clear voice rang out. This pronouncement was greeted with hearty approval. There was much to celebrate this day and no better time than the present!

With Ki'ara and Conall, hand in hand, at its head, the procession made its way back to the castle.

The feast was one that the clan, as well as the attending lords and their spouses, would remember for years. The housekeeper, the cook, and the staff had simply outdone themselves. They basked in all the compliments and the thanks they were getting from just about everyone.

Too many years had passed since the MacClair Clan had a proper get-together. The very last party had been when Ragnald had become the ruler. And, that one had been nothing like this!

Ki'ara and Conall once again sat at the high table, and, one after another, many of the clan folk wandered by to have a brief chat. Their new lord listened attentively to all their concerns. She had her secretary stand by and take notes.

Gawain was also talking to people, and even Lyall was more sociable than usual. The family had agreed that it would be easiest to learn about grievances and problems when people were less inhibited, and their tongues loosened by drink.

The siblings intended to compare notes later and look into possible issues more deeply. The last few days had molded the three together into a unit determined to do right by their people. There was much the family had to atone for after the years Ragnald had been in charge.

The boisterous revelry went on until late into the night. By then, most of the lords and their spouses had long since retreated into the quietness of their quarters. Only Gawain remained in the hall, enjoying himself immensely.

The clan members had always found the youngest son to be the most approachable of his siblings, and he did like to party. They were thrilled to know that he would be the regent whenever his sister was gone.

The kinfolk were exceedingly pleased with the changes that they had been blessed with so suddenly and unexpectedly. If this feast was a sign of things to come, they would be well served by their new rulers.

Chapter 34

An Unwelcome Message

Many a man, as well as woman, woke up with more than a bit of a hangover the next morning. The Highlanders absolutely loved a good feast. It had been a while, eleven years to be exact, since the clan had gotten together. Therefore, the kinfolk had taken full advantage of the offerings.

It had been some celebration! There had been plenty of alcohol of different varieties to please just about every palate! To go along with this had been all kinds of delicious snacks. The castle's staff had continued refilling the plates until late into the night.

The music had also been a delight. A group of skilled performers had played some of the Highlanders' favorite songs. As requested by Ki'ara, the tunes had been more sedate and in the background during the main evening meal. She had been very pleased.

Once the tables had been moved alongside the walls of the hall to make room for the dancers, however, the players had free reign. They had picked up the pace and even more so as drink took effect. All had agreed that the party had been just plain glorious.

The immortals did not suffer as badly. Due to their connection to the land, spirits did not affect them the same way as their mostly human counterparts. They did manage to get inebriated, but, if need be, once they stopped drinking, the Zidarians could sober up rather quickly. Lord Hamish had been proof of that at the wedding.

The Highlanders were tough people who lived close to their land. Sleeping in tents and eating outside were part of their ways. If they were honest, many liked it that way. Ki'ara had anticipated that after a night of steady drinking, they would prefer not to have to be on their best behavior around their new lord or the other Zidarians.

Therefore, breakfast for the ones outside the walls was served in the courtyard. In any case, there was no place in the castle to hold all the guests except the great hall, and it was still in utter disarray. Here and there, revelers who had not made it back to his or her tent were still sleeping in the midst of the mess.

Anyhow, a bit of fresh air after all that drinking the night before was a healthy thing. Also, trying to find one's way around in that castle when one's head was throbbing and felt like it was about to split was not an ideal state of affairs either.

For the nobles, their meal was served in the formal dining room. The chamber was barely large enough to hold all those who had chosen to attend. Due to Ragnald's behavior, there had been years of animosity. As a show of goodwill and to signal that all was forgiven, most of the lords had taken the MacClairs up on their invitation.

Congratulations and a lively discussion about the laws Ki'ara and her brothers had instituted accompanied the breakfast. Some of the new rules had piqued the other leaders' interest, and they wanted to know the details and reasons behind them.

The siblings were only too happy to answer the many questions. Any change for the better in the Highlands was good for them all.

⚜

Ki'ara was genuinely enjoying the meal as well as the company. She was very pleased with the other lords' thoughtful input that gave Gawain, Lyall, and her more ideas for positive changes. Much of the damage that Ragnald had caused had yet to be undone.

Out of the corner of her eye, Ki'ara noticed the sudden appearance of James. The butler looked worried. An unwelcome tightness settled in the pit of her stomach. Something had happened, and it was not good! She could just feel it!

"Milady, Lord StCloud, there is a rider approaching and fast. We believe he is wearing the StCloud colors," he whispered to them. "What are your orders?"

The couple exchanged a glance, and Conall nodded. "Bring him to us as quickly as possible, please," Ki'ara requested in a low voice. James immediately left the room. This was one task he would see to himself.

⚜

The assembled guests had not missed the interchange, and it had grown quiet in the room. The conversation had stopped, and all eyes were focused on Ki'ara and the StCloud. Being Zidarians, they could sense trouble before it ever arrived.

Lord Iain could tell from his niece's pale face that something was up. Ki'ara met his questioning gaze and shrugged her shoulders. She figured that most likely, her brother had something to do with all this. Why else would one of Conall's men be arriving in such a state?

Ragnald would have kept whatever was happening to himself, but that was not her style nor Conall's. Ki'ara was the newest lord and needed these people on her side, not against her. She felt that, in this case, transparency was best.

***

The night before the celebration, Ki'ara and her family had filled the other rulers in on the facts about Ragnald. They had held nothing back. Since most of the lords were in attendance, they had held an impromptu council meeting before dinner.

All present had voiced the opinion that Ki'ara had been more than fair to her hateful sibling. Ragnald was intensely disliked, and the lords felt that he had gotten what he deserved. Her brother was still one of them, however, immortal or not and fell under the jurisdiction of the council.

Ki'ara's eyes met her husband's. Conall gave her an encouraging wave with his hand. Since this was her realm, it was up to her as the Lord of the MacClairs to announce the news. After a brief look around at all the curious faces, she rose to her feet.

"I am sorry for the interruption of such a productive discussion, but we have just been informed that a rider is approaching the castle wearing the StCloud colors. He seems to be in a bit of a hurry. We have given the order to bring him here as soon as he arrives. You, as members of the council, are all welcome to hear what he has to say!" Ki'ara informed them.

A murmur of approval went through the room, and Ki'ara knew that she had done the right thing by being this forthcoming. Depending on the news that was heading their way, she might actually need the help of her peers. Smoothing her dress, she sat back down.

Conall's hand quickly found hers under the table, and he squeezed it reassuringly. Whatever had happened, Ki'ara would not have to deal with it alone. They were a team, and he had her back, always.

⁘

It only took a few minutes before an out of breath James arrived with the tired messenger. From the man's appearance, it was evident that he had ridden hard. He bowed deeply to his lord and lady and then to the rest of the room.

"Permission to speak, my lord!" he addressed the StCloud. "Granted! Please proceed!" came the immediate response.

"My lord, the MacClair you left in our keeping has tried to escape. He pretended to have a seizure, and when your man went to check on him, he murdered him with his own knife," the messenger began.

"The MacClair then tried to set the fortress on fire and did a fair amount of damage. As a result, he was almost killed himself. He has been placed in irons and is under increased guard to keep him out of further trouble. Still, Lord Thomas would greatly appreciate you taking this man off his hands as quickly as possible!" the herald concluded.

Angry mutters broke out as soon as the envoy finished. With another bow to his lord, he asked for permission to be dismissed, which Conall immediately granted. The man looked exhausted and needed to rest.

⁘

Just as soon as James and Conall's clansman left the room, pandemonium broke out. At this point, the assembled lords' patience with Ragnald was exhausted. He had now added the murder of a member of another clan to all his other crimes. Such an act could not go unpunished!

Lord Hamish Fairlie rose from his seat. His usually already ruddy face was now close to purple with fury. "I propose banishment from all clan lands forever. He does not deserve to be one of us! He is a disgrace! Since the Zidhe want him, let them keep him!" he shouted into the chamber.

Lord Lorena Kirkcaldie rose next. "I second this motion! May he rot in hell!"

Lord Iain Elvinstone was the third to rise. "The man is my nephew, but he has gone too far! All in favor, please say 'Aye'!" he requested.

One after another, the lords stood and voiced their agreement. Finally, only the visibly upset Ki'ara remained. After exchanging a despairing look with her husband, her own 'Aye' rung out loud and clear in the room. Ragnald's fate had been sealed.

Chapter 35

The Journey Begins

Very early the next morning, the StCloud and Ki'ara were on their way to his friend's fortress. After the anger over the murder had died down a bit, the assembled lords had called an official council meeting to sanctify their impromptu vote to banish Ragnald. For it to be binding, it had to be done properly.

A short discussion had resulted, and the decision had been made that the couple would move their departure forward a day. Lord Thomas needed to be relieved of his homicidal prisoner. The MacClairs' guests understood that these were unusual circumstances. They would be heading home the following day.

All felt that playing host for a day under the close scrutiny of the lords and their spouses was a good way for Ki'ara's siblings to start their reign. That way, if anything went wrong, there were enough Zidarians around to help smooth things over. Gawain and Lyall were greatly relieved to hear this.

Another concern had been that the MacClair Clan had been severely mismanaged for years. Things were a mess, and this was the first time for the two to govern. Therefore, the brothers had asked Lord Iain as well as Lord Lorena Kirkcaldie to remain behind as advisors. Gawain figured that there was no telling what kinds of problems would pop up while Ki'ara was away.

When the newlyweds and their entourage set out from Seamuir Castle, the couple was comfortably seated in the carriage. But, they had taken horses as well. Neither Ki'ara nor Conall wanted to spend any time in the company of her oldest brother. Once they retrieved him, he and his guards would take the coach. The StCloud felt that this would give Ragnald less of a chance to escape or to cause trouble.

For the first time in years, Ki'ara would have her maid along on her travels. Leana had arrived at the castle several days ago. She had brought with her the luggage that had been left behind in Deansport. The lady was still acting as a servant, and not even her niece knew of her real identity.

With practicality in mind and following her instinct, Leana had packed several riding dresses and even some pants and shirts for Ki'ara. The coffer held only two fancy dresses reserved for the young lady's meeting with the Zidhe.

Leana herself had chosen to travel by horse. She was thrilled to be visiting her home and family, and absolutely loved the freedom that riding brought with it. She had missed this and could not stop the occasional smile from lighting up her face.

To the regret of many of the servants, Shimmer was also leaving Seamuir that morning. The staff had grown fond of the droll creature. The bird had decided to accompany Ki'ara. He had insisted on riding in the carriage and was now happily curled up between the seats. On occasions, he would put his head in his lady's lap and demand the pettings he had come to see as his due.

It would take them several hours to get to the home of Conall's friend. To pass the time, the StCloud was entertaining Ki'ara with tales of his voyages. His wife was fascinated and loved his stories and vivid descriptions of all the locations he had been. There were so many places she wanted to see!

One question finally bubbled back up in her mind. Her husband's recounting of his travels had reminded her again. So much had happened in the last few days that it had not been that important until now.

Ki'ara finally could take it no more, and she interrupted the StCloud's narrative. "The day of the wedding, why were you there? I had heard that you were far to the north!"

Conall laughed. "Yes, that was well planned, wasn't it? I knew you were coming home and that Ragnald would never let you out of the house if he even thought I was in the area!" her husband began with a chuckle.

"I actually was in the far north but managed to conduct most of my business there rather quickly. I left one of my men behind to take care of the rest. Remember the ship you saw when you were heading towards the harbor?" he asked her.

"Yes! It was gorgeous and incredibly fast!" Ki'ara responded. "That was your ship?" she continued with wonder.

"Yes, it had just been finished. I had it built to my specifications, long and rather narrow, so that she can cut through the waves like a blade. She is the fastest ship out there," Conall told her with pride.

"Remember my pet name for you when we went sailing when you were little? I named my new beautiful ship the '*Mermaid*' with you in mind and with the hope that one day we would sail her together," the StCloud continued.

"She got me home in record time. A little magic filling the sails helped as well. That is how I was able to make it to the wedding while your brother still believed me in Narinia. Your uncle was very helpful in the planning of things," Conall concluded, laughing heartily.

"You scoundrel! You fooled Ragnald and had it all planned out, didn't you? Were those clothes really your mother's? They fit awfully well, and I remember her being a little bit shorter and a tad rounder than I!" Ki'ara asked, laughing.

"I confess! I got your measurements from that wonderful Leana and had them made especially for you. There is a whole closet full of them, and I do hope you like them. I guess I will have to wait to find out until we make it home again," he admitted with a rueful grin.

Carefully pushing the bird aside, Conall slid on the bench next to his wife. Lightly cupping her face, he began to kiss her gently. Ki'ara's response was instantaneous. Passion flared to life in her body. Sensing this made him deepen the kiss. Soon, everything but each other was forgotten.

Desire burned hot between them, but this time, there was even less room in the coach with the large bird curled up between the seats. Ki'ara finally impatiently undid her husband's trousers and straddled him. The StCloud moaned as she began to lower herself and took him inside her.

"Thank you, thank you, thank you, my Gods, for this amazing man! I am so grateful that he loved me enough to go through all that trouble to win me! I am a fortunate woman, indeed!" she kept thinking.

Ki'ara sent a silent prayer full of gratitude to the gods and the magic of the land. That was the last rational thought that she was able to string together as Conall began to move inside her.

Their lovemaking was urgent but also gentle and had a sweetness to it that almost moved Ki'ara to tears. When first she and then he found release, the StCloud pulled her tightly against him. Just as their bodies had become one, so did their souls.

What happens on Ki'ara's and Conall's voyage to the Zidhe and their adventures once they arrive is another story altogether. You can read all about it in book three of the Mystic Highlands series.

Appendix

The World of the Highlands

The Highlands are the most northern area of the Mystic Isles and were initially divided into nine clan areas, the realm of the Zidhe, and the border (see Map in front of the book). They are a cold and often windy place, with a rugged beauty that is enough to take your breath away. The land's interior is inhabited by the Zidhe. The elves reside partially under domes as well as in fertile valleys and in beautiful evergreen forests that they keep alive with their magic.

King Richard McCulloch of Cambria acted as a guiding overlord over the kings and queens of the clans for many years until his death. He died without naming an heir and without children of his own. A distant relative, Patrick McCulloch, eventually assumed the rule over Cambria but did not have the presence nor the strength to fill the vacant position as the leader and advisor for all the Highlands.

This set off an all-out war amongst the clans for the coveted position. Several rulers felt that they were best suited to govern over them all. The Zidhe finally had enough and intervened. As a punishment for their intolerable behavior, they forced the kings and queens to give up their crowns and become part of a council of Highland Clans.

More of the history of the Highlands is woven into the tale of Ki'ara and Conall itself in Book 1 of the Mystic Highlands Series. An extended version will be published in a separate volume.

The Ten Highland Clans

Clan Name	Clan Region	Clan Chief	Clan Seat
Alistar	Islandia	Rowena Alistar	Seacrest Tower
Blair	Larinia	Duncan Blair	Killinstone Castle
Elvinstone	Ravenshire	Iain Elvinstone	Birdrell Tower
Fairlie	Kendall	Hamish Fairlie	Kendall Hall
Kirkcaldie	Argness	Lorena Kirkcaldie	Middlesea Castle
Macgillmott	Caithyll	Niall Macgillmott	Gilmockie Tower
StCloud	Summerland	Conall StCloud	Cloudshire Hall
McCulloch	Cambria	Andrew McCulloch	Lockmair Castle
MacClair	Eastmuir	Ragnald MacClair	Seamuir Castle
MacClair	Fairholme	Ki'ara MacClair	Fairholme Castle

This table shows the clans, their regions, the present ruler, as well as the names of the Clan Seats. Initially, there were nine clans, but through an edict by the council, Ki'ara MacClair becomes the Lord of Fairholme and her people the 10th clan.

Places

Arillia

Arillian Continent: a large landmass that includes the Mystic Islands. In times past, most of the population inhabited the warmer parts of the continent. The peaceful societies founded by the Zidhe predominated in these temperate regions. The cold and barren northern reaches were only sparsely occupied until the elves made them their home.

Espanira

Espanira: A country bordered by Frankonia to the north and Portugana to the west, mostly rolling plains with some mountain ranges at the border with Frankonia.

Frankonia

Frankonia: A country to the south of the Mystic Isles. Part of it is mountainous, but it also has a beautiful coast.

Frankic coast: The coastal regions of Frankonia.

Frankonian Mountains: A range of tall mountains situated between Frankonia and Espanira.

De'Aire Chateau: A small dilapidated fortress way up in the mountains of Frankonia. It is home to the wizard Argulf and his few remaining servants. Not much grows there, and the supplies have to be fetched from the lowlands and the harbor of Mercede. The place is completely isolated in the winter, and provisions have to be brought in during the summer. During freak storms, the castle is often cut off for days. The servants raise some goats as well as chickens to supplement their diet. It takes more than 3 days to travel from the castle down to the harbor and an additional 3 weeks to reach the Highlands.

Mercede: The busiest port in the southern region of the Frankic Coast. The sizeable sheltered bay of Mercedeas makes for a deep natural harbor suited for large ships. It provides a safe haven in even the fiercest of storms. The shipping industry has brought prosperity to the port and its people, but crime has increased right along with the wealth.

Bay of Mercedeas: A deep water bay used as a harbor.

The Mystic Highlands

The 10th Kingdom: Until Ki'ara becomes a lord, the elves' realm was known as the 10th Kingdom. After that, the elves domain becomes known as the 11th realm. The Zidhe occupy the center of the Mystic Highlands, a strip along the border with the south, and several valleys leading down to the sea. Rumors have it that it is a truly wondrous place, but not many outsiders get to visit or live there.

The Barrier: An area along the border to the Lowlands created by the magic of the Zidhe. It is designed to keep people from crossing into the Highlands and extends out into the sea. This region is inhabited by all kinds of creatures. It has an area of sentient fog that leads intruders in circles and spits them back out far from where they have started as well as the Zone of Death where nothing grows.

Caithyll: The realm of the Macgillmotts.

Cloudshire Hall: The home of the StCloud clan and its present lord, Conall.

Council Chamber: A magnificent hexagonal space with an adjoining cloakroom on its right side next to the doors. Nine mirrors, one for each clan, are affixed to the three walls facing the entry. The room is subtly lit by magic and an intricate system of small mirrors that channel outside light into the windowless room and provide a luminous glow that perfectly sets off the chamber. A table is placed in a horseshoe shape facing the mirrors with the head of the assembly always seated dead center.

Deansport: The closest ship harbor to Seamuir Castle. To travel by boat from Deansport to the castle, one would have had to go all the way around the spit protecting the bay and then work one's way south along the coast. Usually, this turns out to be an uncomfortable trip since the waters close to shore are rough. Storms blow up without warning. The road to Seamuir, the seat of the clan, is a much faster way to go. It first heads inland to avoid the wetlands bordering the shore. Once past those, it curves and heads up the coast. It winds its way between the heather-covered hills and the deep brown moors. The use of the local gates cuts hours off this journey.

Eastmuir: The realm of the MacClairs. A deep fjord, cutting far into the interior, marks the boundary between the lands of the MacClairs and the StClouds. Tall mountains border each side of this protected inland waterway. Many a ship finds refuge here from the powerful storms which can develop so suddenly on the local waters.

Elvenhorst: The mysterious central city of the elves, built in the shape of a five-pointed star. It is located in an extinct volcano and covered by an energy dome.

Fairholme Castle: A whimsical castle granted to Ki'ara along with the land on her 24th birthday. It is located half a day's ride from Seamuir and not far from Cloudshire Hall. The small but delightfully playful and airy Fairholme Castle is a truly generous gift and one that had been long in the making by Mikael MacClair.

Nor'Dea: Created as a last refuge for the Zidhe just in the case that humanity also overruns the Highlands. It is one of five spots they selected as sanctuaries and has been very extensively terraformed. Nor'Dea was transformed from a place of snow and ice with little vegetation to a paradise of sorts that is a vacation spot for some of the more restless elves and those wanting a child. For some unknown reason, any female Zidhe spending time here is able to conceive. The birthrate among the residents is actually quite high for the Le'aanan, and even multiple births are not unknown.

Seamuir Castle: The home of the MacClair Clan located in the hills above the sea. It serves as a watch station over the adjacent waters as do all the other coastal fortresses in the Highlands.

Zone of Death: A part of the border area created by the magic of the Zidhe. Nothing grows here.

Ships

Mermaid: Conall StCloud's sleek, narrow vessel that he christened after his nickname for Ki'ara when she was little. He had her built to his specifications, and she is the fastest ship out on the seas.

Sea Witch: The ship, a clipper, meets Ki'ara and Mathus at Mercede Harbor to transport them back to the Highlands. Ki'ara is the actual owner of the vessel, and her uncle Iain looks after the business first for her father, Mikael, and now for her.

People

Frankonia

Amara: The Goddess of the Frankonian Mountains. She restores Ki'ara's magic after the young sorceress saves the dragon wraith and the ghost cat.

Milla: The housekeeper at De'Aire Chateau, a woman well up there in years. Milla took to treating Ki'ara like a cherished granddaughter. She was the one who always fixed those wonderful cups of hot chocolate for Ki'ara to restore her after working on the castle.

Argulf: An ancient sorcerer and master of De'Aire Chateau. He is a rather arrogant man who is firmly convinced of his own prowess. When he first meets Ki'ara, he tells her that it would take her at least a lifetime to learn what he knows. Her being immortal, that would truly be a very long time. It takes her less than two years to best the self-important man, something that he does not handle very well. When Ki'ara arrives, the old sorcerer tries hard to give off an air of dignity and grandeur. He wears shoes with blocks glued to the bottoms to make himself look taller and more majestic, his floor-length robes are marginally clean but so wrinkled that they look like he has slept in them. He is continually tripping over the hem. Argulf's stringy, greasy mane is dyed, but, somehow, the magic went wrong, and the hair looks more purple than black. His mean, beady brown eyes are close to his beak of a nose, and the wizard's gaze is cold and calculating. His mouth with its thin lips is usually turned down into a frown, and his face set in a permanent scowl. Argulf goes out of his way to appear imposing but lacks the height to truly pull it off. The short, pompous man reminded Ki'ara eerily of an overgrown rat.

Brianna: The great golden dragon whose spirit was captured and enchanted by the sorcerer Argulf. The dark emanations of the wizard's dungeon turn the dragon wraith evil and into a genuinely frightening being.

Dragon Wraith: A fearsome creature brought into being through dark magic. It can be directed to some degree by its maker but will kill any who cross its path. It takes tremendous energy to bring such a monster into the world, and it will live only a few days or hours unless it feeds.

Hugo: The stablemaster of De'Aire Chateau and Ki'ara's guide up and down the mountains. He is also the one responsible for fetching his master's supplies up to the fortress and, during the summer, makes the long trip at least once a month.

Jacques des Montagnes: The leader of the bandits. He and some of his men are attacked by the dragon wraith and only survive due to Ki'ara's assistance. Jacques and his outlaws have their hideout in the mountains. He is well-mannered and the son of a nobleman.

Mikka: The ghost cat and Taryn's mate. The wizard Argulf finds her close to death and decides to use her for one of his unholy experiments. Planning for bigger and better things, Argulf is no longer interested in this enchantment once it is finished. After placing the enslaved spirit in a vial for safekeeping, the careless man decides to store it down in the dungeons. The malevolent emanations of past atrocities committed here pervert it completely and turn it to evil.

Pierre: One of the few servants at De'Aire Chateau, he functions as a butler when needed.

Taryn: A mountain cat, also called a catamount or ghost cat who befriends Ki'ara and becomes her constant companion.

The Highlands

Ulric: A southern lord's son who sets his sights on the Highlands. His name means wealthy, powerful ruler or Wolf Ruler.

Ziderians

The Zidarians are mix-breeds between elves and humans or one of the other races. They are almost immortal, living well over 1000 years. The more Zidhe blood a person has, the more magical powers they possess. Once despised by all the races, they gained status as lords after the battle with Ulric. To maintain pure bloodlines, the ruling Zidarians only marry each other. The families have magic in their blood and are intimately tied to the land. When a Zidarian reaches 21, their physical body stops aging, but they continue to mature emotionally. Their bodies remain strong and full of vitality until well after their nine hundredth birthday. Nine main families rule the clans.

The Clan of the MacClairs

The MacClairs: One of the ruling Highland families. Ki'ara is born into this clan.

Ali'ana Ard Cymru: The second wife of Mikael MacClair and mother of Ki'ara.

Gawain MacClair: The youngest of the MacClair men and also the most handsome. His hair is of a beautiful dark red color, almost mahogany, not too unlike his sister's copper-colored curls. He usually allows it to fall into his face and cover one eye giving him a rakish air. His features are open and pleasant and beautifully set of his stunning brilliant blue eyes. He is a stocky man with a barrel chest and in great form since he keeps physically active all the time.

Ki'ara MacClair: The daughter of Mikael and Ali'ana. She is tall and slender, and her waist-long, somewhat curly hair shines like bright copper in the sunshine. Ki'ara's startling green eyes, set into a face with clear skin and delicate facial features, are the color of a mountain lake with moonlight reflecting off its waves. Her inner beauty matches her appearance and is so evident that most people instantly like her. Ki'ara has just recently turned 24 when this story begins. By Zidarian standards, she is still considered a child. Her oldest brother, Ragnald, was her guardian until her birthday. Ki'ara was thirteen when her dad passed on the throne to his oldest son. Due to Ragnald's misbehavior, the young lady is made Lord of Fairholme by the council according to her father's instructions. She becomes the 10th lord of the Highlands.

Lyall MacClair: This MacClair's bland personality is very much reflected in his drab looks. Beside his siblings, Lyall is strangely colorless with his mousy hair and pasty face. He also lacks magic and has very little connection to the land. Lyall has been Ragnald's puppet since he was a toddler. He is the least attractive of all the siblings with his mud-colored eyes, slumped shoulders, and plain facial features and moves without the pride in his step common to most Zidarians. This sets him apart from his brothers. Lyall has never developed much of a character due to Ragnald's overbearing influence.

Mikael MacClair: The previous lord and father to Ragnald, Lyall, Gawain, and Ki'ara MacClair, a kind and fair ruler who sees the best in most people. The lord passes on the rule of the clan and its land as well as the magic to his oldest son when Ki'ara is 13 years old. He and his wife, Ali'ana Ard Cymru, also make Ragnald guardian of their minor child, Ki'ara.

Morena Elvinstone-MacClair: The first wife of Mikael MacClair and mother to Ragnald, Lyall, and Gawain. She never recovers fully from the birth of her youngest son, Gawain, and slowly declines over the years. Only the love for her husband and sons and the intense desire to see her small boy grow up keep her alive for as long as it does. She finally dies from lingering complications when Gawain is 18 years of age.

Raghnall MacClair: The father to Mikael MacClair and once lord of the clan, a harsh and bitter man. Ragnald was his favorite grandchild, and he filled his head with his poison from an early age on. The old man resented the loss of the crown and the rules laid down by the Zidhe. He held on to the old hostilities and enjoyed a good fight. Raghnall, along with Daron StCloud, disappeared one night as a punishment for starting a battle.

Ragnald MacClair: The present lord of the MacClair Clan and an immortal Zidarian who has the land's magic at his disposal. The oldest MacClair's hair is raven black and always immaculately cut and combed. His features are even and clean cut. He would have been handsome if not for the perpetual scowl that mars his visage. The name Ragnald is a form of Raghnall and means 'world mighty' or 'great chief.'

Clans People

Arabella: Gawain's date and the owner of the "Seven Sailors" Inn. A very smart and ambitious young lady who has her sights set on the young lord. Being the rebellious daughter of a distant relation, she has enough elven blood to qualify for marriage with a fellow Zidarian.

Berta: The rude housekeeper Ragnald MacClair employs. Her primary job is running people off, which she does rather well until Ki'ara comes along.

Celia: The bride whose wedding Ki'ara attends. She is wed to Rodric.

Gina O'Malley: A female riverboat captain and the mistress of Ragnald MacClair. Gina has terrible manners, she is a true sailor, cusses like a deckhand, and loves to get drunk and belligerent down at the pub. It is rumored that the MacClair is not her only lover. Since she is nothing but trouble, most of the castle's inhabitants avoid her like the plague. Gina is an attractive woman with dark, sparkling eyes and long black hair, but what she has in beauty, she lacks in coordination. She is well known for being accident-prone and getting people hurt. Ragnald uses her in an attempt to harm his sister, and she ends up getting injured by the blaze.

James: The butler at Seamuir Castle.

Kendrick: The healer present at Seamuir Castle during the wave. He is brought in to help Ragnald after James finds the unconscious lord. Due to having a fair amount of Zidarian blood, Kendrick has been affected fairly severely himself and, for a while, has problems even seeing straight.

Leana: Ki'ara's maid who is, in reality, her aunt and Princess Le'anara of the Zidhe. She accompanies her sister Ali'ana to Seamuir Castle to protect her niece and does so first as her nurse and later as her maid. She can see many possible futures and blocks the ones she does not like. Leana is fiercely loyal to Ki'ara.

Marcus O'Rourke: He is and has been the captain of the *Sea Witch* for many years. He is a competent and jovial man with whom Ki'ara has always gotten along well. Under his guidance, the ship runs like clockwork.

Mathus: The Lowlander is Ki'ara's tutor. Ragnald sends him along wherever she goes, and he acts as her watchdog. He is a lanky, gangly, obnoxious man who abuses his position and mistreats Ki'ara. He reminds the young lady of an ill-tempered stork. All the self-centered tutor cares about is his own comfort. It is not surprising that Ragnald's lackey has been fired from his last employment and had to flee to the north!

Rodric: The groom whose wedding Ki'ara attends. He marries Celia.

Athair Thomas: The jovial high priest of the old religion who marries Ki'ara and Conall.

York: The carriage driver, hired by Captain Marcus to deliver Ki'ara to Seamuir Castle. He is a shrewd, middle-aged man who assists Ki'ara in her dealings with the unfriendly housekeeper Berta.

Zertra: The ancient crone is well versed in herbs, the lore of the land, and she is a seeress. She is banned to the stables by Ragnald, who is furious that his father has granted this useless, feeble woman lifetime residency of the castle.

The Clan of the StClouds

Conall StCloud: The present lord of the StCloud clan. He was Ki'ara's fiancé before the young lady's parents set off on their journey, leaving Ragnald in charge of their daughter. He is a tall and very handsome man with dark curly hair and warm brown eyes. Ki'ara loves his smile and has never stopped loving him in all the years they were apart. Conall means 'strong wolf.'

Daron StCloud: Conall's grandfather, a stubborn, willful man who disappeared along with Raghnall MacClair. The two men had remained bitter enemies despite the treaty and could barely stand the sight of each other. They had been furious that the covenant forced them to keep the uneasy peace.

Lord Thomas Dareby: A good friend and distant cousin of Conall's. His castle is the one where the StCloud leaves Ragnald MacClair for safekeeping.

Clans People

Lady Annabella: The housekeeper of Cloudshire Hall.

Robert: The butler at the home of the StCloud Clan.

Willa: Conall's long-time mistress. After the death of her very abusive husband, the young woman found herself on the streets. Another marriage for her was not an option since a midwife had declared her barren. The arrangement with the StCloud had been her idea and gave her a freedom she would have never had otherwise.

Other Important Zidarians

Airon: A young Zidarian messenger who is sent by the council to bring Ki'ara the news of her change in status.

Heather McClintok: She is employed by Lord Rowena Alistar of Islandia to present her at meetings in Eastmuir. A beautiful lady, shrewd, diplomatic, and very astute. Not much gets past her or her friend Shannon.

Lord Iain Elvinstone of Ravenshire: The brother of the first wife of Mikael MacClair, Morena. He is not a blood relation to Ki'ara but treats her as his niece. He is fiercely protective of her, even against his own nephew Ragnald, for whom he, like most people, does not particularly care.

Lord Niall Macgillmott: Lord of the Macgillmotts and of the Caithyll region. He is one of Ragnald's foster fathers and the one who mentions the prophecy to Ragnald, sending him off on a desperate hunt for this proof that Ki'ara is a threat to their clan. He and Lyall search until they finally find that reference in an old book high up on a shelf in Lord Macgillmott's library.

Lord Weatherlin: An old gent who is very gallant and has always been one of Ki'ara favorite people. His white mane looks like he has been through a windstorm, and he has bright blue eyes. Lord Weatherlin, who is sitting in for Andrew McCulloch of Cambria, presides over the fateful council when Ki'ara requests her brother's removal as lord.

King Richard McCulloch of Cambria: The lord acted as a guiding overlord, as had his father before him. While the circumspect man held this power, peace reigned across all the realms of the Highlands.

Shannon O'Leary: She is the local stand-in for Lord Lorena Kirkcaldie of Argness at council meetings in Eastmuir. A beautiful lady, shrewd, diplomatic, and very observant.

The Zidhe

Geradian: He is the leader of the Zidhe and stayed behind during the exodus to call for a council of the races. The Zidhe is a tall, handsome man with long, dark hair. He has a slender built. His bright green eyes are piercing and seem to see right through to the very core of a person. Not much gets past him. Geradian is highly intelligent and intuitive but also kind and compassionate. What makes him so ultimately suited for dealing with the elves' once friends, however, is his ability as a shrewd negotiator and an astute reader of others' emotions. Many years of experience as a circumspect leader has taught him much. He is extremely powerful and surpasses his peers in magical strength and abilities. His connection to the land goes deep.

Jenna: Wife to Geradian and the leader of one of the expeditions into the polar regions that goes in search of shelter just in case the Mystic Highlands are ever overrun by the humans.

Lord Syl'vian: One of the rulers of the Zidhe and Ki'ara's grandfather.

Definitions

The 'Choosing' or 'Becoming': The process of the magic of the land binding with the new lord. Only a select few outside the ruling lords, mostly healers, have been told what to expect.

Council of Lords: The Zidhe establish the main committee to rule the Highlands, the Council of Lords. It handles all major problems affecting one clan or more and acts as the primary body governing the Highlands. The Zidarian lords are allowed to manage the everyday business of their individual clans. All decisions involving the other regions, no matter how small, have to be brought before one of the councils.

First Council of the Highlands: After the clan lords are declared kings by the Zidhe, they realize that they need to be able to protect what was theirs. Therefore, one of the first acts of the new kings is to call a gathering. Zidhe, dwarves, and human alike heed the call, and even a couple of giants attend. Many an idea is born and then discarded or gives rise to a brand-new proposal. Progress is slow but steady. The northerners are all aware that things cannot continue as before. The battle with Ulric taught them that. Their way of life has to change if they want to keep their lives and their homes. The Highlanders understand that it is vital that they band together. They need to learn from each other, be better organized. They have to be prepared to respond more quickly. The days of separate groups living here or there are over if they want to survive.

Gathering of Lords: Minor problems, affecting no more than three neighboring clans, can be discussed and handled at the 'Gathering of Lords.' These meetings are held before weddings, becomings, funerals, and such.

Magic Mirror: A very effective magical communication device. Outside the realm of the Zidhe, these looking glasses are very rare and highly treasured. Each lord, the council, and every gate have one of these items. The mirrors allow for efficient communication as well as for the attending of meetings from afar.

Magical Gates: Had it not been for the network of such doorways all over the Highlands, bringing people together would have been a logistical nightmare. The gates are located at strategic spots in each realm, easily reached but never too close to one of the castles. They are primarily used for official business and connect the nine kingdoms to each other and the council's main chambers. The shortcuts allow the lords to attend meetings and events no matter where they are held. To prevent sudden invasions, only one carriage can pass through at a time, and the travelers have to state their name and destination to the gatekeeper there. He or she will then dial in the desired location, lock it in, and open the portal. An alarm goes off at any nearby fortress whenever someone enters the realm. A magic mirror is then used to determine if friend or foe is on their way to their doorstep. The system was built by the Zidhe and has been functioning perfectly for many a year.

Afterword

I love to write, and even the tiniest little bit of an impression or glimpse can give rise to a story or poem. Sometimes, a new tale will pop into my head while walking, reading a book, watching a movie, or in a dream. Since I have learned how to look, stories are all around me, begging to be shared with the world.

I especially cherish the ideas coming to me in my dreams. The ones I remember vividly feel different. When I put them down on paper, more details flow into my mind, almost as if I had lived them. Some believe that there are many universes and many dimensions. Who knows, maybe in one of those I did have a part in these adventures!

Many of my longer tales start with a dream, as did this one. In 2017, I was actually in the middle of working on the sequels to "Arianna- A Tale from the Eleven Kingdoms" when I had this incredible dream of two lovers kept apart by her brother. She/me was Ki'ara, and he was Connor McCloud. He left quite an impression since he was positively gorgeous, smart, kind, honest, supportive, and just plain awesome. In other words, my ideal man.

At first, I thought this would be just a short story. I had no clue it would grow to this extent. The tale soon took on a life of its own and kept getting longer and longer at a fantastic rate. New twists and turns were appearing all the time that I had never even imagined in the beginning. Still, that is where the story led, and it turned into two books instead of one.

The lover's name had given me the setting but could not stay the same due to the Highlander Series. I finally settled on Conall StCloud. Also, Ki'ara's brother started out as Donald, but since I am not writing political satire, he became Ragnald.

The Mystic Highlands are loosely based on Scotland but have magic, all kinds of mystical beings, and customs of their own. The sitting down with the hands on the table in the council scene came straight from my dream.

All the unexpected ideas made writing this book incredible fun. The words would just flow into my mind. Sometimes I could barely type fast enough to keep up. If I was not in the right frame of mind or it seemed that I was flailing, I stepped back for a few days until inspiration once again sent me back to the computer to continue this continually expanding work.

For me, writing is just as exciting as reading. I have a vague notion of where I am heading with my tales, but, along the way, most of my stories manage to surprise me. Adventures that I never even anticipated flow from my fingertips, and I can't wait to see where this new notion is going.

The suspense is what keeps me enthralled and working away. It is almost like automatic writing or channeling, and I am always eager to find out just what happens next.

I had a fabulous time creating this book and hope you will enjoy reading it as much as I loved writing it for you!

Acknowledgements

A very special 'THANK YOU' to all my amazing friends and family who loved and supported me during the creation of this book but especially to Robbi Baskin, Stacey Brown, and Rhonda Mackert. You were always ready to listen, and to provide feedback. Also, I am immensely grateful to Robbi, who did an absolutely awesome job editing this book. I love you.

The cover took form over several months. Thank you, my wonderful friends and family, for helping shape it with your comments and tips.

And last but not least, a huge thank you to the Divine for sending me this story in a dream and helping me write it.

Author's Biography

GC Sinclaire loves to write and could not imagine her life without it. Her inspiration comes from many places. One of these sources is Sinclaire's vivid dreams. When she commits them to paper, more facts emerge, almost like she has lived them.

Just like her other books, 'Arianna - A Tale from the Eleven Kingdoms' and 'The Shapeshifter's Bride,' the Mystic Highlands Series is the result of one of these dreams. Several other stories, including a sequel to this saga and 'Arianna,' are in various stages of completion. They should be published within the next couple of years.

If you would like to read more about GC and her works, please visit her Facebook page, GC Sinclaire, or her web page at www.gcsinclaire.com. You can check on updates there and connect with the author.